A WELL-PRESSED SHROUD

When Detective Inspector Montague Pluke takes a holiday, it gives him a long-awaited opportunity to go in search of the Lost Giant's Horse Trough of Trippingdale, rumoured to exist in the grounds of Trippingdale Castle. He not only finds the Trough, but face-down in its shallow waters, a dead man. The body is identified as that of the recent heir to the estate, a thoughtful and well-liked man. Why did he, along with several other village people, receive a single pressed snowdrop – a well-known sign of death?

A WELL-PRESSED SHROUD

A Well-Pressed Shroud

by

Nicholas Rhea

Magna Large Print Books
Long Preston, North Yorkshire,
BD23 4ND, England.

British Library Cataloguing in Publication Data.

Rhea, Nicholas
A well-pressed shroud.

A catalogue record of this book is
available from the British Library

ISBN   0-7505-1725-5

First published in Great Britain 2000 by Constable,
an imprint of Constable & Robinson Ltd.

Published in Large Print 2001 by arrangement with
Constable & Robinson Ltd.

Magna Large Print is an imprint of Library Magna Books Ltd.

Printed and bound in Great Britain by
T.J. (International) Ltd., Cornwall, PL28 8RW

1

It was Friday, regarded by some as the most unlucky day of the week. It was also the first Friday in May, not the most fortuitous of months but, in spite of those worrying portents, Detective Inspector Montague Pluke was about to embark upon a week's holiday.

Renowned for his knowledge of horse troughs, in addition to being officer in charge of the Criminal Investigation Department of Crickledale Sub-Divisional Police Station, he was looking forward to a stimulating break from police work. He felt rather tired because his recent crime-fighting initiative had proved somewhat stressful, even if it had been spectacularly successful. As a result of those endeavours the level of reported crime in Crickledale was at its lowest for years and his monthly statistics showed a sixty-two-per-cent detection rate for crimes within the sub-division. It was a superb achievement by Pluke and his team.

He had been proud to report that within the sub-division during the last quarter there had been no murders, rapes, arson, treason, piracy, extortion, bribery, riots, affrays, acts of sedition, offences against the Merchant Shipping Act, cheating at cards, fraudulent mediums, unauthorised hypnotism, personation at elections, forged pawnbrokers' certificates, illegal hairdressing, brawling in churchyards or blasphemy.

The most serious crimes during that period had been an outbreak of seventy-five night-time burglaries in hen houses. That crime wave had been detected following the spectacular arrest of a teenage egg thief. The arrest had proved the value of good old-fashioned detective work, supported by a deep knowledge of the local community, along with a little help from the owner's security camera and his Rottweiler. After recovering in hospital, the thief had been sentenced to community service in the kitchen of a social services hostel where his omelettes were truly appreciated.

Following the submission of that glowing report, which had resulted in a telephone call of congratulation from no less a person than the Chief Constable himself, Detective Inspector Pluke felt perfectly justified in taking a break from the demands of high office, even if the anonymous sender of the pressed-snowdrop letters had not been traced. Pluke felt sure that his deputy, Detective Sergeant Wayne Wain, could cope with the pressures of that unresolved investigation. Apart from the snowdrop mail, which had begun only three weeks ago, there was no other outstanding matter. Pluke's in-tray was otherwise empty. He had cleared his desk and put away his trough-shaped paperclip container; it was time to bid farewell to his secretary.

She was the splendidly rounded and warm-smiling Mrs Plumpton, famed throughout the police station for her frothy and billowing dresses with dangerously low necklines. There were times when the sight of her bending forward to clear his out-tray made him perspire profusely.

On such occasions he found himself trying to calculate the strains and stresses that must severely test some items of her clothing. There were times he wished he could remember or even understand the laws of physics he had learnt at school – he reckoned the stresses involved must be something akin to those affecting the wires that magically supported the road across the Humber Bridge. He did wonder how her clothes, which appeared to float on a cushion of perfumed air around her ample charms, managed to contain so much of her without any of the deeply interesting parts overflowing around the edges. There was quite a lot to Mrs Plumpton, he thought from time to time, and some views of her were rich with magic and mystery.

On this important occasion, however, Mrs

Plumpton wished him a happy holiday and added she'd look forward to his return a week on Monday. She assured him that Detective Sergeant Wayne Wain would be a good and efficient deputy during his absence. She didn't tell him, though, that Wayne Wain had already sneaked into Pluke's office to test the chair for size and to see if the desk was conveniently positioned. He'd even brought a photograph of a current girlfriend, a long-haired blonde in a scanty bikini standing beside a swimming pool. That would be placed upon the desk the moment Pluke left the office, he'd revealed to Mrs Plumpton. At this stage, though, Detective Sergeant Wain had not thought it wise to change the nameplate on the door, although a week was a long time in rural police station politics.

'We are all dispensable, Mrs Plumpton, none of us is irreplaceable.' Pluke tried to assuage the worries she must be suffering at the thought of his absence from the sharp end of operational policing. He reassured her that the vacuum caused by his absence could be tolerated for a week. After all, it was not as if he was retiring from the Force, he was merely taking a few days of his annual leave entitlement. 'I am sure that my brief non-presence will not result in an uncharacteristic crime wave in Crickledale,' he assured her. 'Detective Sergeant Wain is

10

a most capable officer. He will keep the worst of our villains at bay during my absence and will give his full attention to the snowdrop letter mystery. I have given him permission to use my office and to take full advantage of all your skills and talents, Mrs Plumpton, so that he might accomplish his duties in style.'

'Thank you. He is such a nice young man, Mr Pluke,' she oozed. 'I know we shall get on well together. He did say he liked my milk coffee and orange creams, that I had hidden depths and that he felt sure we would function well together.'

'He is absolutely right, of course. He is a most capable detective and somewhat ambitious, Mrs Plumpton, and I am sure you can keep him active and usefully employed. He does need to be kept busy. Well, I must be off. It is after five o'clock and Mrs Pluke will have my tea ready. Fish on Friday, you understand.'

'Are you going far on your holiday?' she asked as he lifted his ancient coat and blue-ribboned panama from their hooks on the office wall.

'I have a very important mission to fulfil.' He spoke in hushed, mysterious and almost reverential tones.

'Really, Mr Pluke?' She wondered if it was something to do with MI5 or international terrorism.

'This week away from work is most opportune because it enables me to undertake the challenge of a lifetime,' he told her. 'It is an expedition of the most dramatic kind, a true voyage of discovery.'

'Are you joining that expedition that's going to look for the Lost Tribe of Machpela ... there was an article in the *Gazette* about a team of local experts leaving next week to trek through steaming jungles, while braving snarling tigers and poisonous snakes as they hunt for a lost civilisation which continues to indulge in human sacrifice with innocent virgins. I can visualise you undertaking that kind of daring deed, Mr Pluke, and your detection skills will be of enormous help in locating the tribe.'

'No, I am not going on that particular expedition, Mrs Plumpton, although I shall be undertaking something of a similarly daring nature. I consider my mission to be of far greater importance than seeking a lost tribe. You see, a lost tribe is not really lost, is it? That is a misnomer. The tribe in question will not consider themselves lost, will they? They know where they are because they have always been there; they're just keeping themselves hidden and secure from the unwelcome advances of so-called civilisation. And someone is going to try to find them and destroy all that. I think that is a dreadful shame, so I will have no part in that enterprise, Mrs Plumpton.'

'You are so right, Mr Pluke, such an intellect!'

'My mission, Mrs Plumpton, is on behalf of the British Horse Trough Society. I shall be endeavouring to confirm the existence of the famous and massive Lost Giant's Trough of Trippingdale.'

'Is it really lost, Mr Pluke, or is it like the tribe? If people know where it is it is not lost, is it?'

'I shall not know if it is truly lost until I try to find it,' he said. 'If it is truly lost, then perhaps I shall never find it. It has not been viewed by the public for many generations because it is within the walls of a ruined castle situated on private land and no access has been granted for centuries.'

'So it is not a lost trough, Mr Pluke, even though you are going to find it?'

'My quest is an attempt to confirm its existence, Mrs Plumpton – that is, assuming it has not been destroyed or removed. Ancient legends told of its existence and its extraordinary size but no one is quite sure whether the stories relate to a real trough or whether it is pure fiction; if it is real, we do not know whether it has survived the ravages of time and climate. The estate that owns it has never allowed outsiders on to the land, so anything could have happened to the trough. If it is genuine, it might have been broken up to make stones for rockeries or road foundations, or it might have been stolen, then resold in a garden centre. But you are right. Perhaps we should not refer to it as the Lost Trough? Hidden Trough, maybe? Perhaps, because it was allegedly used by the Giant of Trippingdale's horse, I should refer to it as the Giant's Trough.'

'Trippingdale? That's just up the road, isn't it?' she commented.

'The dale with its lost village and castle, yes. About three or four miles away. The village was destroyed by the great flood of 1367 and the site has never been excavated or examined since that time, Mrs Plumpton. It now forms part of the parkland of the estate. The castle ruins are also closed to the public and the Giant's Trough is said to be within its walls. My task is to ascertain the truth; I shall determine whether or not Trippingdale Castle contains what is possibly the largest horse trough in the world!'

'The largest in the world? You mean it might get into the *Guinness Book of Records*, Mr Pluke?'

'If I can establish its authenticity, yes indeed.'

'The estate owners must have a reason for not letting people on to their land, Mr Pluke.'

'I am sure they must, Mrs Plumpton, although no reason has ever been given. But so far as the trough is concerned, there are no pictures, no drawings or photographs. This is one of the great horse trough mysteries of the world, Mrs Plumpton. Apart from the estate owners and perhaps their staff, friends or relations, no one has seen the trough for more than six centuries. I think the staff must be sworn to secrecy about it. Ancient records do suggest it was used in Norman times to water the Conqueror's horses; that is how I came to know about it and to associate it with the legend of the giant.'

'Fancy that, Mr Pluke.'

'If it has survived intact, it will be of enormous historical significance, although I suspect the estate owners do not appreciate its importance. The claim is that this trough watered, in only ten sessions, the entire complement of war horses used by William the Conqueror during his Harrying of the North in 1069. Four hundred and eighty horses, Mrs Plumpton. If that account is correct, it means it is capable of watering forty-eight horses simultaneously. One old account says it could accommodate fifteen horses along each of its two sides and nine at each of its two ends, all drinking together. Think of that, Mrs Plumpton, forty-eight horses all enjoying a drink at one and the same time. So, as you can see, if it does exist it is a trough of immense cultural and

15

historic interest, a true part of England's glorious heritage.'

'It is quite a large trough, then, Mr Pluke.' She smiled.

'Truly gigantic in both size and stature, Mrs Plumpton. Bottomless, too, so it is said. It is probably the tenth wonder of the world. If I do locate it I may set in motion the procedures to have it declared a Word Heritage Site, rather like the Taj Mahal, the Great Wall of China and that coalmine in Blaenavon.'

'What an honour, Mr Pluke!' And she sighed at the prospect of her reflected glory in working for a person of such eminence.

'Just imagine,' he went on. 'I could be the first member of the public, and certainly the most informed, to set eyes upon it for more than six hundred years.'

'I had no idea about all this!' She tried to sound very enthusiastic. 'You never know what's on your doorstep, do you?'

'The timing of my quest is perfect, Mrs Plumpton, because Trippingdale Castle and, in fact, the whole of the Trippingdale parkland may soon be open to the public. The elderly and rather eccentric lady owner, Mrs Gallholme, like her predecessors, had constantly refused all requests for public access or information. She would not even allow archaeologists on to the site. No one really knows what gems lie undiscovered within the Trippingdale parkland, so I hope to prove that the Giant's Trough is more than just a legend, Mrs Plumpton.'

'A bit like Robin Hood, eh, Mr Pluke?'

'I suppose so, yes. However, things have changed. Mrs Gallholme, the estate owner, died two months ago and her son, Stephen, is prepared to allow some access to the parkland. I am the first to be allowed to take advantage of that development.'

'Well done, Mr Pluke! You deserve that. You know the rumours about the old lady, do you?'

'What kind of rumours, Mrs Plumpton?'

'I'd heard she was very eccentric, Mr Pluke, that she led a very odd life. Dancing in the moonlight, worshipping at stone circles, that sort of thing. When I was a child the local children thought she was a witch. We were always told to keep away from Trippingdale; nobody ever wanted to go there. We were scared of the place, Mr Pluke. So I have never been, not to this day.'

'I was regaled with the same scare tactics, Mrs Plumpton. I was told never to go into the dale. My parents said all kinds of dreadful things might happen if I did trespass in any of the parkland, especially the castle. I kept away; I was terrified of dragons and giants and things. It's funny looking back on those days. Now I realise it was the estate's method of keeping people out. The whole owning dynasty was very superstitious too and Mrs Gallholme, although marrying into the family, followed that tradition and did everything to ensure good fortune for herself, her family and the entire estate. People might have said she was far too superstitious for a modern woman, but that does not mean she was eccentric. After all, I believe in superstition, Mrs Plumpton, and I am not in the least eccentric.'

'Her desire to lead her own kind of life might explain why she wanted to keep people away?' she demanded.

'Perhaps, but it was something the family had done for centuries, Mrs Plumpton. It is their private property, even if the parkland does contain an entire dale with a deserted village and a castle, as well as moors, fields and streams. And, of course, there was a tragedy in the dale.'

'A tragedy? In addition to the flood, you mean?'

'Yes, the flood was in 1367, the more recent tragedy was in 1966, before I joined the Force.'

'Oh dear, what kind of tragedy, Mr Pluke?'

'A child, a small boy, drowned in the stream near the head of the dale, Mrs Plumpton. A tragic accident.'

'A member of the family, was it?'

'I am not too familiar with the details. I was not a police officer at the time. But I believe the little boy was the son of one of the estate workers. People never talk about it; it's history now.'

'Then I can understand the estate owners not wishing to open to the public,' Mrs Plumpton said.

'Yes, but time moves on, Mrs Plumpton, and Stephen Gallholme has broken the tradition of centuries. That might not please everyone, of course. But whatever the situation in the past, things are changing and I have obtained the necessary permit to visit the estate.'

'What an honour, Mr Pluke. So the truth of the trough is about to be revealed to the whole world.'

'Indeed yes, Mrs Plumpton. You can imagine how excited I was by the estate's very timely change of policy. I think my role as a leading authority on English horse troughs enabled me to be granted access. It offers a wonderful opportunity and it means that the fate of a missing link in our history, part of our English countryside heritage, will be recorded for posterity. Hopefully, if my efforts prove the existence of the Giant's Trough, it will eventually lead to it being available for more detailed examination, documentation and conservation.'

'It is a great honour, Mr Pluke.' She sighed. 'And a wonderful means of ack-nowledging your expertise on this very specialised subject.'

'Well, I am far too modest to say I have earned this privilege, but I cannot ignore what the fates have in store for me,' he said. 'And on the day I made my formal application, I found a four-leaved clover and, in addition, I met a piebald horse face to face on that gypsy encampment at the edge of the town. They are both signs of impending good fortune, Mrs Plumpton, so I will begin first thing tomorrow morning. My understanding is that the trough is buried beneath centuries of debris and undergrowth in the castle ruins, so it might take a long time to locate it. But if it is there, Mrs Plumpton, I shall find it. I shall find it however long it takes and however difficult and dangerous the task.'

'I'm sure you will, with your determination and skill. And will Mrs Pluke be accompanying you?'

'She has some pressing commitments tomorrow, but she will be my driver and my PA. She is worth her weight in gold, is Mrs Pluke. Most supportive.'

'You will send me a postcard, won't you?' Mrs Plumpton smiled. She thought this was the kind of joke that would be acceptable to Detective Inspector Pluke.

'I doubt if there are any postboxes in Trippingdale, Mrs Plumpton. Nor, indeed, are there any shops. As I said earlier, the entire parkland has been closed for centuries.'

'Oh, well, I shall just have to manage without one!' Again, she smiled softly at him. 'Detective Sergeant Wain always sends me one when he's away.'

'He's never been to Trippingdale,' retorted Pluke. 'But I shall be thinking of you when I gaze into the intriguing and unfathomable depths of that legendary horse trough, Mrs Plumpton.'

'It will be like a large bath, Mr Pluke, and they do say that beauty is in the eye of the beholder.' She sighed, wondering if Mr Pluke might dream of washing her back, or some other part or parts of her, in that commodious trough. It sounded as if it would require a lot of bubble bath to cover its water with foam.

'Beauty is indeed in the eye of the beholder, Mrs Plumpton.' He averted his eyes from the area of her splendid chest, which now began to oscillate beneath his gaze. She was moving from her chair as he fastened his calf-length, voluminous, all-embracing mustard-coloured plaid coat with its shoulder cape, epaulettes and ragged cuffs. The coat was a family heirloom, a coaching coat owned by a previous gentleman of the Pluke dynasty. It had been passed down to Montague through the male line of the family, beginning with the original owner who was a coachman on the Highflyer.

21

In spite of its age and crumbling appearance, it went everywhere that he went, invariably with Pluke inside it. To complement his famous old coat he donned his blue-trimmed panama, checked that his spats were fastened and that his blue dicky bow was correctly aligned. With everything correct, he lifted his chin into the air and sailed majestically out of the office with a faint 'Goodbye, Mrs Plumpton' while leading from the door with his right foot. One always started a new journey with the right foot.

With strands of his long, dark-grey hair poking at random from beneath his hat, his large black-rimmed spectacles and his rather short figure, he looked like a comedian's imitation of Sherlock Holmes as he descended the stairs.

Eager for the excitements that lay ahead, he said farewell to Sergeant Cockfield (pronounced Cofield) in the Control Room and walked into the evening air with a sense of impending destiny. He *knew* he was only hours away from being recorded in history as the man who had confirmed the existence of the legendary Giant's Trough of Trippingdale.

2

Millicent Pluke always drove the family car because Montague's driving ability was regarded by his police colleagues as incompetent and dangerous. According to a police driving instructor who had once attempted to guide Montague through a special test, he lacked co-ordination between limbs and brain when behind a steering wheel. He had no concept of planning a route, especially one involving one-way streets and pedestrian crossings, he was unable to anticipate dangers or hazards on the highway and he could not distinguish between top gear and bottom. He did not know his offside from his nearside, his reversing manoeuvres were unknown to modern science and did not appear in any driving manual and he was, at all times, a danger to other road users. This was particularly so when he was trying to negotiate traffic lights or turn right from a main carriageway. In spite of these deficiencies, he had managed to pass a civilian driving test, although that had been many years ago.

Whenever he attempted to drive police transport, however, none of his colleagues would accompany him and this situation was not considered conducive to good and efficient police work. Without doubt, it was disadvantageous when investigating crime and so it had been decreed from on high that someone should act as a driver for Detective Inspector Pluke whenever he was on police duty.

Having survived Montague's driving techniques over the years, Millicent Pluke had eventually thought it sensible to adopt a similar system during his off-duty moments. She became his regular driver and having such capable persons to drive him did, in Pluke's mind, elevate him above the normal strata of society. After all, the Queen was driven by others, as were people like the Prime Minister, foreign potentates, military commanders and leaders of industry. In Pluke's opinion it seemed only right that a person of his prestige should have a driver. It meant he could concentrate on things far more important than gear levers, brakes and steering wheels, and it also meant he could maintain the highest levels of observation from his vehicle. His legendary vigilance for lawbreakers would not be diluted due to worries about winking indicators, hazard lights, other people's brake lights, tyre pressures, motorway regulations, unstaffed railway crossings, wobbly cyclists and death-defying children who leapt off footpaths. It also meant he could look out for undiscovered horse troughs.

On this momentous Saturday morning, therefore, Millicent was his driver. Her task was to deliver him to Trippingdale Castle and everything went smoothly until they arrived at the ornate gatehouse, which formed the entrance to the parkland. The gatehouse was a curious structure comprising two identical towers each built of mellow limestone with a battlemented roof. Each had a series of windows, a door facing the roadway that ran between them and was linked to the other by a handsome carved stone arch, which spanned the highway beneath. The arch was large enough to admit a coach and four, or a medium-sized modern vehicle such as a van or small lorry.

Built into the walls that faced him during his approach were additional carved stones. They formed the distinctive shape of a giant horseshoe; the stone arch was part of that image but Pluke realised the horseshoe was upside down. The points should aim skywards otherwise the good luck would run out. But had this huge horseshoe given rise to the legend of the giant of Trippingdale and his equally massive horse? If so, it was perfectly logical that a giant horse of this size would require an enormous drinking trough.

High walls led from each of the towers to

surround this part of the estate; the immediate effect was to remind Pluke of a prison gate and compound. However, those two towers formed one house – the living quarters were in the left tower as one approached from the public side and the sleeping quarters on the right-hand side. In stone letters across the archway was the legend 'Good Luck with Honour', the motto of the Gallholme family. Bolted to the left-hand tower was a large white-painted notice with black lettering; it said 'Trippingdale Estate. Private Property. Keep Out'. A large green gate blocked the road ahead of them and as Millicent eased to a halt before it, a big, angry-looking man appeared from the tower on the left and an equally big and angry woman emerged from the other. Both Millicent and Pluke lowered their windows to speak to the gatekeepers; Pluke thought they were like those weather-forecasting models, one living in one house and the other in the other. Mr Wet and Mrs Dry, or was it Mr Storm and Mrs Fair?

'You can't go through this gate!' the man called. 'It's private property. Can't you read?'

'I have permission,' countered Pluke, whose subservient and somewhat reticent appearance concealed a powerful but submerged determination.

'They all say that, folks that come at week-

26

ends. Nobody has permission,' retorted the man, at which the big woman disappeared indoors leaving him to deal with these potential trespassers. Clearly, the fellow had no idea that Pluke was a senior police officer.

'I have *written* permission.' Pluke now decided to confront the fellow. In his famous overcoat and panama, he stepped out of the car and fished the necessary permit from his pocket. 'Here.' He flourished the piece of paper beneath the nose of the red-faced ogre, a thickset, powerful, black-haired fellow in his sixties. He towered more than six feet high and sported thick arms with hands like shovels.

The man took the paper and read it. 'Nobody told me you were coming. Where did you get this?' he asked. 'It could be a forgery for all I know.'

'Check with your Estate Office,' demanded Pluke. 'I wrote to them and they supplied me with this document. It allows me unrestricted access to the whole of the parkland but my only intention at this stage is to visit the castle ruin.'

'Nobody ever tells me anything. It says here that Mr Pluke should be given access, it doesn't mention anybody else. You've a woman in the car, I see.'

'That is my wife. She will deliver me to my destination, then she will return. I shall remain for as long as it takes to achieve my purpose. Look, if you object to this official document you can check with your Estate Office,' Pluke repeated.

The man dithered for a moment, so Pluke continued, 'If you do not want my wife to take the car through I shall walk. Please contact your office for confirmation of the arrangements while we all wait here. I suggest you speak to Mr Stephen Gallholme; his signature is on my permit.'

'I can't say I agree with all this laxity, letting all and sundry into the parkland,' grumbled the man. 'But you can go. And your missus as well, just to drop you off. I've no authority to let two folks in when only one is mentioned. So she goes in on condition she comes straight back after leaving you there.'

'She will,' said Pluke. 'On my honour as an English gentleman. Then she will return here later in the day to collect me. I trust you will allow her access on that occasion too?'

'Either me or the missus will. She might be on the gate later. I like to go off on Saturday afternoons to watch football or cricket, whatever's being played. Crickledale cricket team are playing today, first game of the season.'

'Then I hope they win!' Pluke smiled.

'So what will you be doing at the castle?' asked the keeper, mellowing as he began to open the gate. 'Not dropping litter or lighting picnic fires, I hope.'

'I am seeking the Giant's Trough of Trippingdale,' Pluke informed him.

'It's there all right, bottomless they say and covered with briars and things. You can't see it for rubbish, you'd never know it was there unless you really looked. I don't know why you want to see it – it's old, neglected and never used. It's too big to shift and neither use nor ornament. It's an eyesore and dangerous, too, I'd say.'

'I am so pleased to be assured of its existence,' said Pluke, slightly dismayed that he hadn't actually discovered it for himself, but relieved that his mission was now very positive, not merely exploratory.

'Folks should keep away from it. The estate children have never played there, not for years. Warned off, they were, not that there's any children on the estate now. It should have a bomb put under it for all the good it is. It would make good crazy paving for somebody's garden.'

'If that is the trough I think it is then it is of major historic interest. I would have you know that I am Montague Pluke, author of works on Yorkshire horse troughs and an expert on horse troughs of every kind.' Pluke drew himself to his full height.

'Really?' The gatekeeper did not seem impressed.

'I wish to confirm its presence whatever its current state of preservation,' he went on. 'It is important that the trough is recorded for posterity whether it is bottomless or not.'

'And if the new master lets the public in to look at it, that'll mean more tourists and litter and cars and bonfires, and then we'll need toilets and picnic tables...' The other sighed, with the gate now open to its fullest extent.

'I shall treat the castle and its environs, including the trough, with the greatest respect,' Pluke assured him. 'You may come and check me, if you wish, Mr ... er...?'

'Pinder. Aaron Pinder. Gatekeeper to the estate for the past twenty-five years or more. I've got to be careful, you understand, my job's keeping trespassers out.'

'Of course, Mr Pinder. I am sure you do an excellent job. Now, we must be off. My wife has some urgent appointments in Crickledale so I must not detain her. How far is the castle?'

'A shade over a mile from here. The deserted village is another mile or so beyond that. There's just the one road through the parkland. You'll have to use it to come back but you can park beside the castle. You'll see a kissing gate. Park there.'

'My wife will return shortly, Mr Pinder, and I have a mobile telephone to call her when I require transport home.'

'I'll warn the wife,' said Pinder.

As they passed through the gate, Pluke was aware of Pinder's wife looking at them from the opposite side of the road. She was standing in the open doorway of that part of this peculiar cottage and she had a yellow duster in her hands. She was almost as large as her husband and equally formidable, a grey-haired sixty-something who looked as if she'd been an Olympic shot-putter. Pluke did wonder if she would really allow Millicent back into the dale. If this gatekeeping team turned awkward he could always walk to this gatehouse – a mile wasn't too far. After negotiating the narrow twisting lanes, however, Millicent eventually parked on a conveniently wide verge, switched off the engine and said, 'Well, Montague, there it is. Your castle.'

'Trippingdale Castle at last,' he breathed. 'It's like being allowed into deepest Tibet for the first time. So, Millicent, am I about to make history or not?'

'Well, from what that man said, it seems the trough is well known to the workers on the estate even if no one appreciates its historic role, but I am sure you are going to identify it as something very special and then record it for posterity, dear,' she said.

'Troughs of such eminence cannot be ignored!' he stated.

'Of course not. Now, I have placed a pick

and shovel in the boot, along with your hiking gear, flask of coffee, sandwiches, an apple and an orange, some secateurs, gardening gloves and your notebooks. They're all in the haversack. There's everything you need, whether for digging deep holes or cutting your way through undergrowth. Your mobile telephone is in the pocket of your greatcoat and so is your camera, with two spare films. And don't lose your letter of authority. It seems that this estate does not welcome visitors!'

'You do look after me, my dear.' He smiled as he prepared to disembark from the car. 'I shall be fine, I will spend the day here, searching with the utmost care. I'll see you later.'

'I have to go to the supermarket,' she said. 'And I promised I would join Mrs Mayweed for lunch, a long-standing promise to her. There is something she wishes to discuss, a matter of great confidence, she said. As you know, she has been proposed as the new president of the Ladies' Knitting Circle so perhaps she wants to discuss it with me before deciding whether or not to accept. I hear she is rather concerned about the duties it might carry. I get the impression she's not sure about undertaking another spell of rather heavy public responsibility.'

'So when shall I expect you?' he asked. 'I have no idea what kind of efforts I shall have to make, but I will need sufficient time for a sustained search and examination. That is, assuming the trough to which Pinder referred is the one I am seeking. There may be other troughs in this unexplored dale.'

'I have no wish to rush you, Montague. Shall we say four o'clock? It is just after ten now, so that gives you about six hours. You can always call me on your mobile if you finish early or need to stay longer. What will you do with the trough once you've confirmed its existence?'

'I don't think I shall be able to do anything with it, Millicent, it belongs to the estate. My task is merely to prove its existence and to determine its current state of repair, then I need to decide whether it is of special historic interest.' He went to the boot of his car, lifted out all his paraphernalia, put on his famous old overcoat and bade farewell to Millicent. 'I shall be over there,' he told her, pointing to the imposing ruin on its bleak hilltop site. 'When you return, you could either walk up to the castle and find me there, or pip the horn and I shall hear you. You might, of course, be keen to share my triumph.'

'I could always take a photograph of you beside the trough.' She smiled. 'When you've found it, that is. For the family album. So goodbye, Montague, and good troughing. See you later.'

'Goodbye, Millicent.'

He watched her drive away, soon passing out of sight among the walls and hedges. Quite suddenly, he was alone with his castle.

And then he was dismayed to observe a magpie as it flew across the field before him. It was a solitary bird, fluttering along on short wings with its long tail protruding behind, and in vain he sought a companion for it. But there was none. A single magpie. He thought of the old verse: 'One for sorrow, two for mirth, three for a wedding and four for a birth...' He spat on the ground, bowed towards the departing bird and crossed his fingers. All those instinctive actions were to avert any of the misfortunes threatened by the sight of the lone magpie. But it was an ominous sign, not the sort of thing anyone would wish for at the beginning of an enterprise of this magnitude. How he wished there'd been two magpies! Taking a deep breath and trusting that his counter-actions would repel the bird's bad luck, and that his crossed fingers would remove any hint of misfortune in his forthcoming venture, he placed the haversack on his shoulders, collected his pick and shovel and began to walk toward the distant castle. It was about a hundred and fifty yards away and he began his journey with his all-important right foot.

He saw the kissing gate that led into the

field. On the wall beside it was a large sign which said 'Trippingdale Estate. Private Property. Keep Out. Trespassers will be Prosecuted' but from the appearance of the wooden gate it seemed to be in regular use because there was a track across the field and it led towards the castle. The path was not a paved route, however, merely a muddy track, now dry, but its condition told him that people did walk regularly across the field and into the castle ruins. Estate workers, perhaps? Friends of the estate owner?

He wondered whether other people had been surreptitiously searching for the Giant's Trough of Trippingdale or whether the tracks were made by free-range ramblers intent on trespassing to the annoyance of the landowner, but sight of the well-used path did make him realise he might not be alone in this remote and deserted place.

As he surveyed the building ahead, he saw that Trippingdale Castle remained glorious and dramatic. Dating to the eleventh century, it was silhouetted against the bright morning sky and comprised four huge towers, one at each corner to form a large square. Each tower was linked to its neighbours on both sides by a high stone wall, which rose to a height of more than forty feet and was topped with battlements. Each of those walls was dotted with window openings at varying heights, indicating internal stairs or small rooms. For a castle that had not been maintained by English Heritage or any other formal authority, it was in surprisingly good condition considering its age, with all four walls mostly intact and each of the towers virtually complete except for their missing roofs. Weeds were flourishing in some of the fissures among the stones and small trees sprouted from the most unlikely places.

The main gate faced south, a graceful arched entrance in the centre of the wall. It lacked any doors and there was no formal route leading to it. Above the gate he noticed a coat of arms; it was carved in stone and very worn due to the weather but he could recognise three horseshoes arranged in a triangle, each with its points towards the sky. Underneath were the faded words 'Good Luck with Honour'.

The modest footpath led to that gate and as he approached he could see that the ground in the gateway itself was muddy, as if people or animals habitually congregated there. Drawing closer, he noticed that the interior floor area of the castle was grass-covered; cows had once grazed here, he thought, probably wandering in from the surrounding field, and there was no sign of a cobbled or stone courtyard. If there was one, it was probably under several inches of grass and earth. When he drew closer to the main gate, he saw that the entire castle was open to the elements; not a shred of roofing timber remained on the towers or the main building and he could hear the wind sighing through the exposed stonework as he walked into the imposing entrance. As he crossed the threshold a jackdaw flew from its perch. He saw it the moment it took flight. It launched itself from the mantelshelf of a stone-built medieval fireplace at the base of the south-west tower. With its distinctive *chackchack* call, it flew into the higher reaches of the tower, soared above the roofless heights, then vanished over the wall to take to the skies beyond. First, a single magpie – and now a single jackdaw! The omens were not at all good this morning.

But had the jackdaw come down the chimney into that fireplace? When a jackdaw comes down a chimney it is an omen of death, he realised with a shudder. Shivering in a sudden breath of chilly wind, he decided he must be extra careful where he placed his feet – there might be hidden wells or underground dungeons with rotten covers and if he tumbled down one of those, he might never be found alive. Was that the message of the jackdaw?

Jackdaws liked old buildings, he knew, but usually there was a colony where they made use of holes among the stones for their nests. Here there was just the one. It was most ominous. He felt himself grow cold as another shiver, a deep one, rippled down his spine while he peered into the gaunt and awesome ruin. The jackdaw called raucously from somewhere beyond his vision, the wind increased a fraction to sigh and moan through the exposed stones and, quite unexpectedly, the sky darkened as black clouds moved across in the strengthening breeze. The brave Montague Pluke felt just the tiniest tremor of fear, the irrational fear of something unknown or a deep sense of foreboding, but he told himself there was nothing here that could or should frighten him – detective inspectors must not be afraid.

After all, it was only a ruined castle, just a pile of old stones without a life of its own, jackdaw or no jackdaw. He decided he must not permit outside influences to deter him in his quest. He walked into the huge court-yard as the jackdaw returned to settle on a high wall to call down at him in defiance, then halted to allow his eyes to grow accustomed to the gloom and to acquaint himself with his shadowed surroundings. The far corners of the interior were lost in the dark-ness; he wished he'd brought a torch. Had Millicent packed a torch, he wondered?

She hadn't mentioned it and besides,

who'd think you'd need a torch in broad daylight during a sunny day in May? But those far corners did seem as if no one had visited them for centuries. Looking at things logically, he thought that previous visitors probably had approached the castle via the route he'd taken – the track across the field told him so – but few appeared to have entered those ancient walls.

It seemed most had come as far as the gate, then stopped to look inside without venturing any further. While the corners of the castle were deep in gloom, the spacious centre of the vast courtyard was smothered beneath a massive tangle of briars and undergrowth comprising weeds, convolvulus, small trees and other assorted rubbish, which was several feet deep. The tangle covered a large area and appeared to be the result of countless years of unchecked growth. Among it all he could even discern some fallen roofing joists, stones and beams. The entire place looked like a medieval rubbish dump, the accumulation of centuries, and not the sort of place to welcome visitors.

When he looked more closely at the robust tangle before him he could discern some recent tracks across it. Pinder had said the trough was under such a tangle but most of it consisted of a very dense matting of briars at least four feet deep or more and it looked as though people had stomped across parts of it, rather like they do when picking blackberries from bramble patches. They walk on top of the briars to crush them beneath their feet and this had apparently happened in several places. Judging by the way sections of the briars had been depressed, and taking into account the damage to fresh new shoots, it did appear as if someone had made a recent excursion into the depths of Trippingdale Castle.

Trough hunters, he wondered? Was the trough really under there? Or were the visitors mere tourists? Or trespassing ramblers?

The path across the tangle had not been cut, he noted. Maybe those tracks were left by fruit pickers after last season's brambling expeditions? Perhaps bramblers – estate workers probably – came to pick the rich crop this clump must surely produce?

Remaining in the framed gateway, Montague Pluke did not move any further into the depths until he had surveyed all before him. It was almost like studying the scene of a murder or serious crime, with the senior detective absorbing all the visual information prior to making any movement on to the site. And that is precisely what he was doing because he hoped no one was here, he hoped no one had sought the Giant's Trough ahead of him and, worse still, he hoped no one had tried to move it to another site or break it up for reconstruction elsewhere. But if the trough was as large as legend had led him to believe, no one could move it.

They'd never get it through that kissing gate or out of the castle gateway. Not even the entire complement of the Conqueror's horses could drag it away and there was no way a mobile crane or heavy lifting gear could gain access to the castle. He did not think anyone could have stolen the trough, although he did appreciate that very determined thieves could steal massive objects to sell to keen gardeners. Pinder had said it was still here and, if it was as large as legend suggested, then the castle might have been built around it. That suggested the trough was older than the castle. This being so, it was a true piece of history, yet it had never featured in any national survey, newspaper or magazine article – it was England's best-kept secret, the kind of special structure known to very few. But one could not be complacent.

Pluke had no private rights to this trough and he realised that, bearing in mind that others had tramped across the briars ahead of him, he must consider the possibility that there was some other interest in it, whether for commercial, academic or tourism reasons.

Alone with his thoughts in his position of surveillance, he could now distinguish more of the interior. His eyes had become accustomed to the gloom and he could make out a row of smaller buildings against the west wall. They were stone buildings with doors and some had windows. Several did bear their ancient tiled roofs. The tiles were made of stone, he noted; they'd be worth a lot of money, he told himself but he was pleased they had so far evaded the unwelcome attention of thieves. The outer section of each tower appeared to be complete and there were window openings on every floor, although none of the towers had a roof. More than likely, every floor within them would have collapsed too, due to the effect of weather and age. Each had a doorway at its base, and he could see the beginnings of flights of stone stairs inside, but at this stage did not intend to venture into any of the towers. There were more buildings around the interior of the other walls, some in a derelict condition and others in a surprisingly good state of repair, although none had doors fitted. There were spaces for the doors so perhaps they had rotted due to the combined effect of the passage of time and the onslaught of the elements.

As he studied the spacious interior from this static position, though, he could not see any part of the famous horse trough. In fact, he could not see any part of any horse trough. The place appeared to be a horse trough desert.

Pluke felt that was rather odd because a castle of this size would surely have had its complement of horses along with stables, a smithy and several troughs – or one very large trough. Such water troughs would not be indoors – unless more recent generations had constructed those small buildings over the sites of ancient troughs. Those small buildings, he decided, might have served as stables in bygone times.

Somehow he felt this was unlikely – the little buildings looked the same age as the castle itself and were probably storerooms, ammunition shelters or even accommodation for the guards. In the centre of the courtyard, however, was that challenging, colossal and deep mass of briars, fortified by entangled weeds and other growths. There was even a hawthorn bush growing among it all and he noticed that the briars had grown high by climbing a structure. Then he saw, in the centre of the tangle, a stone pillar, which was barely discernible through the mass of stems and leaves. The briars had used it as a support. They grew all around it in dense clusters, which must have begun decades ago – it was a true wild paradise, especially for bramble pickers. This was

precisely the kind of problem he'd antici-
pated, hence the secateurs and gardening
gloves among his carefully assembled
trough-hunting kit. It would be like trekking
through a jungle looking for a lost tribe, he
thought. But there was no sign of the horse
trough that Pinder had said was here.

As Pluke studied the trough-concealing
wilderness of briars and undergrowth he
pondered the purpose of the stone tower. It
looked like a centrepiece of the castle interior so he decided to make a closer
inspection.

The small tower had an edifice on top and
as he tried to identify the design through the
mass of leaves and branches clinging to it he
realised it was a sculpture consisting of
three horseshoes. They were standing in a
close triangular group, each touching the
others as their horns pointed skywards in
the traditional manner. Clearly, good luck
symbols were important to this estate.

It was while thinking these thoughts that
Pluke felt a growing excitement because, he
reasoned, the tower might be the ornamental centrepiece of the giant trough. It
might even be a former fountain but, from
his position, whatever lay around the foot of
the tower was totally concealed. Centuries
of briars obliterated everything, but removal
of the tangle would present no problem,
thanks to the gardening gloves and pair of

secateurs Millicent used for pruning her roses. Early explorers had hacked their way through jungles with far less equipment than this and he would take as long as necessary to finish his task.

Having completed that all-important initial assessment of the scene, he decided he should venture along one of the routes already evident among the entanglement. He hoped it might lead him closer to the stone tower. Leaving his pick and shovel against the wall of the gateway, therefore, he began his precarious, thorn-ridden trek across the deep layer of briars. It was like walking upon a bed of thorny springs with spikes catching the skirts of his coat and snagging his trousers as he manoeuvred himself between the waist-high garden of thorns and foliage.

The route took him to the left of the tower along a semicircular path and then moved around to the rear. He was delighted to discover the track turned towards the tower. He followed it until it reached what looked like a stone wall, which ran in front of the tower, a wall about three feet high and some distance away. Then he halted. There was a pair of human feet ahead of him. The ankles were resting on the wall and the toes were pointing towards the ground ... well, not feet exactly, but boots: riding boots. Their soles were towards him and the boots were sloping downwards beyond the wall, so much so that he could not see their tops. It was almost as if someone had hung up the boots by their toes, leaving them there to drain or dry. But they couldn't remain in such a position without some support. He moved forward, ever so carefully now, crunching the stems beneath his feet and cracking the thorns that dared to wrestle with his own footwear and clothing.

As he moved closer he was alarmed by a snorting sound. In the hushed atmosphere, childhood memories and inbuilt fears came flooding back as the unexpected noise made his hair stand on end. It had come from behind him. He whirled around to see a horse standing in front of one of the small buildings. It was untethered but wore a bridle and saddle. It lifted and lowered its head repeatedly, whinnying nervously as he looked at it. Then it began to trot towards him, but halted after a few strides to stand expectantly at the edge of the briar patch. It was a handsome chestnut-brown gelding with a white diamond pattern on its forehead, a beautiful black mane and black tail. A Cleveland Bay. Then it pawed the ground with its right forefoot as it looked at him, whinnying all the time.

'Steady boy,' he said, wondering if those words sounded sufficiently like horse talk to calm the animal, but the sound of his voice did have some effect. The horse stopped pawing the ground and ceased its whinnying, then trotted around in a circle to return to the same place. It halted to look at Pluke as if expecting him to do something. Those boots must be somehow associated with this horse, Pluke told himself. But why would anyone suspend a pair of riding boots over the side of a wall like that? And especially a wall smothered with centuries of thick briars in the middle of an old castle courtyard.

'Stay, boy,' he said to the horse, thinking that was more like the command one gave to a sheepdog and, rather surprisingly, the horse did not move. It continued to watch him with its head going up and down as if saying, 'You're doing all right, Mr Pluke. Just keep looking...'

'Are these your owner's boots?' he asked the horse, while edging yet closer to them.

But before he reached the soles he realised there was someone in the boots. It was a human figure, a man or a woman dressed in riding gear comprising a dark velvet jacket and light-coloured jodhpurs. He or she was lying at the far side of the narrow wall, with his or her feet on the top of it. Worse still, Pluke could now see that his or her head was under several feet of water.

The head was towards the pillar of the horseshoe tower, the hands were out of sight and there were no air bubbles in the water.

Pluke realised he had found the Giant's Trough of Trippingdale.

The problem was that it contained a human body.

3

During those first micro-seconds of dreadful realisation Pluke did not know whether the person was dead or alive, man or woman, black or white, old or young, or whether the tragedy was the result of murder, suicide or accident. If only that horse could talk. It was still watching Pluke with its ears erect and head bobbing up and down, and its harness jangling. So had the horse thrown its rider?

The position of the body did suggest it could have stopped sufficiently suddenly to pitch its rider headlong into the trough. Or had the horse unexpectedly lowered its head to drink, so that the surprised rider had somehow slithered forward head first, dropping off the animal's front end rather like an otter skidding down its slide on the river bank? Upon reflection, though, that seemed unlikely because the horse would hardly be able to reach the edge of the trough due to the depth of briars; a man might walk along the surface of the entanglement, but not a horse.

It did look as if he or she had hit the water head first at high speed, rather like a torpedo or someone sliding down a chute in a swimming pool, but in this case it had been done while fully dressed. The feet had ended the zooming effect when the toes caught the edge of the trough to halt the forward rush.

Pluke did not think the casualty had collided head first with the stone pillar with the horseshoes on top – it was too far away. Nonetheless, a head-on collision with it could have knocked out the victim, and then he or she might have rebounded to this position and drowned while unconscious.

A crash helmet, the sort riders wear, should have prevented severe head injury but it might not have prevented unconsciousness followed by drowning.

At first sight, thought Pluke, this seemed to be a terrible accident. As a detective of enormous experience, the fact that it had all the appearances of an accident meant his subsequent actions were much easier and infinitely more simplified than those necessary to deal with a suspicious death. For example, he could move the body without worrying too much about destroying any evidence of wrongdoing. If this had been a murder, the body would have had to remain in situ until the forensic and pathology experts had examined it. But then it dawned upon Pluke that, in spite of the absence of air bubbles from the nose or mouth, the person might still be alive. People could survive for long periods in very cold water, even when they were not breathing. And his priority, as a police officer, was to save life. He must act quickly and with great precision.

All these thoughts flashed through his razor-sharp brain in the smallest fraction of a second and, within an instant, he was standing beside the body and doing his best to haul it out of the water. The first task was to extricate the head so that the nose could absorb some air, but from his position outside the wall of the trough he could not gain sufficient leverage. The helmet-covered head was too far away; he couldn't reach it. It meant he had to climb into the trough. But didn't legend say it was bottomless? And there was the old superstition that one should never save a drowning person – if the water wanted a victim it would have one. If you saved a person from drowning, the water would take its revenge by claiming you.

Pluke knew that lots of people had drowned while saving others; that superstition was not without foundation. But he was a police officer, sworn to do his duty, and part of that duty was to save life ... but should he, a very senior officer, risk his own life to save someone who might already be dead? He peered into the cold depths to see if there was a floor of any kind. After all, the horseshoe-topped tower must be standing on something. From this distance it was impossible to see whether or not the central area was bottomless but close to the rim where he stood, he could see what appeared to be a wide stone ledge or base directly below him. It was just inside the wall. In spite of the blackness of the evil-looking water, he could see it was wide enough for him to stand on and it seemed about waist deep. He could hang on to the wall with one hand as he hoisted the still form from its watery grave.

With immense bravery, therefore, and wasting not a fraction of a second, Pluke threw off his heavy overcoat, shinned over the rim of the trough and lowered himself into the filthy, icy, foul-smelling cold water. It rose to his waist and took his breath away; he seemed to be sinking too far and for a fleeting second wondered if he was going to drown. Then, thankfully, his feet met solid ground. Even though he had learnt to swim as a young constable, he found himself ter-rified and so he hung on to the rim with all his strength as he reached towards the person's head. Holding the rim with one hand, he managed to seize the clothing behind the head with the other, then lifted. Fortunately, neither the head nor the upper torso was tangled in the briars that flourished beneath the surface and up it came with foul and dirty water running from the clothing and helmet.

It was a man, Pluke noted in those moments.

Finding superhuman strength from somewhere, he manhandled the body towards the edge of the massive trough and managed to heave it on to the rim, where it rested with the head at one side and the feet still in the water. As the horse became increasingly restless, Pluke toppled the body over the wall so that it came to rest on the thick carpet of briars. Even now, the animal did not venture on to the covering of briars but neighed and whinnied as it began to trot around the courtyard.

Pluke could see that the casualty was a very tall man in riding gear complete with black crash helmet, riding boots, black velvet jacket and white jodhpurs. Sadly, he looked very dead. Nonetheless, Pluke had to see if breathing was possible; a spot of artificial respiration and a kiss of life were necessary. He clambered out of the water, still wondering if parts of this trough were bottomless, then placed his beloved old coat on the flexible carpet of briars. He hoisted the body on to it, rolled it into a firm position for artificial respiration, loosened the clothing and helmet, and with all his might began to pump the man's chest and, despite the touch of froth around the mouth and nostrils, tried to apply the kiss of life as taught by the very best of the rather old first aid manuals. But the body was so wet, dirty, cold and smelly, so lifeless. True, there was no rigor mortis but that could mean he had either died recently or more than thirty-six hours ago. But in the hope that there was still a flicker of life in this chilly body Pluke worked at his respiration techniques for a long time, before eventually having to admit defeat.

This man was not breathing; not a whisper of breath came from his body. He had drowned in this magnificent and historic horse trough.

Perspiring from his unproductive activities, Pluke decided to call an ambulance. Although the ambulance service would not remove a dead body, Pluke would insist that the man might be alive and in need of emergency treatment with the attention of skilled paramedics or a doctor. By that ruse the body would be removed from the scene and it would reach hospital where the fellow would receive life-saving treatment even if he was beyond recovery. Pluke decided first to inform Sergeant Cockfield (pronounced Cofield) in the Control Room; he would instruct the sergeant to call the ambulance as a matter of urgency and also to despatch a uniformed police officer to the scene as a 'sudden death' report would have to be completed. On his mobile telephone he punched out the number for Crickledale Police Station. It was just like being at work – but unfortunately the excitement of discovering the huge and legendary horse trough had been diminished in the face of his professional responsibility.

'Pluke speaking, Sergeant,' he said when Sergeant Cockfield (pronounced Cofield) answered. 'I'm with a man who has apparently drowned in the horse trough at Trippingdale Castle; I need an ambulance urgently. I'll continue with artificial respiration; there may be a chance of life although to be frank I am sure he is dead. I don't think he's been in the trough very long. The ambulance crew will have to walk from the road into the castle, there's no access for vehicles. And the presence of a police officer is needed to compile a sudden-death report.'

'No sooner said than done, sir,' said Cockfield (pronounced Cofield), knowing better than to waste time asking for unnecessary details. 'What about a doctor?'

'You could arrange for one to be standing by in Casualty when the ambulance arrives.'

'Yes, sir.' The sergeant disconnected the call, used the internal line to telephone Crickledale ambulance service and within seconds they were *en route*. By chance,

55

Detective Sergeant Wayne Wain was in the Control Room when Pluke called.

'This could be one for you, Wayne,' said Cockfield (pronounced Cofield). 'Pluke's found a body.'

'I don't believe it! He took some leave to go looking for a horse trough, not to go finding bodies.'

'Well, it seems he's found his horse trough and it's got a body in it. It's at Trippingdale Castle and it looks like a drowning. The body's not been there long in his opinion so there might be a chance of life. He says he'll continue with artificial respiration. The ambulance will have oxygen on board so that might bring him round.'

'It's not murder, is it?' asked Wayne Wain.

'He didn't suggest anything like that although he did ask for a police presence.'

'That's routine for any sudden death. I wonder if this is something more sinister? How can anyone drown in a horse trough?' asked Wain. 'OK, I'll go and have a look.'

'You?'

'Why not? There's nothing else happening. And I'll take Detective Constable Helston. If it's a routine sudden death we can always hand it over to uniform.'

Within minutes the tall, dark and handsome Detective Sergeant Wayne Wain, with the delectable and desirable Detective Constable Paula Helston at his side, was hurtling through the peaceful Yorkshire countryside towards Trippingdale. Wain knew the way – in recent days he'd tolerated Pluke's constant effusions about its significance in trough history.

Wayne Wain spent the journey trying to visualise the means by which someone could drown in a horse trough, and his detective acumen was at fever pitch by the time he and Paula reached the imposing horseshoe-embellished double-towered gatehouse. In their unmarked car, they arrived immediately behind the ambulance. Wayne could see that the gatekeeper was having an animated conversation with the ambulance driver but after some loud and frantic shouting, accompanied by a great deal of energetic arm-waving, he allowed the ambulance through. Rather than waste time explaining his presence to the gatekeeper, Wayne Wain followed directly behind. Aaron Pinder waved his arms and shouted for him to stop, yelling that it was private property and they were trespassing, and they hadn't got permission, but Wayne ignored him and drove on, saying to Paula, 'We're police officers; we don't have to explain ourselves to job's-worths in this kind of emergency!'

'He doesn't know that, Sergeant,' she said sweetly. 'It's an unmarked car and we're not in uniform.'

'It's too late now,' was his response as he

accelerated to maintain his close position behind the speeding ambulance. With blue light flashing, it threatened to leave them but soon both vehicles were halting near the kissing gate below the castle.

At the sound of their arrival the dishevelled, smelly and coatless figure of Montague Pluke, with his trousers dripping wet and clinging to his legs, appeared in front of the castle. He waved his panama at them. 'Over here!' he called, his voice sounding faint on the strengthening wind and his hair waving around like stalks of barley in a gale.

The ambulance men opened their rear doors and seized a stretcher, a portable defibrillator and an oxygen cylinder. With these encumbrances they managed to negotiate the kissing gate and began to run up the hill towards the castle. Wayne did likewise, with Paula lagging behind; she was no match for the ultra-fit, squash-playing fitness freak that was Wayne Wain.

'Through there.' Pluke directed the ambulance men into the castle courtyard.

As they hurried around to the far side, with Wayne and the panting Paula forming a small procession behind Pluke and the others, Wayne saw the horse. Surprisingly, it had not wandered away. It seemed content to linger within the confines of the castle. 'Yours, sir?' he asked, not in the least out of breath.

'It is not my horse, Detective Sergeant Wain!' snapped the breathless Pluke. 'It is possible that it belongs to our casualty. It may be our only witness to this unfortunate occurrence.'

'I'll call the Mounted Section to come and interview it, shall I?' Wayne Wain chuckled. 'And we can get a statement straight from the horse's mouth.'

'This is no time for undue hilarity, Detective Sergeant Wain,' chided Pluke. 'I am saying that horse is a witness just as these four silent walls are witnesses and they're saying nothing. But they could reveal vital forensic clues, Detective Sergeant, as you should know. And we have a dead man here, so we need to display a little decorum and respect.'

'I thought he might just be alive – the ambulance, you understand...'

'I doubt it, but let us see what our paramedic friends think.' Pluke led his team of officers to the place where the body rested on his overcoat. The horse was still there, standing patiently in the background with its head hung low, observing events as if considering everything that was happening. Pluke wondered if it knew the man was dead. Some animals did have a sense about such things, but did horses?

'Too late,' said one of the paramedics after briefly examining the man. 'Much too late.

He's been dead some time, Mr Pluke, a few hours, I'd say. Drowned, by the look of it, but you'll need a doctor to certify that.'

'But you will take him to Casualty, won't you? An emergency admission?'

'No way, Mr Pluke, he's been dead too long for that. It'll be more than our jobs are worth to carry this corpse in our ambulance. Ambulances are for living folks, hearses are for bodies. You need a hearse or one of your own shell coffins. Sorry, but rules are rules. Come on, George. There's nothing we can do here.'

Thinking his mission was being plagued by a succession of job'sworth types, Pluke watched in some disbelief and much dismay as the pair packed up their equipment, turned their backs on him and walked away.

'Sorry we couldn't save this one, Mr Pluke, but he's too far gone,' was George's parting comment.

'Well, Detective Sergeant Wain.' Pluke never addressed subordinates by their first names, although he did sometimes make an exception with the sergeant because his forename and surname sounded so alike. 'It looks as though you will have to arrange for the removal of this body. I'm not on duty. I'm on leave, remember.'

'Me, sir? Routine sudden deaths are jobs for the uniform branch. We do the tricky ones.'

60

'We are all police officers, Detective Sergeant Wain, whether or not we wear the uniform. Happily, I have my mobile telephone, you can use that. Perhaps a situation report to the Control Room? You'll need to arrange a shell in which to place the body, then you must call a doctor to come to the scene to certify death before the body is moved and then you should telephone the coroner to say we are dealing with a sudden death for which a post-mortem will surely be necessary. I doubt very much if any doctor could or would certify the cause of death in these circumstances.'

'I came only because Sergeant Cockfield (pronounced Cofield) said you'd found a drowned man in a horse trough, sir, and I couldn't see how a man could drown in such a small container.'

'So you suspected something suspicious and came along, like a good detective?'

'Yes, sir.'

'Well done. That shows sound initiative.'

'But I see no trough, sir.'

'Detective Sergeant Wain, and you, Detective Constable Helston. Take a look at that wall behind the body. That is no ordinary wall; that is one rim of a gigantic horse trough. Examine it carefully. Then you will know why I was so keen to come here in my off-duty moments. This is a trough of staggering proportions, a wonder of the world, a true part of our heritage.' And with the body lying nearby on his old coat, Pluke showed Wayne and Paula the rim of the trough. Three feet high, some thirty feet long by fifteen feet wide, they could just discern the length and breadth of the enormous rectangular trough through its smothering covering of briars and undergrowth. They could also see that it was full to the brim with the dirty water of countless decades, water which was now giving off a ghastly smell because it had been stirred and activated by Pluke's actions.

'It has always been said the trough is bottomless, but I think that is pure fallacy,' Pluke said. 'There is a central ornamental tower, which must have foundations and I did rest my feet on some kind of base inside the wall. Nonetheless, the water is at least three feet deep, perhaps more. It is claimed that forty-eight horses can drink at one and the same time from this trough, Wayne, a legend that dates from the time of William the Conqueror.'

'It's very old then, sir?'

'Old and big. This is Britain's biggest horse trough, the famous Trough of Trippingdale, the Giant's Trough.'

'It's like a swimming pool, sir,' Wain breathed. 'So how did you find the casualty here? Now I *can* understand someone drowning in a pool of this size, especially with all those briars and weeds to snag them and hold them under the water. You say you think this man fell in? But what has the horse got to do with all this? And who is the dead man?'

Taking a few steps back from the rim of the trough, and standing on solid earth instead of the briary cushion, Pluke told Wayne and Paula how he had come to find the body and then explained his theories about how the fellow came to be head first in the trough with his feet on the top of the rim. He added that he had not touched the horse; if he'd attempted to approach it, he felt the animal might have fled the scene. Both detectives listened carefully as he provided his account.

When Pluke had concluded, Paula said, 'With all due respect, sir, I don't think this is a riding accident.'

'Oh, really, Detective Constable Helston, and why do you come to that conclusion?'

'No experienced rider would leave his horse untethered like this, sir. If the rider had dismounted with the intention of staying here, even for a short while, he'd have tethered the horse with a head collar, not the reins like they do in films. And if he'd intended staying a longer time he'd have loosened the saddle girth, too. In this case, none of that has been done. The reins are draped across the horse's neck, just as if the man had dismounted momentarily. If the horse had thrown him off, or if he'd fallen off, you'd expect the reins to be dangling or in some kind of disarray. But they're not. Besides, dangling reins are dangerous to the horse; it could get its legs caught in them. If the man had fallen off or been thrown, the horse could not replace the reins in this position, sir, and you did not touch them. It seems to me that the rider dismounted in a perfectly ordinary way, perhaps to come across to the trough to look closer at something. Even if he'd done that only for a brief moment, he would have retained a hold on the reins, for safety reasons, that is, and to stop the horse wandering.'

'Would the horse walk into those briars?' asked Wayne Wain. 'I can't imagine anyone trying to persuade a horse to do that.'

'I'd have thought not,' considered Pluke. 'No rider would risk damaging his horse's legs. Apart from any likely injuries from the briars, you can't see what lies under them where they cover the ground. There could be potholes and all sorts of dangers. But with long arms and long reins, our man could have approached very close to the trough while leaving the horse on the circumference of the briars. In my mind that would suggest something had caused him to release his hold of the reins after dismounting.'

'In that case, sir, someone has replaced the reins,' said Paula. 'How else would they come to be over the horse's neck?'

'We are saying there was another person, here, are we?' whispered Pluke.

'It does seem a logical explanation,' admitted Wayne Wain. 'And if that was the case, it might explain how he came to be head first in the water.'

'Go on,' invited Pluke.

'Well, if he was standing close to the rim of the trough, it's hardly likely he would suddenly topple over and fall in,' continued Wayne. 'And if he did fall in or stumble for any reason, you'd think he would be able to recover sufficiently to extricate himself before pitching in. And even if he did fall in you'd think he'd be able to climb out. You go in and out at the same point, sir.'

'I agree with that assessment, sir,' chipped in Paula.

'You said his head was lying towards the centrepiece, sir, with his ankles on the rim of the trough?'

'He was.'

'But that doesn't sound possible, sir, not if he fell in. And was he tangled up in the weeds?' asked Wayne Wain. 'When you extricated him from the water, I mean. Was he held down by briars and weeds?'

'No, he was not.' Pluke began to ponder the situation anew at this point. 'He was just

65

lying there on the surface weeds, which had sunk with him on top of them. I must admit that I rushed into things. My first thought was to rescue him and save his life. I did think he might still be alive.'

'So he wasn't drowned through being caught in the weeds. The paramedics felt he had been in the water for some time, sir,' Wayne Wain reminded Pluke.

'I think so too. So if he did not fall off his horse and was not thrown from it, how did he come to be in the water in such a peculiar position?' Pluke was talking softly now, almost addressing himself with a new set of questions. 'And there was another person here, we think, someone who replaced those reins, so did that person cause him to be in the trough?'

'A veritable puzzle for us, sir,' agreed Wayne Wain.

'Then we must rethink the whole situation. Let us look at this scenario,' suggested Pluke. 'He dismounts from his horse, comes to the side of the trough to look at something, say the central tower, while retaining a hold on the reins. Perhaps the other person persuaded him to approach the side of the trough to look at something? The reins have a long reach so the horse does not venture on to the tangle of briars. The man is then struck heavily on the back of the head, either with or without a blunt instrument of some kind. The effect is to topple him into the trough or, of course, he might have been pushed or forced into the water. Whatever happened to him, he released the reins but, once in the water, he is held down in some way ... something powerful, other than the weeds, stopped him from getting out.'

'There'll be marks on him if that happened, sir,' said Wayne Wain.

'He is wearing a riding helmet, sir,' added Paula. 'Maybe that would prevent injury if he was attacked and the fact he is still wearing it might mean there are no marks on his head...'

'There could still be bruising. But we need a post-mortem,' said Pluke. 'And in view of our reappraisal of the possible circumstances, I think we need to have our experts examine the scene, and the body before we move it any further. I am not happy with things now that we have reconsidered the matter and I thank you both for your contribution. On reflection, it is a great blessing those ambulance men refused to take him away. I fear we could have a mysterious and suspicious death here. I shall treat this as a murder investigation until the contrary is proved.'

'So who is he and how did he get here?' pondered Wayne Wain.

'We do not know but I am assuming he

arrived on that horse,' said Pluke.

'It might be the attacker's horse, sir.' Wayne Wain smiled.

'It might not belong to either of them,' added Paula, who continued, 'you can't get a horse through that kissing gate, sir, nor would any horse be able to leap those drystone walls, they're too high. The presence of a saddled-up horse means there must be another route into this field, another way to this castle.'

'I am sure there must be. It will surely come through the Hall grounds. The Hall is some distance from the gatehouse, a mile at least,' admitted Pluke, adding, 'but such a route would not be used by strangers, would it? Strangers would use the route we took, through the gates into the parkland – that's if they could get past that gatekeeper. If the deceased man used another route it suggests he knew his way around the place. He might be an estate worker, for example. But that is a matter for our investigative teams to determine.'

At that point Pluke, Wayne and Paula, having gravitated towards the castle entrance during their conversation, were shaken by an awesome shout from a large, tweedy, red-haired man who was puffing and panting as he climbed the field. He was heading rapidly in their direction. It was not the gatekeeper, they noted. 'Oi,' he shouted in a bellowing voice. 'What the hell do you think you are doing? This is private property ... now get out...'

'Leave this to me.' Pluke advanced towards the fellow. It was evident the man had no idea that a body was lying in the castle, or that those present were police officers.

'Right, out I said, all of you!' snapped the man, advancing towards Pluke. 'Clear off, we want no riff-raff here, no bloody ramblers claiming roaming rights, no tourists dropping litter, lighting fires and having picnics...'

'I am Detective Inspector Pluke, the officer in charge of Crickledale Criminal Investigation Department, and I have a letter of consent from this estate. It is signed by Mr Stephen Gallholme, the new owner. I was allowed here to seek the Giant's Trough of Trippingdale. I can produce the letter if you wish, it is in my overcoat pocket, inside the castle.'

'I know the name, I dealt with your permit. I didn't know you were in the Force. So who are these other people? They're trespassers. Your permit was for one person.' The man pointed to Wayne Wain and Paula Helston. 'They did not stop to explain themselves when our gateman requested it, but drove straight through without halting. It's no good saying you were with the ambulance, it's gone. It was a false alarm,

69

somebody fooling about by calling them, wasting their time and mine. The country's full of idiots now and I'll have you know this is private property...'

'And who are you?' asked Pluke.

'I am the Estate Manager. Broadbent is the name.'

'Basil Broadbent,' said Pluke. 'I recognise the name. We have spoken in the past on the telephone, Mr Broadbent.'

'Mebbe we have. I speak to all sorts of folks in my work. But what are these people doing here, Mr Pluke, and why did they not stop when requested?'

'Mr Broadbent, in my search for the trough I discovered a dead man inside it, drowned, so it would seem. I called the ambulance and the police – they came through your gates not many minutes ago; it was a genuine emergency. But we were too late. The man is dead. He is lying near the rim of the trough.'

'A drowned man?' Broadbent's attitude changed. 'Who is he?'

'That is what we must determine, Mr Broadbent, and then we must endeavour to discover how he died.'

'Then where is he?'

'He is lying on my coat at the far side of the trough, Mr Broadbent, out of sight from here behind all that growth of briars, which covers the trough. There is also a horse, fully saddled-up ... you can see it, over there in the shadows.'

'Oh, my God, it's Bayleaf. He'd never leave his horse loose like that...'

Without waiting for any further explanation, Broadbent raced past Pluke towards the animal, which turned and trotted away for a short distance.

Then Broadbent saw the body on Pluke's old coat. He dropped to his knees beside it and said, 'Oh, God, it is him ... it's the master...'

Pluke was at his side within seconds. 'The master?' he asked.

'My boss, Stephen Gallholme, the new owner of this estate.'

4

'The master rides Bayleaf at dawn every day.' Broadbent, his country-style clothing looking perfectly right for this setting, had recovered somewhat from the shock of finding his master dead and was now talking rationally to Pluke in one of the small shelters beneath the castle's west wall. He had managed to catch the loose horse and it was safe in another of them within the castle, secured by a length of rope he'd found hanging on a wall. His initial anger had subsided and he was trying to be helpful. Pluke and he had adjourned to the shelter, leaving Wayne and Paula to guard the body while awaiting the support services, the first of whom was expected shortly.

Broadbent was saying, 'I didn't see him this morning. He didn't come into the office at the time I'd have expected him – nine o'clock or so – but with it being Saturday that's not unusual. It never occurred to me he might be in trouble.'

'He hasn't been living here long, has he?' asked Pluke.

'Only three weeks or so, but he's no

stranger to Trippingdale, Mr Pluke. He was brought up here as a boy and young man, living in the Hall with his parents. Then, after university he went off to London to pursue his career as a financial consultant. His father died about twenty years ago and he continued to come home for the occasional weekend or sometimes for a longer break. His mother liked him to come to see her when he could get away from work.'

'Was he close to his mother?'

'Not particularly. She was a bit odd, eccentric and very superstitious – a difficult woman in many ways, bossy and determined to have her own way. She wouldn't listen to her son's ideas for improving things here; she didn't like change. She was like someone from the Middle Ages. He coped by keeping out of her way for most of the time.'

'But it was always assumed he'd come to live here when he inherited the estate, wasn't it? Is he an only child?'

'He is. Everyone knew he'd take up his responsibilities when she died or became incapable. He always said he would live in the Hall; he was determined not to run the estate from a distance. Since her death, he's been very much the new boy, Mr Pluke, learning to cope with his role, but I must say he's – was – a bright individual, quick to learn and to identify areas for improvement.

73

I'm so sorry this has happened, we were all expecting great things. He had some good ideas for modernising the estate and increasing its productivity by making use of our natural assets.'

'And you helped him settle in?'

'Yes, of course. It's in my interest to encourage him and to teach him as much as I can. He's my employer ... er ... was my employer. He was a nice man, Mr Pluke, a very nice man; all the estate workers liked him even if he was a bit on the quiet side. He got around and met them all. There was no snobbishness in him, not a scrap. It was his idea to open up the parkland, if only in a limited way at this stage, but I think he had plans for the castle, the deserted village and even the dale head. He saw it all as a potential money-spinner, tourists you understand, with school trips and things like archaeological surveys. It is a very historic site, the whole of our parkland.'

'That kind of progress is all right so long as it doesn't ruin the place.' Pluke smiled. 'Now, was he married?'

'Not at the moment, but he was in the past. There was a divorce five or six years ago, quite amicable, but with no children. I have his former wife's address in the office. She'll want to know about his death; they did keep in touch. Caroline is her name. But he came here alone, Mr Pluke, there's no live-in girlfriend or anything like that.'

'So how old is he?'

'Forty-two,' said Broadbent. 'I know that because I had some legal forms to fill in when he assumed responsibility for the estate.'

'And what about his horsemanship? Would you say he was accomplished?'

'Yes, he was. He brought Bayleaf with him, he was his favourite. Bayleaf would never throw him off, Mr Pluke, if that's what you are thinking, and Mr Stephen would never risk injury to his horse by leaving him untethered. I thought that very odd. So do you think this is more than an accident? With those detectives being here...'

'At this very early stage we are merely trying to find out what happened, Mr Broadbent. So what was a normal day for him? Or to be precise, what is a normal Saturday?'

'He hadn't really settled into a firm routine yet, Mr Pluke, being so new to us, but he did go riding at dawn, setting out at six o'clock or thereabouts. He said it was one way of getting around the land he owned, checking for things like blocked drains, damaged fences or walls and the like. Then he'd go home, attend to Bayleaf, have a shower and breakfast, and come into the office around nine. We'd deal with estate matters, with me taking him out as much as

I could to meet people with whom he would have dealings in the future.'

'You got on with him, did you?'

'I did, and very well too. He was a bit younger than me, ten years or so, but he was totally charming and likeable. I could have worked with him quite happily, I reckon he'd have been a very good boss and very good for the estate.'

'And Saturdays?'

'I work Saturday mornings, Mr Pluke, usually in the office. I like to get things tidied up for the weekend and found Saturday mornings were quiet enough to allow me to complete any outstanding work. My wife goes out to work too, on Saturdays, at a newsagent's in Crickledale, so it gives me something to do while she's away. He said he would do the same: come in on Saturday mornings at least until he got properly settled in. He'd take his morning ride and come into the office about nine; that's what he's done for the past two Saturdays. But I must admit I was not worried when he never turned up this morning. I just assumed he was having a morning off.'

'Did you see him go out at six?'

'No, I wasn't up then. Besides, I live in a cottage about a mile away from the Hall. There is no way I would be able to see his movements without actually going to the Hall.'

'The Estate Office is part of the Hall's complex of buildings, I believe?'

'Yes, it is. You can come and see the Hall and the entire complex if you wish.'

'I will do that later. So would anyone have seen him leave this morning?'

'I doubt it. Our cowman's at work early too but he's at Home Farm, nearly a mile away from the Hall. He'd not see Mr Stephen.'

'And no one lives in the Hall except him?'

'Right. There is a lady who goes in to clean and to prepare him an evening meal, Lily Preston. She's the widow of one of our retired workers and it gives her a bit of extra income. But she wouldn't be there at six this morning, Mr Pluke. Not being a Saturday.'

'Does she go in at six on weekdays?'

'No, not as early as that. She gets there about half past eight as a rule, to be given instructions by the master for her day's work. He sees to his own breakfast and always has a light lunch, which he does for himself. Soup and a roll, a ham sandwich and yoghurt, something like that. She'd never see him leave on his horse anyway, not even during the week.'

'I am very anxious to know when he was last seen alive, Mr Broadbent. We need to trace his movements, you see, and timings of those movements.'

'He was in the office yesterday evening,

77

Mr Pluke, around five thirty. Then he left to go home. He said he was going to have a night in, looking through estate files and then listening to some music. He was a big fan of Mozart. He said he would not be going out and he had no engagements last night, private or official. I can only assume he went to bed, then set off this morning for his daily ride, around six as usual. But I can't prove that, Mr Pluke, nor do I know anyone who can. You are at liberty to ask all the estate workers, of course, just in case some of them were out and about. I can give you their names and addresses.'

'I shall talk to them in due course and I shall conduct my preliminary investigation on the assumption that he did set off this morning for his daily ride on Bayleaf. If that did happen, as we believe, then it means he died some time after six this morning. I found him shortly after ten. It seems reasonable to assume he died within those hours.'

'It looks that way, Mr Pluke. So far as I know, he did not ride Bayleaf in the evenings. It was always during the early morning.'

'Thinking about his riding, there must be another way into the castle field, is there, Mr Broadbent? Other than the kissing gate? He'd never get his horse through that gate.'

'Yes, our own people, estate workers and

of course the owners, always use the back lane to reach the castle. It leads through the Hall grounds and emerges at the rear, then crosses the rising ground until it comes into the castle field. From there you've access to the surfaced road, which leads up to the dale head. Between the Hall and the castle, though, it's an unmade track, but it's suitable for horses and motor vehicles. A four-wheel drive would have no trouble and on a dry day, like today, a conventional car could use it. We've run cattle in the castle field in the past. We use other fields, too, and we alternate them, to stop the grass getting sour.'

'It would be helpful if our vehicles could use that route, we like them as close as possible to the centre of operations. But first I would like our Scenes of Crime officers and forensic scientists to examine the entire area around the castle. We shall seal off all routes for the time being. Now, did your master have enemies, Mr Broadbent?'

'I don't think he's been here long enough to make enemies, Mr Pluke, and I know of no one who resented his presence. It's not as if there was anyone who had a stronger claim to the estate – it was his and his alone. We all hoped he would marry and produce an heir. We like working for Trippingdale, you see.'

'So you can't think of anyone who might

have hated him sufficiently to kill him or who might benefit from his death?'

'I'm sure there's no one who would do such a thing to Mr Stephen. It must have been a terrible accident, surely?'

'We have to consider every possibility. Now, he is a very tall man, I notice,' said Pluke. 'Well over six foot and very slim. If his horse nudged him in the middle of the back while he was standing and looking into the trough, it might cause him to pitch headlong into the water, and if he was knocked unconscious in his fall he might then drown. That would be a tragic accident; a smaller man would hardly tumble forward over the rim of the trough in that way; a tiny man certainly would not,' considered Pluke. 'The height of the rim would prevent such an accident to a small or medium man, like me. It might be different for a very tall man, his centre of gravity would be higher. But let us suppose someone knocked him in. Let us say the horse did not butt him into the trough. I don't think it would venture on to the covering of briars. So let us consider it was the action of an enemy of some kind. It might be that he disturbed someone, perhaps – a trespasser, a poacher – or it could be someone who was waiting for him even, someone who knew he'd be there, who pushed him into the trough and held him under the water.'

'You *are* thinking of murder, aren't you?'

'We must consider every possible angle and we trust the post-mortem will help. It is most important, therefore, that we know of any incident in the recent past that might have some bearing on his death. I appreciate he has not been here very long but you, as one of the people closest to him, might have noticed something unusual, something different or out of the ordinary such as odd phone calls, indications of jealousy or anger, that sort of thing.'

Broadbent paused a moment, then said, 'He did get a strange letter last week, Mr Pluke. It went to his home at the Hall, not the Estate Office, but he brought it in to show me. It wasn't sinister by any means and most certainly it did not give either him or me any cause for concern. Curiosity, perhaps, but not concern. That's the only odd thing I can recall.'

'A letter? In what way was it odd, Mr Broadbent?'

'It contained a snowdrop, Mr Pluke. A dried one; pressed in fact. You know the sort that ladies used to do – they'd preserve. flowers by pressing them between the pages of a book, sometimes with tissue paper around them, sometimes without. This one was without. It was just a pressed snowdrop in a plain brown envelope bearing a second-class stamp, but with no message inside and nothing to indicate who had sent it.'

'Did he keep it, or the envelope?'

'No, he burnt them on his office fire.'

'Was it a single flower?'

'Yes, just the one.'

'In full bloom?'

'Yes, in full bloom, Mr Pluke.'

'And it went to his home, not his office?'

'Yes, is that significant in some way?'

'It is, Mr Broadbent. In recent weeks, several people in and around Crickledale have received identical missives, all posted locally in plain brown envelopes and all anonymous. All went to home addresses, not places of work or hotels. Around a dozen people received them. And they are the ones we know about, there may be others who have not reported the matter to the police.'

'But those people have not died, Mr Pluke, surely? Not all of them?'

'No, none as far as we are aware. Mr Gallholme is the first to die. His death means, however, that I am now very concerned about the others.'

'So what's it all about, Mr Pluke? Why send snowdrops to those people, or to Mr Stephen?'

'Snowdrops are out of season just now, Mr Broadbent, they die in March as a rule. So these are preserved flowers, but snowdrops nonetheless. You may or may not know that a single snowdrop in the house is considered a token of death, because the white flower looks very like the shroud that covers a corpse.'

'But surely the person who is sending these is sick … it doesn't make sense. I mean, if they believe this rubbish and if they have snowdrops in their own house...'

'They could have lots of snowdrops in their own house, Mr Broadbent. It is a single snowdrop that is a token of death, not a bunch of them.'

'So you're saying that someone has picked a stock of these flowers, dried them and is now sending these to people as a warning that they might die?'

'It looks that way, Mr Broadbent. Of course, not everyone who receives one will understand the message of the flower.'

'Which makes it worthless in their minds and therefore ineffective as a threat?'

'Yes, but if they start to ask around and talk to the older folk who know about these things, the message will be conveyed to them, albeit indirectly, and then it will create concern, Mr Broadbent, even in our modern society. After all, how many people like to think a witch doctor has stuck needles into a wax model of themselves and how many, even in this day and age, would like to know they have received what can be interpreted on the one hand as a death threat and on the other as a warning that they might soon die from natural causes? Make no mistake about it, Mr Broadbent, this is a death token; it has been received by your new master and now he is dead. Need I say more about the efficacy of this emblem?'

'I never thought I'd hear a modern detective inspector say a thing like that! So what are you going to do about the snowdrops? You're not going to waste police time and resources trying to seek out some little old lady with a bookcase full of pressed snowdrops and a dislike of certain people, are you? Not with a real killer to find?'

'I shall investigate whatever I feel is necessary,' said Pluke, who then added, 'Ah, I see the first of my support services has just come. Now we can get things moving.'

'Do you need me any more? I don't want to get in the way,' said Broadbent.'

'If you could remain a while, I would appreciate it,' answered Pluke. 'Among the people just arriving will be our forensic pathologist and he might want to ask you some questions about your master.'

'Right, I'll stay.'

Within minutes, the surrounds of the castle had become a hive of activity: Scenes of Crime officers, a doctor, police photographers, a pathologist and forensic scientists all appeared and Pluke's first task was to assemble them in some kind of order, away from the body, so that he could brief them about his discovery.

He gathered them just outside the gateway of the castle and stood on a stone mounting block to address them, while Bayleaf remained in his temporary stable, occasionally whinnying in his boredom. Wayne Wain, Paula Helston and Basil Broadbent stayed with the body as Pluke provided a lucid and very detailed account of what he had found.

Afterwards, the first formality was to have the body certified dead; it took but a few seconds with Dr Andrew Carruthers, the local GP, certifying that Gallholme was dead while adding he could not estimate the time or the cause of death. Pluke asked Wayne Wain to take a written statement of formal identification from Basil Broadbent and then the forensic pathologist, Dr Simon Meredith, began his work, with the police photographers taking both stills and video recordings of the examination. Pluke watched with deep interest.

Meredith worked in silence, beginning with a visual study of the body from a distance and following with a physical examination, testing for simple things like broken bones or obvious wounds from objects like knives or bullets. As he worked he quizzed Pluke about the position of the body as Pluke had found it, asking how much of it had been in the water, questioning the position of the arms, legs and ankles, and the whereabouts of the horse when Pluke had arrived, and finally asking if the body could be replaced in that original position with its feet on the rim of the trough and the head under the water.

Fortunately, Broadbent was not present to witness that unbecoming rearrangement of the corpse. He had been taken into another of the small buildings to make his statement to Wayne Wain and so he did not see what might be regarded as irreverence towards the deceased. But once Gallholme's cadaver had been replaced in a position as similar as possible to that in which Pluke had found it, it was photographed, videoed and examined with infinite care. Eventually, Meredith was satisfied and the body was hauled out of the trough and replaced on Pluke's old coat.

'What is the purpose of that large stone water container?' asked Meredith of Pluke. 'Is it a medieval water supply? A well of some kind? It's mighty large for a well!'

'That is probably the biggest horse trough in the world, Mr Meredith.' Pluke beamed. 'Certainly the biggest in Britain, the legendary Giant's Trough of Trippingdale, capable of watering forty-eight horses at one time.'

'So you think this fellow's horse somehow jettisoned its rider so that he flew head first into the water?'

'There are several possible explanations,' said Pluke. 'But in view of what I have learned this morning I am of the opinion that the fellow did not fall from his horse. I think he was murdered, Mr Meredith, forced into the water. He is very tall, as you will note, and I feel it is possible his head was forced under, perhaps while he was unconscious.'

'And what gives you that idea?'

Pluke explained about a rider's care and attention to his horse and also his theory that a tall man could be attacked from behind to finish up in the trough in the rather unlikely pose in which Gallholme had been found. Such a pose was unlikely to happen to a smaller person; a short person could not fall into the water due to the height of the surrounding rim. In Pluke's view a tall person could be made to overbalance and topple in by a severe blow from the rear.

'You could be right, Mr Pluke. There are marks on the sides of his neck, which cannot be readily explained. Now I shall begin to remove his clothes. Photographs and videos of my actions, please.'

He began by removing the riding helmet, raising the victim's head slightly as he loosened the strap and eased it away.

'The helmet will need to be examined, Mr

Pluke. For signs of attack, especially from the rear, fractured fibres, deposits in the fabric and so on.'

A Scenes of Crime officer came forward to take the helmet; he placed it in a plastic exhibit bag, labelled it and put it to one side for future examination. But Meredith was already looking at the back of the man's head, fingering it gingerly and peering at some marks, which were evident at each side of the neck.

'I think the back of his skull is broken at the base, Mr Pluke, in spite of the protection provided by the helmet. I suspect a blow to the lower part of the rear of the skull, a very severe blow indeed, close to the top of the spine. That is a most vulnerable area, even while wearing a riding helmet. Now, these marks ... see them?'

On the left of the neck, looking at it from the rear, just below the ear, Pluke could see an elongated bruise. Midway along it was a spot of blood, which marked a puncture wound, a small one. On the other side of the neck there was what appeared to be an identical mark, again with tiny skin wounds along its length.

'What do you make of those marks, Mr Pluke?'

'It looks as though there has been something very tight around his neck, Mr Meredith, hardly a starched collar in this day and age. A noose, do you think?'

'I don't think a noose would nick and puncture the skin in the way this has been done,' said Meredith. 'I think those nicks have been caused by something metallic, sharp and pointed, nicking the skin *en passant* as it were. Whatever it was, it was a tight fit and, if you look very closely, you'll see corresponding marks at the back of his neck as well as the sides. Not nicks, but bruises of the same width and caused by something of the same texture. Metallic, I'd say.'

'So the object was pressed on to his neck from behind, is that what you are saying, Mr Meredith?'

'That would equate with him being held under the water by something pressing down on his neck from the rear, Mr Pluke,' said Meredith. 'Something which was strong enough to keep his head down there in spite of his struggles – if he was not unconscious, that is.'

'You think he drowned?' asked Pluke.

'I'm sure of it,' agreed Meredith. 'Look at his hands. They've clutched at weeds and scraped along the bottom of the trough. There is some evidence of white foam around his nostrils and mouth. He was alive when he went in, Mr Pluke. I think you are right – I think he was attacked from behind, hit with considerable force at the back of the

89

head, which may or may not have rendered him unconscious but which was sufficiently powerful to knock him over the rim and push his face into the water. Then he was immediately held down or pushed deeper by some instrument that fitted around the neck...'

'Murder?' asked Pluke.

'Yes – although I qualify that by saying I must conduct a post-mortem in laboratory conditions, just to satisfy myself that death was due to drowning; if he was alive when he went in there will be water in the lungs and micro-organisms from this water. Diatoms they are called. If he was dead when he went in there will be no water or diatoms and we might have to consider some other cause of death. But yes, Mr Pluke, the preliminary indications are that he died from drowning, that he was forcibly held under the water and that he did not enter the trough by his own actions.'

'So am I seeking two murder weapons?' mused Pluke. 'Or just one? It seems one was used to strike him on the back of the head and another to hold him under the water ... that one must have required a long handle, mustn't it?'

'Like a hay-fork, Mr Pluke. A two-pronged hay-fork or straw-form, a pitchfork, a very common implement in this part of the countryside. That would fit this scenario, with another to strike him with like a walling hammer or sledgehammer.'

'Could just a single implement have been used?' asked Pluke. 'To knock him off balance and thrust him under, all in one sweeping movement?'

'That is very possible. I will bear it in mind, Mr Pluke, when I examine the body for injuries. If you do find any likely murder weapon or weapons, it might be possible to prove their involvement by evidence left on the riding helmet or his neck. Science can prove a lot, Mr Pluke, contact between two surfaces can be proved scientifically. Now, I must examine the rest of his body for injuries, then our forensic people will want to examine him *in situ* and after all that I shall conduct a post-mortem in my laboratory.'

'So are we looking for one murderer or two?' asked Pluke.

'I feel that one man could be capable of doing both deeds, Mr Pluke, one immediately following the other, provided he had both weapons close at hand. A quick surprise attack from behind with the sledgehammer might have knocked him into the trough; if not, it could render him unconscious or helpless for long enough for the killer to hoist him completely or partially over the side and then pin his head to the bottom with the hayfork. Or, of course, only

91

one weapon might have been used to deliver a very swift blow and then to pin him down beneath the water. Whatever he did use, Mr Pluke, I think this is the action of a single attacker.'

'Obviously a very strong man?'

'A very determined and rather skilful man and, I might suggest, aided by his strength. I'd say skill or deftness was more evident here, probably more of that than sheer strength.'

'An agricultural worker?' asked Pluke.

'Such people can be very skilled in man-oeuvring heavy weights and coping with powerful animals, Mr Pluke.'

'And one who knew the victim was here?'

'It looks like that, yes. The killer could have been waiting for the victim or he could have arranged a meeting here.'

'No accident then?'

'Not in my opinion, Mr Pluke.'

No further injuries were evident on Gall-holme's body, nor did his clothing reveal any further information at that early stage; Pluke realised, of course, that detailed examinations of both the naked corpse and its clothing in laboratory conditions might reveal additional evidence. As Simon Meredith was preparing to leave, Pluke addressed the small contingent of investigators and confirmed they were now involved in a murder investigation.

At this stage Broadbent returned, having completed his written statement and, upon being asked by Pluke, said there was a large room within the estate complex, which could be utilised as the Incident Room.

And so began Montague Pluke's investigation into the Giant's Trough Murder.

5

'So your leave has been cancelled, sir?'
Wayne Wain wondered if he could get back
to Pluke's office ahead of the Detective Inspector so that he might remove the bikini
blonde's photograph from Pluke's desk. He
and Pluke were waiting patiently in a corner
of the courtyard while, following the pathologist's examination, the forensic expert
studied the body. The Scenes of Crime
officers were already prepared for their
meticulous searching but likewise awaited
the forensic expert's comments in the hope
he could provide some kind of lead. Outside, teams of police had sealed off the
castle with yards of yellow tape but inside,
the central portion was a veritable hive of
activity.

Having managed to get past Pinder on the
gate, police vehicles had assembled in the
lane, although some had been directed
through Trippingdale Hall grounds. A
uniformed officer stood on guard near the
kissing gate to prevent unauthorised access.

'When I rang Headquarters to order the
call-out of CID teams, I volunteered to can-
cel my leave and to take charge of the

94

inquiry, Sergeant,' Pluke told Wayne. 'And the Chief Constable understood – not that I mind returning prematurely to work because I did find the object of my quest rather more quickly than I had expected. I must admit, though, I hadn't bargained for what it might contain.'

'It is hardly the sort of thing one likes to find on holiday, sir, except in crime novels.' Wayne Wain beamed.

'A police officer can never escape the heavy responsibilities, which are inseparable from the office of constable, Wayne. When all this is over I shall take my leave allocation and seek permission from the estate to clear all the vegetation from in and around the trough. I want to examine it in detail, to determine its method of construction and its age, and I need to photograph it and make sure it is recorded in all the learned and academic journals that feature items of archaeological and historic interest.'

'Our Task Force will clear the rubbish for you, sir.' Wayne smiled. 'They'll have to drain the trough to examine the bottom, if there is one, and they'll shift all those briars and that tangle of undergrowth covering the surface, to say nothing of draining the water. They'll save you hours of work – after all, it is part of their work on this investigation. With a bit of luck we might find the murder weapon as well.'

'I must take great care never to allow my leisure pursuits to impinge upon the responsibilities of duty, Sergeant; I cannot be seen to be taking advantage of police procedures to further my private academic interests, but most certainly we shall have to examine the bottom of the trough. As for getting the water out I don't suppose there is a plughole. Not many stone horse troughs, even those of conventional size, have plugholes.'

'Don't they, sir? I am not very knowledgeable about the finer points of horse trough design or construction.'

'I shall contact the Fire Brigade, Sergeant. They may regard the draining of this trough as a useful exercise for their officers and appliances. They are always keen to practise their drainage skills. Now let us consider our own strategy.'

'You have a plan, sir?'

'There is one matter that will provide a starting point for our enquiries, Sergeant. I refer to the anonymous letters containing preserved snowdrops.'

'I have studied the file, sir, but I did not view these incidents as a matter for the police. It's not as if there's an offence against the Post Office Act – snowdrops in the post can hardly be considered indecent, obscene or grossly offensive, nor can they be regarded as explosive devices or dangerous, noxious or deleterious substances.'

'I fear they *could* be considered offensive, Sergeant, in certain circumstances.'

'But there's no law that says it's illegal to post a snowdrop, pressed or otherwise. Sending flowers through the post is now big business, so how can a mailed snowdrop be offensive? They don't smell like garlic, do they? But are you suggesting those snowdrops have anything to do with this murder?'

'That is what we must determine, Sergeant. You must agree that it is odd that Mr Stephen Gallholme received such a snowdrop before he died.'

'Did he really? That is news to me. Are you saying there's something sinister about snowdrops in general, sir? Or these snowdrops in particular?'

For the second time that day, Pluke explained the ancient superstition surrounding a single snowdrop within a dwelling house, emphasising its shroud-like appearance and its role as a death token.

Wayne listened carefully and understood. 'You're not suggesting that all the recipients are destined to die, are you, sir? Is there a serial snowdrop killer at large in Crickledale? We can't afford to provide police protection to all the recipients, can we?'

'No, we cannot, but let us consider this matter with care. I think it is more a case of the sender wishing the recipients were dead, Sergeant, not that he or she intends to carry out lots of murders, or even one. I am sure he or she wants the recipients to die naturally, but the implied desire is for them to reach that stage before they would normally do so. It's a case of bringing forward a death, rather like a witch doctor pricking a wax model of his enemy so that the enemy expires before his due time. Frightening the victim into a death situation, in other words. In our case, of course, once the recipient understands the message revealed by the snowdrop, he or she could develop genuine fear and anxiety. So there is a mischief maker at work, Sergeant. And he or she sent a snowdrop to our murder victim in addition to all those other people. It means the snowdrops are relevant and that the sender must be traced and eliminated from suspicion – or otherwise.'

'Then I agree. It's a nasty idea, sir, frightening folks like that.'

'Indeed it is, Wayne, but even if such a snowdrop did result in a premature death, it is hardly murder. In some ways, the snowdrop packages are rather like anonymous letters, albeit of a particularly threatening and scurrilous kind.'

'Under these circumstances, then, surely the snowdrops can be regarded as illegal postal packets?'

'That would be a matter for a court to decide, Sergeant. In the mind of the sender there is an implied threat, a form of revenge, perhaps, or a desire to cause undue anxiety in the mind of the recipient. At the very least that is mischievous conduct and I am sure we could persuade a court to have the sender bound over to be of good behaviour.'

'I can understand that now, sir, but we are not totally sure who has received them, are we? Not everyone will have informed the police.'

'Then we must publicise the fact, Sergeant, we must persuade other snowdrop recipients to come forward. There must be a common link between them all and we must find it.'

'Shall I take up that line of enquiry? I'd have thought it was more for your skills than mine.'

'Then I, with my deep knowledge of such matters, will do that, Wayne. Perhaps you could concentrate upon the recent movements and personal contacts of the deceased?'

'Yes, I'll do that with pleasure, sir, with Detective Constable Helston's assistance. She is a very good detective.'

'She did acquit herself well during our investigation into the death of that nun, Wayne, so I shall be pleased to encourage her to develop her detective skills. You may consider your request approved.'

Millicent Pluke and Molly Mayweed, each sporting a rather outlandish hat and speaking with her finest accent, had enjoyed a most delightful lunch. Mrs Mayweed knew how to impress her guests. The meal had been preceded by a few sherries and accompanied by a glass or two of wine, and was held in the sumptuous setting of Forest Hall Restaurant on the outskirts of Crickledale. (Occasionally, Millicent would accept a glass of wine when Montague was not around.) Forest Hall Restaurant was a very superior place, somewhat beyond the financial circumstances of Millicent and Montague Pluke but well within the price ceiling that Mrs Mayweed expected to pay. Happily, Mrs Mayweed had paid. This was not surprising because Mrs Mayweed considered herself a lady of great substance in the town, a role model, the sort of person other ladies tried to emulate, generally without success.

She enjoyed a considerable status within Crickledale's social societies and, among her multifarious duties, she had been secretary of the Crickledonians, chairman of the Crickledale Flower Arranging Society, chairlady of the Crickledale and District Embroidery Club, chairperson of the Lib-

Lab Lobbyists, chair of the Ladies' Right-to-Roam-on-Private-Land Committee and president of Crickledale Ladies' Bowls Club. She had also been secretary, treasurer, speaker finder and a committee member of dozens of other organisations.

As with all lunches where important business was to be conducted, the participants had skilfully refrained from formal discussions during the main courses, not allowing such seriousness to detract from the mutual enjoyment of good food and companionship. Mrs Mayweed had entertained Millicent with stirring tales of looking at new Jaguars and BMWs, shopping in Bond Street, London, going to the theatre in the West End, visiting art galleries and museums, going around Buckingham Palace while the Queen was on holiday, actually speaking to Lord and Lady Boltorium during a month-long cruise in the Mediterranean, and having her hairdresser comment on the fact that she looked younger every time she paid him a visit. She had decided to increase the frequency of her visits to the hairdresser, she told Millicent.

Millicent, on the other hand, told of Montague's current and dramatic quest for the legendary Giant's Horse Trough of Trippingdale, how he refused to change his old coat, how his work with the police had resulted in the district's lowest crime rate since records began, how he studiously avoided walking under ladders or meeting people with flat feet on Mondays, how he disliked beginning new enterprises on Fridays and lived in hopes of finding a black cat with double claws, although he did quite enjoy sneezing on Thursdays. Thursday was an excellent day for sneezing, she informed Mrs Mayweed, it heralded good fortune. 'Montague is on holiday this coming week,' she told Mrs Mayweed as the coffee was delivered. 'He really deserves a break, he's been working so hard in recent weeks.'

'Let us have a liqueur with our coffees, Millicent, to round off a most delightful occasion.'

'Well, I have to drive the car because I have to collect Montague...'

'But that is not until four o'clock, Millicent, so you told me earlier. And you've done your shopping, haven't you?'

'Not all of it, there was an overnight power cut at the supermarket, so it did not open this morning at all. I managed to get some essentials from Watkinson's, though, before I joined you but it was rather a rush.'

'But you do not have to rush away immediately, Millicent. Waiter, a brandy for me ... and, Millicent?'

'Well, yes, a brandy then, a small one.'

As the brandies were being organised and as the waiter poured coffee, Mrs Mayweed lowered her voice, no longer speaking so that the entire restaurant clientele could hear her: 'It must be wonderful, being a policeman and being able to cope with heavy responsibilities without signs of stress, Millicent. Men of the law are such decent people. My own dear father, the late coroner, you know, and a solicitor in this town, was such a fine man, a real example to others. An honourable profession, the law, Millicent. It embraces such a variety of interesting and responsible work. I am not surprised your Montague chose a legal career, he was such a fine young man. And I can call you Millicent, can't I? It is such a nice name,' oozed Mrs Mayweed. 'That is why I wanted to talk to you, as the wife of such a prominent person.'

'Montague has rather made a name for himself.' Millicent blushed.

'He is the epitome of wisdom and calm reassurance – as, indeed, are you – which is why I wanted to discuss a matter of an exceedingly delicate nature with you, Millicent. I can be assured of your discretion, can I?'

'Of course, but perhaps you should have talked to Montague, he is always willing to share his advice. He has such a broad experience of most things. He is a very capable person. You said you knew him as a young man, Mrs Mayweed?'

'I have known him ever since I was a young secretary for Heathcock, Hockday and Haydock, the solicitors, you know. They are still functioning. They are a very well-established and respected firm.'

'I do know of them, but Montague has never said he knew you then.' Millicent smiled. 'The coroner's office is part of the practice, I believe. I have heard Montague talk about them.'

'That was my father, Royston Heathcock,' continued Mrs Mayweed. 'He was the coroner when your husband was a young constable on the beat. Those were the days, Millicent! And do call me Molly. But I have come to you because I felt I should not trouble such a busy and prominent person as your husband with my little worries.' Mrs Mayweed beamed.

Millicent sipped the brandy, wondering if the smell would linger on her breath as Mrs Mayweed eased her chair closer to Millicent. She leaned forward in an attempt to confine her conversation to her guest, whereupon Millicent had a clear view of the top of her head.

She was a lady whose hair was a beautiful shade of light-blue with a nest of deep-grey on the crown. She had fleshy cheeks, too, which tended to sag a little over her expensive blouse collars, rather like a bulldog, thought Millicent.

'Now, as I am sure you know, I have held many positions of responsibility over the years, no doubt because of my own skills and perhaps because of my husband's success in his business – Mayweed Kettles. I am sure you know of them.'

'I do believe we used a Mayweed Kettle for years,' said Millicent. 'A really good boiler with a heavy, solid base, nice fat feet and such a reliable model.'

'People never throw them out, you know, they just keep going for years and years, rather like me ... chortle, chortle, chortle. However, I wanted to speak to you about the Ladies' Knitting Circle. I know you have some strong links with the Circle – and with other important societies and clubs in Crickledale, not to mention being organiser of the Flower Rota for the parish church and a leading member of the committee of the Women's Institute.'

'I am deeply involved with many aspects of the social life of the town,' agreed Millicent. 'It enables me to mingle with the people and I do enjoy it. I think it is all due to Montague's prominence in our community. So how can I help you?'

'It is a rather delicate matter.' Mrs Mayweed leaned even further forward towards Millicent, her jowls preceding the rest of her face. 'Now, Millicent, are you aware of any cliques or raging jealousy within the Knitting Circle? Someone – or several someones – who might resent my success at being nominated president elect?'

'Good heavens, no!'

'It's not that I intend any radical change, like admitting men members or recommending nude calendars to be posed by our members, but I fear there are worrying elements of jealousy within the Circle.'

'The Knitting Ladies are really nice, er, Molly. There's not a hint of jealousy among them; none will resent your success, they'll all be very proud for you, and *of* you. I'm not so sure about admitting men members, though; I don't think the Women's Institute were too happy when such a radical change was suggested – a Persons' Institute doesn't have quite the same ring, although a Knitting Circle could be just a Knitting Circle without any hint of sexual preferences.'

'How nice of you to say such lovely things...'

Millicent was continuing, 'I do know that in some circles jealousy can manifest itself among the ladies, resulting in bitchiness, backbiting, gossip and other unladylike behaviour, but our Knitting Circle is renowned throughout Crickledale for its sense of fair play, innovative patterns, outsize balls and wonderful cups of tea.'

'And that is exactly how I see its future: an oasis of calm within a turbulent and demanding modern lifestyle,' mused Mrs Mayweed.

'Do I detect some reason for your concern, Molly? It's not like you to worry about accepting a position of influence and responsibility within the community. You are so experienced in such things, so self-assured, confident and capable.' Millicent alternatively sipped her coffee and brandy, and wondered why she could not be so assured as Molly Mayweed. But her observations and powers of deduction told her that Mrs Mayweed had something very important to say.

At this, Molly hauled from the floor her handsome leather handbag with its gold-coloured clasp in the shape of a kettle, opened it and pulled out a small brown envelope. She passed it to Millicent, who noticed it bore Mrs Mayweed's name and address in blue ballpoint handwriting, a second-class stamp and a local postmark.

'Open it,' invited Mrs Mayweed.

Millicent did so. 'Good heavens, Molly, a snowdrop! Pressed and preserved like they used to do in my mother's time ... is it yours?'

'It arrived by post last week, just like that. No letter, no explanation, just a pressed snowdrop in that cheap brown envelope.'

'And?'

'Well, I'm of the generation that knows a

107

single snowdrop in one's house is a token of death, Millicent. I threw it outside immediately but I did wonder if one of the Knitting Circle ladies had sent it, in a fit of jealousy or as an act of revenge. Then I thought about it and wondered if there might be some other explanation. I retrieved it from the dustbin and decided to talk to you, with you knowing most of the ladies in Crickledale. Really, Millicent, I would like to know who sent it. It is rather disturbing.'

'Molly, other people have received these, Montague was telling me over tea the other night. It is very rare that he talks about his work when he comes home but he is an expert on superstitions, you know, and was puzzled by this act. He did say it was not really a police matter – a snowdrop sent by post, even anonymously, is not, in itself, offensive nor is it a clear offence against any of our laws.'

'There must be something to prevent people doing this kind of thing!'

'Possibly, but quite honestly, I don't think any of the Knitting Ladies would stoop to this sort of underhand behaviour.'

'So what should I do, Millicent? Report it to the post office, the police or the vicar so that he can exorcise it, or forget it?'

'I will take it from you, Molly,' said Millicent. 'I would like to show it to Montague to see what he feels about it. If I were you I should ignore it – it is not in your house now, anyway, so what power it might have been able to exert is ineffective.'

'I didn't really believe it was harmful...' Mrs Mayweed blushed.

'Rest assured, Molly, that I cannot think of any knitting lady who might have sent this. I am sure it is someone well outside the refinements of those ladies, so you must accept the position of president. We are all depending upon your leadership as we begin the new millennium.'

'I find your common sense so reassuring, Millicent, and of course take it away and show it to your husband. And I will take your advice – I shall accept the post of president, with all the pressures and responsibility it might carry!'

'Well,' said Millicent, tucking the envelope into her own handbag. 'I must leave you now. I have some visits to make, then I must go and collect Montague from Trippingdale Castle. I do hope he has found his trough. He left home with such a sense of destiny!'

'You will contact me with your husband's comments on the snowdrop, will you?' asked Mrs Mayweed. 'And especially if he knows the identity of the sender?'

'Yes, of course. Now, a walk around the town should help to clear my head and my breath. I have some friends to see about the arrangements for tomorrow's service in church and I should then be fit to collect Montague from the castle. I do hope he found his horse trough without too much trouble.'

Because Millicent did not want to trouble Montague with trivial police matters at home during his annual leave, she decided to visit the police station where she could leave the snowdrop and its envelope in Montague's in-tray. He could deal with it upon his return or else another officer could take care of it in his absence. Opting to walk rather than drive, she climbed the hill to the picturesque police station, entered and was immediately recognised by the constable behind the counter of the Enquiry Office. He waved at her without speaking because he was coping with ringing telephones, a burbling radio and a computer screen, which appeared to blink and flash all the time. He was clearly extremely busy, covered the mouthpiece of the phone with his hand and said, 'Won't be a minute, Mrs Pluke. These phones never stop. It's all go in here today!'

'I won't bother you. I just want to leave this in Montague's in-tray,' she said, waving the envelope. 'I know the way. I don't want to drag you away from your work. It all sounds very busy, especially for a Saturday afternoon. So I'll just pop up to his office.'

'Right,' he mouthed, as he scribbled down some message coming through the telephone. 'Thanks.'

She climbed the stairs and opened his office door. It was empty and very tidy but she cried, 'Montague! How disgusting...' the moment she spied the bikini-clad blonde on his desk. 'How dare you display such pornographic pictures in your office ... this is most unseemly ... you wait until I get you home.'

And she snatched the picture from the desk, stuffed it deep into her handbag and stomped out of the office, then realised she had forgotten to leave the snowdrop in its brown envelope. She stalked back, dropped the snowdrop and envelope into his in-tray, then left, flushed and angry, and hurried down the stairs to the main door.

'Everything all right, Mrs Pluke?' called the constable, still holding the telephone to his ear as she sailed past his counter.

'Men!' she snapped. 'They only think about one thing! And I never thought my Montague was like all the others. Just you wait until I get my hands on him!'

'Mrs Pluke?' But she ignored him, hurried out, slammed the door and stomped back to her car. Rare trough or no rare trough, Montague was about to receive a severe ear-bashing from his loving wife. She had not calmed down by the time she reached her car and in that frame of mind she started it and drove off with a flourish, accompanied by a squeal of tyres.

Several minutes later she was approaching the gatehouse and was relieved but rather surprised to see the gate standing open.

As there was no one in attendance – clearly she was expected – she drove through with her foot hard down on the accelerator and her face flushed with suppressed anger and amazement at her husband's secret lust for scantily clad females. When she approached the castle, though, the sight of the assembled police vehicles, yards of yellow tape and lots of police officers, both in uniform and in civilian clothes, caused her to ease her foot from the throttle. Something was wrong; instinctively, she knew that.

Had something dreadful happened to Montague while she was sipping sherry and being decadent? Now very worried, she drove as close as she was able, eased to a halt, grabbed her handbag, climbed out of her car and was calming down with astonishing rapidity as she approached the constable who guarded the kissing gate.

'I'm sorry, madam,' he said with firmness. 'The castle is out of bounds.'

'I'm here to collect my husband,' she told him, not recognising the man. He was not a member of the local constabulary; she knew them all.

'I cannot allow you past, I'm afraid.'

'Why? What's happened? Why are all these police officers here?'

'There's been a murder, madam. The body of a man has been found inside the castle. I cannot say more.'

'A man's body... oh, my God ... Montague! Let me through, young man, you must let me through!'

'I'm afraid not, madam.' And he moved in front of the kissing gate, effectively blocking it with his large frame. 'As I said, the castle is out of bounds.'

'But you said a body had been found. My husband came here this morning to see a legendary horse trough in that castle. He came alone ... if he's been killed I shall complain to the Chief Constable about your conduct, Constable.' Millicent had found a new authority within her due, probably, to the brandy and wine she had enjoyed not long ago. Certainly, her face was flushed.

'Orders are orders, madam...'

'Who is the dead man, Constable? Answer me that...'

'I am not at liberty to disclose confidential information, madam. Now if you would please go away...'

'I am Mrs Detective Inspector Montague Pluke of Crickledale CID,' she said, drawing herself to her full height of five feet three inches and forgetting all about the blonde bombshell who had graced Montague's desk. 'And I have a right to know if my husband is the victim.'

That seemed to have some effect because the guardian of the gate said 'Just wait there a moment, madam' and activated the personal radio set, which clung to his shoulder like a small monkey. Soon he was speaking into the microphone. 'PC Smithers here, on the gate. I have a lady with me, claiming to be Mrs Detective Inspector Pluke. She says she's here to collect him and is asking for the name of the deceased.'

Happily, it was Wayne Wain who responded. 'Yes, Mrs Pluke is expected, but please tell her that the detective inspector is not the victim, that he has been recalled to duty after finding the trough he sought. In addition, though, he found the body of a deceased male person and he will be spending some time here on the murder investigation. I suggest she goes home and awaits his return. It could be quite late.'

'I heard that,' Millicent said to the constable. 'Dear me, whatever next. Montague does get himself into some terrible quandaries. But I am pleased he is not the victim, Constable.'

'Sorry I could not be more helpful,' he apologised. 'But rules are rules and orders are orders.'

'I shall go home now,' she went on. 'If my

husband does mention this to you, tell him I shall see him when he returns. Now, who is this lady, do you know that?' She pulled the photograph of the bikinied blonde from her handbag and waved it before his eyes. Clearly, he much appreciated what he saw.

'She was sitting on my husband's desk,' she said, the effect of the brandy still working wonders for her confidence. 'Can you imagine it, Constable? A happily married and highly esteemed man of Crickledale having such pornographic illustrations in his office!'

'He's clearly a man of taste, I'd say.' The constable immediately wished he had not said that, eyeing the small, grey-haired and rather prim lady before him whose pinched face was flushed red. 'But no, Mrs Pluke, I do not know who that is. I am not a local man, you know, I've been drafted in from Easingwold at short notice.'

'I shall not rest until I discover her name,' stated Millicent as she returned to her car. 'I shall carry out my own criminal investigation into this matter.'

Moments later, she was roaring away down the dale. The constable watched her go, wondering for a fleeting moment whether he smelt just a whiff of alcohol on her breath, but decided his gatekeeping duties were more important than breath-

alysing Mrs Detective Inspector Montague
Pluke.

But he did admire the detective inspector's taste in young women.

6

By seven that Saturday evening, Pluke was ready to deliver his first major address to the teams of detectives in the Incident Room. Preliminary work within the grounds of the castle had been virtually completed; the pathologist had concluded his examination at the scene and the body had been removed to the mortuary for a post-mortem. That would be conducted tomorrow morning. The Task Force had made a fingertip search around the castle, both inside and out, Scenes of Crime had concluded their examination of the scene and Wayne Wain had already begun his enquiries into the recent background of Stephen Gallholme. The draining of the trough had not yet been undertaken, however.

Standing on a chair so that he could be seen by all forty or so detectives, Pluke began with a brief history of Trippingdale, making reference to the privacy of the parkland, the abandoned village, the castle, the legendary trough, the estate and the Hall. He told them about the known eccentricities of the late Mrs Gallholme and then added an explanation for his own presence earlier today, with due emphasis upon the circumstances in which he had found the body.

'I am aware that the person who reports finding the body is the first to come under suspicion,' he said without smiling. 'I am sure you will eliminate me during your enquiries. But now to the facts of the case.'

After providing the little that was known about Stephen Gallholme, Pluke confirmed that his former wife had been traced and informed of his death. She was living in Norfolk and had been at home this morning.

She could not have been involved in his death and had no idea whether he had any enemies in this part of the world. She was willing to be further interviewed if subsequent enquiries showed it was necessary.

Pluke then addressed today's events. 'It seems,' he said cautiously, 'that Stephen went riding early this morning, probably leaving the Hall at six o'clock, which was his normal practice. It is not known which route he chose or whether he met anyone. His departure and the timing of it have not been confirmed, neither has the route he took to the castle. They are matters for us to determine.'

He went on to outline his own actions upon finding the body, adding, 'We are sure he did not fall from his horse, ladies and

118

gentlemen. The horse was present, so he had dismounted but he had not tethered the animal. That is not the practice of a competent rider. I think something or someone prevented him doing what was normal practice. The horse is now back in its stable at the Hall. It has been examined by Scenes of Crime, but nothing of evidential value has been found. The pathologist is confident that the suspected cause of death – drowning – will be confirmed, but because the death was not accidental we are treating this as murder.'

He told them the theories about the weapon or weapons used and the marks on the victim's neck, adding that pitchforks were very common agricultural tools in this vicinity. He followed by telling them of his plan to drain the trough, his requests for sightings of Stephen Gallholme during the relevant times and the need to ascertain whether he had established any friendships since his return as squire.

'Have we any idea of a motive yet, sir?' asked one of the detectives.

'At this stage we have no idea,' Pluke admitted. 'I doubt if it was robbery or done with any sexual overtones. Let us ask this question: Who would kill a man newly responsible for his family estate – and why? Jealousy? An old score to settle? Revenge for some past action? A motiveless attack even?

He did live here when he was a youngster and came back during his days at university and occasionally while following his career in finance – so he has firm links with the district. There may be something there for you to unearth, some secret from the past to discover.

'Now, one unusual piece of evidence that should not be ignored: Stephen received a pressed snowdrop in his personal mail. It arrived last week in a plain brown envelope without any message. For those of you unfamiliar with the importance of this, a snowdrop in one's private house is a death token. A single snowdrop, that is, due to its similarity to a shroud. Not a bunch. Just one flower.

'Several people in Crickledale have also received pressed snowdrops anonymously through the post in recent weeks and some have complained to the police. I do not have a full list of the recipients here nor can I show you an example of the snowdrop. They are in my office at Crickledale Police Station and I shall make sure they are brought here. During your enquiries, I want you to ask everyone you talk to whether they have received such a snowdrop, or whether they know of anyone who has, or, of course, anyone who might have sent one. That is one vital piece of evidence at this early stage. Who sent it to Stephen and why? The scene

120

itself has provided nothing – there are no identifiable footprints or clues. The thickness of the briars and undergrowth took the weight of both Stephen and me when I arrived – and also of the killer, of course. There are no discernible footprints in and around the castle, the ground is too dry, although there is evidence of the movement of cattle, people and motor vehicles. Unfortunately, there is not enough detail for us to isolate and identify, but we shall take samples of the earth in case we do find a suspect vehicle with mud on its tyres, or mud on a suspect's footwear.

'And that, ladies and gentlemen, brings you up to date. We shall work a twelve-hour day until further notice, nine until nine including weekends; overtime will be paid. The nearest place of refreshment is the Trippingdale Arms a mile along the road towards Crickledale where you can get bar snacks. It is just after seven now – you have two hours left tonight. Detective Inspector Horsley over there' – a hand was raised – 'is in charge of the Incident Room and he will allocate your actions.'

As Pluke stepped down from the chair upon which he had been standing to deliver his address, the teams of officers began to filter across the room towards Horsley, but Pluke reached him first and asked, 'Is Inspector Russell here, Mr Horsley?'

Inspector Paul Russell was the Force Press Officer and it was his task to liaise with Pluke so that decisions could be made about precisely what could be released to the media.

'Over there, Montague,' said Dick Horsley.

'Ah, good, I need to discuss the release of information about the snowdrops. If we get the media to highlight those letters, we might get lots of copycat letters, although that could be difficult because snowdrops are out of season now.'

'True. Not many people will have a stock of ready pressed snowdrops, Montague,' said Horsley who invariably used people's first names. 'I think, in view of the fact that we are not in the snowdrop season, we can make reference to them in our news releases. It will be a good topic for the press, radio and television to use. Publicity might help us with this one. It doesn't sound a very easy inquiry, out here in the wilds with no one to see what happened. We need all the help we can get. The snowdrop story might divert attention from any lack of positive lines of enquiry.'

'Well reasoned, Mr Horsley. I shall ask Inspector Russell to make due reference to them. Now, have you any queries about your role?'

'No, not at this stage. I'll set up house-to-house enquiries to start things off, Montague. We need to get under the skin of the estate workers and local yokels, find out what Stephen's been up to in his private life, check on local nutters, people with criminal records for violence or blackmail, the usual stuff. And we'll try to find anyone with a propensity for posting snowdrops, pressed or otherwise, to strangers. So what will you be doing?'

'I shall spearhead the snowdrop line of enquiry,' said Pluke. 'Detective Sergeant Wain is already investigating the background of our victim, along with Detective Constable Helston.'

'He's chasing her now, is he? I hope she knows what she's letting herself in for. Wayne Wain's a ram, you know.'

'His birth sign is of little consequence to me, Mr Horsley, but he does do an extremely good job. Now, I shall visit my office to locate the files on the snowdrop letters and to secure samples. I will update you in due course.'

'You'll need a driver, won't you, Montague?'

'Oh, yes, of course. Mrs Pluke kindly conveyed me here this morning before attending to her social commitments. Consequently I am somewhat marooned and without transport of my own. She should have arrived here some time ago to collect me – I do hope someone thought to tell Mrs Pluke about my involvement with the murder.'

'Yes, she does know, she came to the castle to collect you at four but was told what had happened. We didn't like to drag you from your work, so she went home without troubling you. She knows you will be late home.'

'Good then if you can find a driver for me, I shall go to Crickledale Police Station without delay.'

Moments later, Montague Pluke was being whisked towards Crickledale at high speed by one of the detectives who fancied himself as Grand Prix driver. He dropped Pluke outside the police station. Locally, it was called the Plukedom, but the officers never knew whether or not Pluke was aware of that. The driver received due thanks from his esteemed passenger, then roared back to his work on the murder inquiry. Pluke advanced towards the station, then realised the front door was locked.

It wasn't often he had to work this late on a Saturday night – that was the task of the uniformed branch who maintained the peace in spite of drunks, vandals and drug takers – and it had slipped his mind that many rural sub-divisional police stations closed their doors at six o'clock.

Emergency calls were dealt with by the

Headquarters Control Room. Its staff contacted officers on patrol in motor vehicles – rapid response vehicles, as they were known – but they were usually somewhere else when they were required. That was a fact of modern policing, mused Pluke. Government cutbacks were having a detrimental effect upon policing, he decided as he searched for his key to the Plukedom. Being a senior officer, he did have his own front door key; that was just one of the many privileges – and responsibilities – of rank. Then he realised that he had started the day while on holiday. Because he had left home in holiday mode he had not taken his police station key with him. Thus he was locked out of his own office. There was no point in ringing the bell because there was no one in the building.

Sergeant Cockfield (pronounced Cofield) had booked off duty and left his own Control Room, all incoming telephone calls would be transferred to a central number at Force Headquarters and people arriving at Crickledale Police Station with requests or in need of assistance could press buttons in a hole-in-the-wall system (known locally as cop-in-a-rock) when they would receive advice instead of bank notes.

They were advised: press 1 if you need the personal attendance of a police officer, 2 if you have an item of found property, 3 if you have lost any property, 4 if you have found

125

a stray dog, 5 if you have found any other kind of stray or injured animal or bird, 6 if you want a passport photograph signing, 7 if you have to produce driving documents, 8 if you wish to complain against the police, 9 if you want to report a crime, traffic accident or other serious incident, 10 if you are lost and 0 if you don't know what to do next.

Pluke therefore found himself in something of a dilemma. He needed to gain admission because the snowdrop complaint file was in his office but the cop-in-the-rock system didn't give access to the building nor did it cater for senior police officers who had left their keys at home. He could break in, he mused, but that would create all kinds of problems or, like a member of the public, he could summon a local patrol through number 1 in the cop-in-a-rock system. He needed a constable who might have a key to the office, or he could ask to be driven home to collect his own key. That would create undue hilarity among the ranks, he realised, a senior detective being locked out of his own establishment, and then he remembered his mobile telephone. He could ring Millicent and ask her to bring his office key and other artefacts of duty. She could be at his side within five minutes. Far better than calling a police officer who would take half an hour or more to respond. So he rang home.

'Mrs Montague Pluke,' said the sweet voice in response.

'It is Montague speaking, dearest,' he said softly into the mobile, not wishing local residents or dog walkers to share his dilemma. 'I am outside the police station and do not have my key... I was wondering if I could prevail upon you to get my keys from the drawer in my bedside cabinet and bring them down to me by car? And my notebook and things. I do need to gain access to my office, you see, and it is rather urgent...'

'You want to get into your office to ogle that bikini-clad strumpet on your desk!' was the somewhat surprising retort.

'I beg your pardon?' Montague was extremely shocked at the uncharacteristic tone in Millicent's voice. Clearly, something of a most serious nature had upset her.

'I've seen her, it's no good denying it, Montague. You are a dirty old man. I am ashamed of you, a man of your age...'

'Dearest heart,' he tried. 'I do not know what you are talking about. What bikini-clad strumpet on my desk? I work in a police station, not a pornographic film maker's studio...'

'Your office is just like a pornographic film maker's studio; it is disgusting, Montague. You ought to be ashamed of yourself! I have a good mind not to make your cocoa tonight and to sleep in the spare room. I can hardly

believe that my own husband would succumb to such filth, let alone enjoy it ... it's
not as if I don't show you my deepest and
most enduring love, day in and day out, and
I do wash your socks and all your collars
and I iron your shirts...'

'Millicent!' He decided it was time to be
firm. 'I have no idea what you are talking
about.'

'I am talking about that profane photograph on your desk, Montague.'

'There is no photograph on my desk,
profane or otherwise, Millicent, and if there
is it is not one that depicts a half-naked or
near-naked or even fully naked person of
the female gender.'

'Don't you lie to me, Montague Pluke! I
have seen it...'

'When did you see it?' he asked, hoping
that no one could overhear his private and
rather embarrassing conversation.

'This afternoon, when I took an envelope
in, one that Mrs Mayweed had received,
with a pressed snowdrop inside... I saw it
then, on your desk.'

'Millicent,' he said once more with
firmness. 'I think you should show me what
you saw, then things might become a little
clearer. And if a snowdrop letter is involved,
I regard the matter as very serious indeed.
So, will you get into the car and bring my
office keys to the police station? It is not a

lot for a husband to ask of his wife, especially a husband of my standing in the community and one who is currently actively engaged in a murder investigation, having given up his annual leave to return to duty. I do have rather more to concern me at the moment than obscure and unsubstantiated allegations of debauched behaviour.'

'Montague, I'm sorry, so sorry to bother you when you are so heavily committed with duty matters,' she whispered. 'But I am so upset … it's not every day that someone learns something so distressing about her loved one…'

'Then come down here and we can talk about it, in my office and in front of the offending object!' And, somewhat abruptly to prevent further discussion or argument, he switched off his mobile telephone. That will teach her a lesson, he thought to himself. If Millicent did not come very soon, he would walk home and retrieve his key, and if she refused to make his cocoa tonight he might have to go to bed without it. In his present mood he was quite prepared to do that. Minutes later, Millicent's car appeared at the entrance to the police station yard, drove in and parked. Millicent, by this stage somewhat subdued and even surprised at Montague's reaction to her allegations, emerged with a sheepish grin on her face and walked slowly to meet her husband. He went to meet her too.

'Montague,' she said. 'I am so sorry I behaved like that ... but it was such a shock. I have been brooding about it for hours ... it is so distressing... And what on earth have you done to your trousers? You smell terrible. Did you fall into your trough? And your coat is covered with broken briars and leaves and thorns!'

As he explained things to her he noticed the change of expression in her face. For a moment he thought she was going to throw her arms around his neck and kiss him in an attempt to make up their momentary split, so he backed away. He did not want any such display of raw, sexually charged emotion in a public place and certainly not on the forecourt of his very own police station, particularly with his being such a prominent personage within that station.

'Let's go and inspect the offending object,' he said rather coldly, taking the key from her.

He noticed she had brought her handbag. Why did women take their handbags everywhere with them?'

'It will help me to understand...' she simpered.

'There is nothing to understand, my dear. You had better come in. And you must tell me about Mrs Mayweed's pressed snowdrop, too.'

'You sound very officious, Montague.'

'Official, you mean. I sound very official because it *is* very official and I am on duty, remember. Furthermore, I am far from wishing to discuss private matters during my duty periods, but as this matter has some bearing on what is allegedly on my office desk, I shall attempt to clear it up immediately.'

He opened the office door and stepped inside, admitting Millicent and then closing the door to ensure no member of the public rushed in to report something urgent like a hole in the road or a found racing pigeon. In stern silence he led Millicent up the stairs to his office, passing the deserted Control Room *en route* – he found it odd to be here without the calm presence of Sergeant Cockfield (pronounced Cofield). Finally, they arrived at his office easily identified with a sign on the door which said 'Detective Inspector M. Pluke, please knock and wait'.

He led her inside, entering with his right foot and removing his damp overcoat. He hung it on a peg and followed with his panama.

'Here!' Millicent cried, taking the photograph from her handbag. 'This is it...'

'Good heavens.' Montague Pluke blinked. 'She's a fine-looking young woman, Millicent, if I may be so bold. But she is not

131

mine, I assure you. Where was she?'

'She was on your desk, Montague. This is your office, isn't it? She was here, on this very desk! Don't you have control over what happens in your office?'

'I vacated my office on Friday evening, Millicent, and gave Detective Sergeant Wain permission to use it during my absence. I suspect this belongs to him. Let me see.'

He took the photograph from her, pressed the release catch at the rear of the frame, and allowed the glass and the photograph to fall into the palm of his hand. On the rear of the photograph were the words, 'This is me fully dressed, I know you like me better without all this on ... love to Wayne from Debbie. xxxx.'

Without a word, he showed it to Millicent, at the same time experiencing a fleeting vision of Mrs Plumpton similarly clad.

'Oh, Montague, I am so sorry... I over-reacted... I was so jealous, thinking another woman was claiming your affections ... and one so much younger.'

'I shall return this to Detective Sergeant Wain's office before I leave the building.' He reassembled the picture, admired the shapely extent of Debbie's fine display, then replaced it on his desk – temporarily of course.

'I am so sorry, Montague. I have had a very frustrating day ... first the supermarket was shut due to a power failure and when I went to Watkinson's they had only small packets of your cereal. Then Mrs Mayweed wanted to discuss the pressed snowdrop she'd received. She said how wonderful her father was, the coroner, you remember, and I had no idea you knew her when you were young, but she did say how she'd enjoyed working for the solicitors you used to visit, and then I found that picture and now, instead of you and I celebrating your horse trough triumph you've got a murder to deal with ... what a day, Montague. What a day! I am so sorry I was jealous, but I will make cocoa tonight as usual, I promise,' said Millicent.

'I shall endeavour to conclude this evening's investigations by nine o'clock,' he said. 'And I need to expand the enquiries into those pressed snowdrops...'

'You mean they are associated with the murder?' She sounded aghast at the thought.

'The deceased received one,' he told her. 'And what about Molly Mayweed? What did she tell you? You have left an envelope here, one she received? Does she know who had sent it?'

'No, that was the whole point. She wondered if it might be a jealous person in the Knitting Circle. It's in your in-tray,' she said, pointing to it. 'I thought you'd better have it. She told me over lunch and wondered what to do. I said you should be aware of such things, but as you were on holiday I would drop it in to your office.'

'A wise decision, Millicent, and much appreciated. Now, I shall examine Mrs Mayweed's snowdrop along with the others. It may take me some time.'

'Shall I go home, then? And come back for you?'

'Yes, you go home, Millicent, and I shall walk. The evening fresh air will be a delight after a long and hard day, and it will air my trousers.'

'It was such a shame that your trough hunting was interrupted by work,' she said. 'I was planning a nice celebratory meal this evening.'

'But I did locate the trough, Millicent. It is no legend and I am sure it is the largest trough in the kingdom. It's just unfortunate there was a dead man inside it.' And he provided an account of his activities at the castle.

She listened, enthralled, wondering how a man could keep so calm under such pressure, then said, 'Montague, I must leave you to concentrate on your enquiries. I do love you and I shall see you soon. Shall I prepare a late meal and perhaps we could enjoy a sherry together?'

'Thank you, my dearest, that is a wonderful idea, although I don't want you to think I am an alcoholic,' he said as she left the office. 'Make sure you close the door as you leave. We don't want people thinking the police station is open for business, do we?'

As she left him, he glanced at her departing figure, then looked at the photograph, which stood proudly on his desk. Had Millicent ever looked like that? he wondered. He'd never seen her in a bikini, or even in her underwear. Women were such mysterious creatures, he realised, but a good man must never succumb to their charms. However, it was time to examine the file on pressed snowdrops. He opened his filing cabinet, took it out, slipped Mrs Mayweed's letter among the others and began to concentrate.

7

Fortunately, Pluke's efficient secretary, Mrs Plumpton, had compiled a list of recipients of the snowdrop letters, exceptions being Mrs Mayweed and Stephen Gallholme. With the file before him, he settled at his desk with his damp trousers clinging to his legs and knees, and his shoes still squelching every time he moved. They should have dried themselves by this time, he told himself, while all around him there was the foulest of smells, which accompanied him everywhere.

Knowing that he could not allow such minor distractions to deter him from the task in hand, he relegated his discomfort to the deeper recesses of his mind and opened the file. The list before him showed the date and place of the postmark on each letter; all had been received within the last three weeks, he noted, albeit on varying dates. The date that each had arrived at the recipient's address was included, as well as the name, address and sex of the recipient, a description of the envelope in which each snowdrop had arrived and whether or not each recipient was aware of the sinister message imparted by the pressed snowdrop. All those recorded by Mrs Plumpton did appreciate the implied threat and that now included Mrs Mayweed. They wouldn't have bothered the police otherwise.

Stephen Gallholme had not understood the message although the letter was sufficiently puzzling for him to mention it to Broadbent. Without doubt, his death had elevated the snowdrop letters into a matter of serious concern and Pluke had to determine whether or not the mailings did conceal something more sinister.

It was with that in mind that Montague Pluke began to study the list of recipients, hoping that he might recognise some kind of pattern or trend, which would enable him to identify the sender. The chief question was, of course, why would anyone send this kind of veiled and superstitious threat? Why not send fresh snowdrops earlier in the year? Why bother to preserve them before mailing them? Indeed, why not write an ordinary anonymous or threatening letter if there was some kind of grudge to be aired? So what had the recipients done to attract this unusual kind of attention? Had they antagonised or annoyed the sender in some way? If so, how?

It was a pity Gallholme had disposed of his, but Pluke felt sure it had come from the same source as the others. The coincidence was too great for there to be any other explanation. He emptied them on to his desk, counting a dozen to make sure he'd got them all, then added Mrs Mayweed's and Gallholme's names to make the list of fourteen complete. He added a relevant handwritten note to Mrs Plumpton's work, amending the file to show there were now thirteen small brown envelopes each containing a pressed snowdrop. The fourteenth had been received but disposed of by the murder victim. He shuddered at the unlucky portent of that total of thirteen in his file, then tried to disregard it on the grounds that others had been sent, probably, apart from the fourteen about which he knew.

Pluke studied the envelopes – each was a small brown manilla type, one of the cheap variety, six inches long by three and a half inches wide in old measurements, or fifteen by nine centimetres in modern terms.

These envelopes could be bought from any stationery shop, they were the kind that businesses often used to send out invoices or receipts, although none had windows. Each bore a handwritten address in capital letters, written in blue ballpoint ink. In Pluke's opinion, all were by the same hand. That was particularly evident in the way the postcodes had been written – every 'O' in the YO portion had a curious curly tailpiece at the top where the circle of the 'O' had been completed. YO was the postcode for the York district, embracing the city and a large area around it. All the addressees were given a prefix of Mr, Miss or Mrs – there was not a single Ms among them, Pluke noted – and each address was given its full postcode. The sender must have access to these details.

All were in Crickledale and district – the remarkably efficient Mrs Plumpton had photocopied a large-scale map of the locality and highlighted each address on the map. None was more than three miles from the centre of Crickledale; a large red circle encompassed the original twelve. Pluke added two small red dots to mark Trippingdale Hall and the residence of Mrs Mayweed. Mrs Mayweed lived in a large detached house of stylish character on the outskirts of Crickledale. Her residence was well within Mrs Plumpton's red circle, as was Trippingdale Hall. All the letters in the possession of the police had been posted within the York postal area on varying dates within the last couple of months; some had been sent on the same dates, he noted, wondering whether the person posting them had done so in different mailboxes. Crickledale and Trippingdale were located within that same postal area but he did not know whether all the letters had been despatched

139

within Crickledale itself.

There was no way of determining precisely where they had been posted because mail from all the postboxes in this district bore the same postmark. Clearly, the addressees were all Crickledonians, but what else had they in common? There were men and women on the list and, to his personal knowledge, among them were retired people and others still working. There were professional people and working-class people too, with married and single persons among them – he recognised some of the names. So, apart from their place of domicile, what else had they in common – and did that common factor, whatever it was, provide a reason for someone to send them tokens of death?

The file contained nothing that might lead to the identification of any common link between the recipients and, in spite of Pluke's wide-ranging knowledge of Crickledale and many of its inhabitants, he could not identify any such factor. But the sender of the letters must be associated with all of them and all must have caused him or her some annoyance or created a desire for revenge. In Pluke's opinion that suggested a very close knowledge of the persons to whom the letters had been sent. In turn this suggested the sender was a Crickledale resident with whom the recipients might be on quite familiar terms. The murder victim, even if he had returned to live in the locality only three weeks ago also had to fit into this scenario. So whom had he befriended or become acquainted with during that short time? Pluke did not forget, of course, that Gallholme had lived in the district some years ago, consequently he could not ignore the likelihood that his killer was someone from those days.

Equally, it might be someone from his later life and professional career. Wreaking revenge for some past act, perhaps? But he must not lose sight of the fact that killer and snowdrop sender were not necessarily the same person.

Two further matters came to Pluke's mind as he studied the file. First, where had the snowdrops come from? Not everyone in Crickledale had a garden let alone one containing snowdrops; now, of course, being May, the snowdrop season had finished and consequently it would not be easy to locate such gardens without prowling around every holding in the district looking for dead snowdrop leaves. He was aware that they also grew in the wild – there were several colonies around the outskirts of the town – and another possibility was that they might have been purchased from a flower shop or garden centre. He could arrange teams of detectives to make those kinds of enquiries.

Some shopworker might recall a bulk purchase or someone repeatedly buying snowdrops.

And second, where had the snowdrops been pressed? Pluke knew that heavy books were frequently used for this ancient craft. The newly plucked flowers were placed between the pages, sometimes between sheets of additional tissue paper, and the books were then firmly closed. If they were kept on a tightly-packed shelf, the immobility of the volumes on either side pressed the flowers beautifully, although the time-scale might vary considerably. Some flower pressers left their blooms within the books for months or even years, and in many cases the pages became stained with their colour. The result was a pressed and dried flower, which retained the colours, albeit slightly faded, of a freshly picked specimen.

But these snowdrops looked fairly fresh – he guessed they had not been pressed for long, possibly being retained only since the most recent snowdrop season before being posted to their destinations. There were more sophisticated methods of pressing flowers, he realised – you could even buy a specially constructed press made of wood with screw-down bolts and hinges, but such a thing was very expensive, unless flower pressing was one's business. Books were still the favourite method – and the cheapest – in this part of Yorkshire.

He wondered if the month of May had been specially chosen for this postal campaign of terror? Or was that mere coincidence? May was an unlucky month for some purposes – getting married in May is often considered unlucky, for example, while kittens and even baby humans born in May were regarded as potential weaklings and never likely to thrive. Pluke studied the file for a long time, searching for the elusive factor linking all the snowdrop receivers, but failed to find it.

He realised he would have personally to interview each one of them in an attempt to ascertain the common factor. But he would not do so tonight. It was after nine o'clock, the Incident Room would be closed, the teams would be either having a drink and a meal in the Trippingdale Arms or heading for home and he knew that Millicent would have his cocoa ready. In her present mood of reconciliation she might even allow him to have a nibble tonight. Something covered with chocolate would be wonderful.

He tucked the file under his arm, donned his famous coat and panama, made sure his desk was tidy, then left his office with a last and somewhat lingering look at Wayne Wain's bikini-clad friend. He would deal with her later. Thus fortified, he emerged from the police station into the cool night air.

143

There was no moon tonight, he realised, while ensuring the door was locked, but as he strode damp-legged into the blackness beyond the station, he spotted a lone star in a dark patch of sky. That was a wonderful sign of good luck – that's if you made a wish the moment you saw that first star of the evening. Very quickly, therefore, he said to himself:

Star light, star bright, first star I've seen
  tonight,
Would it were that I might, have the wish I
  wish tonight.

And as he squelched towards his home in the knowledge that the stars governed the lives of all living creatures, he wished for a successful conclusion to this very peculiar murder investigation.

Detective Inspector Montague Pluke always looked under the bed before settling in for the night. His mother and his grandmother had done likewise, and so had his father and his grandfather; they had encouraged him to emulate their example just in case there were any nasty things hiding in the dust or darkness. As a child he had never questioned the example set by the adults in his life and he had continued the practice into adulthood. He had never found anything or anyone hiding under the bed.

Having performed that ritual, therefore, he had settled down to a relaxed sleep with Millicent at his side and awoke at seven next morning, refreshed and ready to continue his hunt for the horse trough killer. Taking several deep breaths as he always did, he made sure he climbed out of bed on the correct side, the right side; to emerge on the left was to get out of the wrong side of the bed, not the best way to begin any day, let alone one that included a murder hunt. He first put on his right sock, then his right slipper, following with his left sock and his left slipper before heading for the bathroom.

During these manoeuvres Millicent snoozed contently; she would rouse herself once he had completed his ablutions. In the privacy of the bathroom he did everything that was necessary to transform him into a fit, healthy and recognisable crime-fighting whirlwind, donned his clean shirt, blue bow tie, drew his belt tight around his trousers, now dry but not pressed with new creases, and went down for breakfast. Millicent then climbed out of bed after crossing to the right as instructed by Montague so that she could emerge at the correct side to ensure a pleasing mood throughout the coming day.

He consumed a sensible breakfast; he liked eating alone with his thoughts and enjoyed his cereal, fruit and black coffee. Millicent came to join him as he reached the coffee stage, noting the snowdrop file on the table. She was allowed to talk to him once he'd sipped a few mouthfuls.

'You found Mrs Mayweed's snowdrop, didn't you?' she asked, in case the matter was mentioned by Mrs Mayweed at church this morning.

'It is in this file,' he said, patting the cover. 'There are twelve further recipients, Millicent, a total of thirteen counting Mrs Mayweed and fourteen with the deceased. Mr Gallholme received a snowdrop before he was murdered...'

'Why Montague, how dreadful ... that is very ominous ... you don't think all those people will die, surely?'

'I do not, Millicent. I do not believe the killer and the snowdrop sender are one and the same. That is my professional viewpoint. But I cannot ignore the fact that fourteen people have received snowdrops in their mail.'

'It does seem very ominous, Montague, very ominous indeed.'

'I consider it more baffling than ominous, Millicent. However, I shall publicise the matter. I need to know whether anyone else has received one. I want all recipients to notify me.'

'I can ask at church,' she offered. 'During

146

the coffee afterwards, I mean, not during the service.'

'That would be very useful,' he had to admit. 'Yes, Millicent, I should be very pleased if you could do that small task on my behalf. You may mention the fact that the murder victim – Stephen Gallholme – received one. He has been formally identified, which means his name can be released, and it might persuade witnesses to talk to us. Do so without referring to Mrs Mayweed, I would suggest. If she wishes to tell the world she has received one then that is her decision.'

'I think she will be at church, Montague. She likes to show her new hats to the congregation and she did buy one yesterday. I know she will want to make sure that Mrs Fibboner notices it. Mrs Mayweed's new hat is much bigger and far more colourful than the one Mrs Fibboner wore last week.'

There was a long silence, which was an indication that Montague was thinking deeply, then he said, 'Millicent, my love, you know that I do not mix my work with my pleasure moments, neither do I impose my work problems upon my precious off-duty time, but in matters of grave concern, one has to make exceptions.'

'Very true, Montague.' She wondered what he was going to say.

'I am engaged on a very difficult murder

investigation, as you know, and I do need help from whatever sources I can muster.'

'Of course, Montague. And you know I shall be pleased to assist in whatever way I can, even in addition to asking the congregation about those snowdrops.'

'Thank you, my dear. Well, before I head for the Incident Room, I wonder if you might cast your eyes down this list of people who have received pressed snowdrops. It is confidential, of course, and I must ask that you do not divulge such official secrets to the press or the public, but I would be interested to know whether you recognise any link between the victims and whether you can think of anyone who might be tempted to send such an object to these particular people, not forgetting Stephen Gallholme.'

'Of course I will do it, Montague. You go and clean your shoes and by the time you are ready I shall have finished.'

It was a blessing she had mentioned his shoes because they were still considerably damp from yesterday's exertions but he did have a second pair of similar appearance. They were in the cupboard in the scullery and so he pottered through, found them, decided they did need to be cleaned of mud and grime, and set about the task with some gusto. After all, his mother had often said that a person with tidy hair and clean shoes was always well dressed. In cleaning them, he took care not to place them on the scullery table because that foretold a quarrel and he had no wish to create a quarrel with Millicent or anyone else, but he did find a knot in one of the laces.

This was a sign of good fortune, he realised, then he wondered what would happen to Stephen Gallholme's boots. The footwear of a murder victim was often hidden to prevent him walking after death ... but that was a very old belief. Nowadays, footwear of murder victims was retained for evidence.

When he returned to the kitchen in his clean shoes, Millicent smiled and said, 'What a pity you have not had time to press your trousers, Montague, you do look smart with those clean shoes on.'

'My trousers are quite dry and look no different from any other day, dearest,' he responded. 'Now, have you examined my list of snowdrop victims?'

'I have,' she said.

'And?'

'Well, I do know them all, as I am sure you realise. That is through my contacts and work among the social life of Crickledale. They are all so very nice, Montague, I cannot think why anyone would wish to send any one of those people something like a token of death.'

'Would you know if any of them have made enemies, Millicent? Or rather, it looks as if they have collectively made enemies and yet they do not all belong to the same social class, or the same club or society, and the list includes men and women. And each of them, in some way, antagonised our snowdrop sender.'

'I was very aware of that, Montague, as I was reading the list, but I cannot see any link between them. I don't know of any upsets within any of the organisations to which I belong – and many of those ladies belong to the same groups as myself.'

'I might want you to detail those in due course, but first I wish to examine the list collectively, seeking a common factor, you see.'

'I understand, Montague, but your Mr Gallholme was not a member of any local society, was he? His name has not cropped up in any of them to which I belong, either as a member or potential member.'

'That is a very good point,' he had to admit. 'Yes, Millicent, that is a very good point indeed. I did recognise people on the list as being prominent within Crickledale society and I did think there might be someone who had been rejected by all or some of those groups, someone who decided to avenge herself for the snub by sending snowdrops. But considering the murder victim, that might not be the case.'

'You need to know whether other people,

not members of local societies or groups and not even prominent in the town, have received snowdrops, Montague.'

'I do indeed, Millicent, so I shall publicise the matter at this morning's news conference. Sadly, it will not reach the local papers, radio or regional television news bulletins until tomorrow. Sunday is a poor day for publicity and not a very good day for detecting crime, Millicent.'

'But I know you will find your murderer, Montague. Well, you must be off. You have important work to do. How are you getting to the Incident Room this morning? Do you want me to drive you?'

'I had not given it a thought, my dear,' he admitted. 'Silly of me, forgetting such a basic necessity... I was thinking I would be going into my office as usual...'

'I shall drive you, then I can go straight to church,' she said with firmness. 'Come along, it's Sunday and that is a busy day for me. I have to make sure there are flowers on the altar, that someone is there to hand out the hymn books and take the collection. So what about lunch? I have not packed anything for you.'

'I might join my colleagues for a bar snack, Millicent. Although I am not one for frequenting public houses, I need to pick up information from the local people and bar room chatter can be very important in the world of crime detection.'

'So long as you do not over-indulge in alcohol, my dear,' was her response.

Minutes later, with the sound of Crickledale church bells ringing in his ears, Montague was being driven to the Incident Room in its manorial setting. For this journey they did not have to pass Aaron Pinder at the gatehouse, something that pleased Millicent. In the car park, Montague bade farewell to Millicent, saying he would ask one of the detectives to drive him home tonight. He looked forward to a busy and fruitful day detecting crime – but he could not forget Millicent's claim that only the deceased had not been a prominent member of Crickledale society and he was the one who had been murdered.

But then, as he walked across the courtyard to the door of the Incident Room, he thought: 'If the local squire, lord or owner of the manor is not prominent in local society, who is?'

It meant all the known snowdrop recipients were, in one way or another, very prominent in Crickledale society. So why had he, the officer in charge of Crickledale CID *and* an authority on horse troughs, not received one of the snowdrops?

Puzzled and rather deflated, he opened the door and walked in.

152

8

'Good morning, sir.' Several detectives bade him welcome as he made his way to the desk he would use during the inquiry. He would have preferred an office for his sole and private use but that was not possible in this limited accommodation. However, the desk was in one corner of the large room, far enough from his subordinates' work stations to permit a degree of confidentiality, and it was positioned at an angle that enabled him to view all the assembled officers and their work places. He would feel quite important, sitting there.

Even at this early stage the Incident Room had all the appearance of an efficient and functional office with desks, chairs, computers, telephones, fax machines, a photocopier, two blackboards and tea/coffee-making facilities. In these functional surroundings, some forty detectives of all ranks were milling about as they waited for Pluke to address the morning conference.

As Pluke reached his desk he noted that someone had placed a sprig of heather in his in-tray, a sign of good fortune. He put his snowdrop file beside it. He knew, of course, that the surrounding moors were covered with a blanket of heather, which would bloom in a rich and royal purple during the autumn, but even in such a heather-rich locality the 'lucky' white variety was uncommon. In fact, it was non-existent on the moors at this time of year. This must be a cultivated variety ... nonetheless, the gift was a very nice touch, he felt, and he wondered who had made this thoughtful gesture.

As if in answer to the puzzle, the tall, dark and handsome figure of Detective Sergeant Wayne Wain materialised from the crowd. 'Good morning, sir.' He sounded cheerful and eager for work as he joined his boss. 'A very nice morning.'

'Good morning, Sergeant,' returned Pluke as he began to remove his heavy coat and blue-banded panama. 'A very good morning indeed. Might I ask who has so kindly presented me with this white heather?'

'I cannot tell a lie, sir, it was me.' The sergeant beamed. 'I found it growing on the roadside this morning, a large clump, I might add, so I picked a small sprig for you, to bring us all good luck during this investigation. Every murder inquiry needs a spot of good luck. I know you regard any means of encouraging luck to be important.'

'I do indeed, and white heather is just as

efficacious as a four-leaved clover, even if it is cultivated and probably from someone's garden, Sergeant, but thank you very much indeed. I am surprised, though, that I did not notice it during my own journey here this morning.'

'Perhaps I came from a different direction, sir,' said Wayne Wain, having last night sampled Detective Constable Helston's cooking, hospitality and ample charms.

'That would not surprise me in the least.' Pluke chuckled at the thought of Wayne Wain getting lost on these moors. He was hopeless without a map. 'So, what have we this morning? Any overnight developments about which I should be aware before I address the teams?'

'Just one, sir. It arises from my preliminary enquiries into the antecedents of the deceased.'

'You speak just like a police officer, Wayne,' chided Pluke. 'So what have you discovered?'

'Quite by chance, I was speaking to a gentleman in the Trippingdale Arms last night, a visitor to the area. He and his wife are staying in a holiday cottage, which belongs to the pub, and he likes early morning walks. He has been there all week and is due to leave tomorrow, Monday. A couple of days ago, so he tells me...'

'Friday?' suggested Pluke.

'No, two days back from yesterday, sir, Thursday.'

'Ah, so on Thursday your contact saw something of relevance to our inquiry?'

'Yes, sir, Thursday last, around six forty-five in the morning. He was on his morning walk and was passing the gates of the Hall when he saw a woman leaving in a small car. A dark-green colour, he said, but he didn't get the number. He had no reason to consider it unusual until my enquiries jerked his memory. He is not sure of the make or model, but it might have been a Vauxhall Corsa. It was that kind of size, a small vehicle. She was alone, by the way.'

'An early morning visitor? Delivering milk or papers, perhaps?'

'No, sir, she's not one of the regular callers or delivery persons. I checked. The suggestion is she had stayed overnight with Stephen Gallholme. It seems she left shortly after he went for his morning ride. He was alive at that time, remember. She was in her late thirties, dark hair, smartly dressed from what the witness could see, white blouse, dark-green skirt, dark hair, either black or very dark-brown, cut short and very well cared for. That's all he could tell us, it was just a fleeting glimpse.'

'And who do you think it might have been Wayne?'

'I have spoken to Broadbent, sir, and that

surly individual on the gate...'

'Pinder,' Pluke reminded him.

'Yes, Pinder, and also the lady who cleans and cooks for Mr Gallholme, but none of them knows who the lady might have been.'

'Maybe a search of the house is necessary straight away, Sergeant? Surely it will reveal something? An address book, perhaps? List of telephone numbers? Make a thorough search of the bedroom, office and domestic quarters used by Mr Gallholme. That must surely produce something of value to our investigation.'

'It shall be my task for today, sir.' Wayne Wain beamed. 'With Detective Constable Helston to help me – she is very good in bedrooms, sir.'

'Make sure you get what you need, Sergeant.'

'I will indeed, sir. Now, did you discover anything last night when you examined the list of people who had received snowdrop letters?'

'Nothing of significance, Wayne, I must admit. The file is on my desk and I shall arrange for a list of recipients to be placed on our Incident Room notice board, along with a sample of the flowers and envelopes. Their names will be programmed into HOLMES, too, but the only salient point that I have been able to discern is that all the recipients are prominent in Crickledale society. Among them is the secretary of the Crickledale Apostle Spoon Collectors' Society, the chairman of the Literary and Philosophical Society, the chairwoman of the Budgerigar Breeders' Club, the former president of the Hollyhocks Society, the secretary of the Primrose Club...'

'Oh, I see. That kind of person.'

'They are people of renown in the community, Sergeant.'

'Is that why Mr Stephen Gallholme was sent a snowdrop, do you think, sir? Because he was locally renowned?'

'Well, in his position as owner of Trippingdale Hall, he was a person of considerable stature. So yes, on the face of things and having due regard to the information in our possession at this stage I think that is why he received one.'

'But with all due respect, sir, you haven't received a snowdrop. You are a person of stature within this community. People know of your family links with the town through the ages. Then there is your horse trough expertise and your horse trough authorship and, of course, your eminence as the officer in charge of Crickledale Criminal Investigation Department. So why have you not received a snowdrop, sir?'

'That is an exceedingly good question, Sergeant, but I have to say that I am sure there are personages of greater, equal or

158

even lesser stature than myself who have not received snowdrops. Status alone is not the reason for this insidious campaign, I am sure. However, that is the object of my enquiries today.'

'You're not suggesting all recipients are at risk of being murdered, are you, sir? Does it mean there is a serial killer about to start work in the area?'

'I doubt it, Sergeant.'

'I thought you regarded Gallholme's snowdrop as highly relevant to his murder?'

'Relevant, yes, but I do not think it is the *sole* consideration. We must not adopt a blinkered attitude by believing the snowdrop sender is the killer, Sergeant. The killer might know nothing about the snowdrop campaign and the snowdrop campaigner might be unaware of the murder – or might have been so unaware at the time the snowdrops were despatched. What I am trying to say, Sergeant, is there may be other vital elements to this investigation, even if the snowdrops do provide important clues. There might be other clues if only we can recognise them. So how much do you know about snowdrops, Wayne?'

'Not a lot, sir.'

'Then prepare to learn a little. They are wild flowers, but they are also cultivated and are said, by tradition, to bloom on Candlemas Day which is the second of February.

159

They all die before this time of the year, but they can blossom even during a snowfall, hence they are sometimes known as the snowpiercer...'

'It sounds like something to do with drugs, sir. Snow. Cocaine, I mean.'

'That association cannot be overlooked, Sergeant. However, the day the flowers bloom – Candlemas Day – came and went quite a while ago, I might remind you. That day is also the Feast of the Purification of the Blessed Virgin Mary, Cradle Rocking Day, Groundhog Day in the United States and Wives' Feast Day in some parts of Britain. The snowdrop is often called the Fair Maid of February; they were worn by virgins as a sign of purity and in some areas it was traditional for wives to hold a feast in commemoration of the Virgin Mary. That is Wives' Feast Day.'

'And Groundhog Day?'

'That is when the groundhog, an American rodent, pops his nose out of his burrow for the first time after his winter hibernation. If the sun is shining and he sees his shadow, he goes back for a few more weeks; if it is stormy, though, he comes out because it is a sign that winter is over.'

'Just like our old verse about Candlemas being fair and bright, sir? A fine and sunny Candlemas means a severe second half of winter to follow? And a wet and miserable

Candlemas means a pleasant second half of winter.'

'Exactly, Sergeant. And finally, Cradle Rocking Day. That occurred at Blidworth in Nottinghamshire when the last male child born in the parish was placed in a wooden cradle inside the church and rocked twelve times on the altar – it represented the child Jesus in the temple.'

'But none of this is of relevance to our investigation? Except that the snowdrop is a token of death.'

'Yes, because of its shroud-like appearance.'

'So all our victims have been presented with well-pressed shrouds, sir?'

'I suppose they have, Wayne.'

'So does this mean we are going to put twenty-four-hour security guards on the people named in your file?'

'We are not, Sergeant! I see no need for that. Apart from the expense, I do not think it is necessary. Now, it is time to gather my teams for the conference.'

During the conference Pluke reiterated the facts of the case. Where necessary, he updated the facts and after an address of almost fifty minutes he handed the teams to Detective Inspector Horsley, the officer in charge of the Incident Room. Horsley would allocate further actions to each team of two detectives; matters like house-to-house enquiries, interviewing estate workers and people who were regular visitors to the estate and its office, or who had business dealings with it. There was the need to trace the woman in the small green car, endeavouring to discover any other recipients of pressed snowdrops and any sightings of likely suspects.

Determining the last-known movements of the deceased, along with any contacts he might have made, remained a priority and equally vital was the finding of the murder weapon or weapons. Because it was apparent that people had been in the habit of walking around the castle and even elsewhere in the private parkland, it was necessary to trace any recent visitors. Early morning hikers, dog walkers, horse riders or naturalists might have seen something; they might even have seen Stephen out riding yesterday morning before his death.

Today, the Task Force officers would intensify their search of the castle and its grounds, then empty the waters of the giant trough with the help of the Fire Brigade; forensic experts would continue to examine the entire scene with customary care. Trippingdale Hall would be searched too and meanwhile Stephen's body was in the mortuary at Crickledale General Hospital awaiting its post-mortem examination. It was scheduled for ten thirty this morning. His clothes and any personal belongings would be carefully scrutinised, in laboratory conditions if necessary.

Having completed his conference, Pluke called Inspector Russell. 'You have announced the time of a news conference, Inspector?' he asked the young man.

'Ten o'clock, sir. The press know about it. We can use the garage area for the time being; it's a former coach house and is large enough. And it is dry.'

'Good man. Now, this is what I want to highlight in the press,' said Pluke. He told Paul Russell that he could publish the name of the deceased because he had been formally identified and his ex-wife had been informed, but added that the cause of death had not been established. The press could be told that forty officers were engaged on the inquiry, that house-to-house enquiries were being made, that the police wanted to trace anyone who had seen the deceased on Saturday morning riding his bay horse between around six and ten o'clock, and that any information about the deceased's personal contacts since his arrival in Trippingdale would be valued.

Then he came to the pressed snowdrops. He told Russell as much as he knew about them, adding that the dead man had been one of the recipients. Then he explained to

Russell, 'What I want to do is this. I want anyone else who has received such a missive in the mail to contact the Incident Room, either by telephone or in person. If possible, I would like recipients to bring along their specimens for laboratory analysis.'

'Is there a danger of crank calls, Mr Pluke? That's one risk of publicising something as offbeat as this.'

'Cranks will always make a nuisance of themselves.' Pluke seemed philosophical about that likelihood. 'I think we can distinguish the cranks from the genuine.'

'Ideally, I'd like a specimen of the snow-drop, with an envelope, for the press and TV to photograph. They'd love that and it might be useful to our enquiries.'

'Then I shall make one available. Now, is there anything else I need to consider?'

'The only question I can anticipate, Mr Pluke, is whether this is trivialising the investigation. You know what the tabloids are like when they get hold of some story that is out of the ordinary. They can place all kinds of wrong interpretations on it and make silly headlines, which do more harm than good.'

'If it keeps the murder in the public eye, Inspector, then it is not all bad; I need to inform the people of Crickledale of the importance of this and I know that very few of them are silly enough to believe what they read in the tabloid newspapers. They are Yorkshire people, Inspector, country folk. They have more sense and I am sure they will make a very positive response.'

'I hope you are right.'

'To be honest, Inspector, I am not too worried what the tabloids do with the story – the kind of people who read them are not the sort one finds in Crickledale; they are not the audience I wish to contact.'

'Well, so long as you are aware of the possibility of some reporter or headline writer drumming up a weird story...'

'Such newspapers will very soon be wrapping fish and chips, Inspector; they are of no lasting consequence.' Pluke smiled. 'One should ignore them.'

'That is not always possible but I do make the point that I have drawn your attention to the risks of trivialising our investigation.'

'Detective Sergeant Wain is fearful that some might interpret the snowdrop as having some links with cocaine, Inspector. We need to bear that in mind.'

'Cocaine is sometimes called snow, Mr Pluke, as I am sure you know. That might be a genuine link, one worthy of investigation. I would think that if the snowdrops do get the public interested in our inquiry for whatever reason and if the publicity does produce some good results, then it will be worth it.'

'Then we shall do it,' said Pluke, looking

at his watch. 'Right, I will take the news conference and I will let them see a sample of the mailed flower, then set about my own enquiries.'

As Montague was preparing for his news conference and planning his subsequent enquiries, Millicent was having coffee in the parish hall with the vicar, the organist and about twenty members of the congregation of Crickledale parish church. Being a polite lady, she had asked the vicar if she could address the small gathering on a matter of some gravity and he had agreed; it was far more practical to address them as a group than to make individual approaches.

As the munching of biscuits and sipping of coffee got under way, therefore, the Reverend Hywel Abbeyfield rapped on the table with a spoon handle. 'Ladies and gentlemen,' he called. 'Mrs Pluke would like a few words. Millicent?'

'Ahem,' she began, her face flushing crimson as she faced her audience. 'Thank you, Vicar. My husband has asked me to mention this matter to you, as responsible members of society. As most of you know, he is Detective Inspector Pluke, the man in charge of the Crickledale CID. Some people in the town have received anonymous letters, which consist of pressed snowdrops sent in plain brown envelopes. Some of the recipients have referred the matter to the police but others may not have taken that action. My husband has asked me to request any of you who have received such a piece of mail to inform him – you can tell me here, of course, I will take your name and he will then come to interview you.'

'I got one,' the vicar beamed. 'A couple of weeks ago. I thought it was some kind of advertising stunt.'

'And I got one at about the same time,' Miss Emily Bampton, the pretty young parish magazine editor who worked for a local printing company, smiled. 'I put mine in an eggcup of water, thinking it might revive. It didn't, so I threw it out.'

'You know about mine, Millicent,' piped up Mrs Mayweed. 'I did tell you and I trust you informed the detective inspector with all due speed?'

'Yes, I did, Mrs Mayweed, and he has taken possession of your envelope and its contents. He has more than a dozen such letters in his file already.'

'I received one too,' added Mrs Hortensia Keysmith, the tall lady with the dyed blonde hair and rather too much make-up for a fifty-year-old. 'A fortnight ago, I had no idea why it arrived. There was nothing else in the envelope, but I think I kept it on the mantelpiece behind the clock, in case there was some kind of follow-up. I thought it might be part of a competition or something.'

'Thank you,' said Millicent. 'Any more?'

No one else admitted receipt of such a piece of mail, so the vicar enquired, 'Mrs Pluke, might I ask why the detective inspector is interested in what appears to be such a trivial matter?'

'You might not have heard the news, any of you, but there has been a murder in the locality...'

'I did hear it on the news yesterday evening, just a snippet, with no name or anything,' someone muttered.

'My husband is in charge of the investigation.' Millicent pumped out her modest chest with some pride. 'He is interested in your snowdrops because one of the odd things is that the dead man also received a crushed snowdrop through the post.'

'Oh, my goodness me...' Mrs Mayweed clutched at her heart but failed to find it beneath the coating of flesh upon her rather substantial chest. 'Oh, dear ... this is dreadful...'

'Mrs Pluke ... please enlighten us,' pleaded the vicar with fear in his voice. 'Why should a murder victim receive one of these letters?'

'A single snowdrop in one's house is a token of death,' said Millicent in her innocence.

'You mean we've all got death threats?'

168

shrieked Hortensia Keysmith. 'You mean we are going to be murdered, all of us?'

Quite suddenly, there was pandemonium in the parish hall.

'I got one as well!' cried a woman's voice from the depths of the high-pitched volume of excited conversation. 'I got one ... I'm going to be murdered ... oh, my God' And she ran screaming from the hall.

'Please, all of you, keep calm,' beseeched the vicar with hands raised like Moses parting the waves. His intervention did, however, quell the advancing tidal wave of emotion and fear. 'Please, keep calm, I am sure there is no need for panic.'

'Please!' shouted Millicent above the din. 'Please keep calm, just listen...'

And, rather surprisingly, they obeyed. She exerted some kind of authority, did Mrs Pluke, probably because she was the wife of the detective inspector in charge of Crickledale Criminal Investigation Department.

'Thank you,' she said, lowering her voice so that the others would have to remain silent in order to hear her. 'Thank you. Now, my husband says there is no need to fear. He does not think the sender of the letters is the murderer, nor does he think those who receive the letters will necessarily be murdered. All he wants to know at this stage is who has received such a letter and, preferably, he would like to take possession of it to see if there is any link between the murder victim and the others.'

'Is it in order to ask the name of the murder victim?' enquired the vicar.

'His name is being announced at a news conference this morning,' Millicent said. 'He is Stephen Gallholme, the new owner of Tippingdale Estate.'

'Oh, dear.' Mrs Mayweed sighed. 'Oh, dear, how awful, the poor man...'

'Dreadful!' cried the vicar. 'He came to see me only last week. He wants to maintain good relations between the parish and his estate. I buried his mother, you see, but this is dreadful news, quite dreadful.'

'I have no further details of him or the cause of his death,' Millicent said, as if reading the minds of the silent crowd now standing motionless before her.

The vicar now took control of this emotional gathering. 'This dreadful event does provide a wonderful opportunity for the people of Crickledale to co-operate with the police,' he told them. 'If any of us have anything to contribute to the investigation, however insignificant we think it might be, we should not be afraid to say so. So, Millicent, I am sure anyone who has received a snowdrop will come forward and if all those recipients who have kept their snowdrops would take them to the police station they would be doing a service to the community.

Am I right, Millicent?'

'That is exactly what the detective inspector would wish.' She smiled with gratitude. 'With the envelopes, of course. They have the names and address on them.'

'And we should perhaps mention that other people who are not members of this congregation and who have received similar snowdrops should do likewise?' suggested the vicar.

'Yes, everyone. We need to persuade everyone to hand in their snowdrops. Perhaps you could all pass the word around among your friends and neighbours?'

'An excellent idea,' the vicar agreed.

And all the people standing before him nodded before rushing home to lock their doors against the snowdrop killer. Only Millicent and Emily remained because Millicent wanted to say a personal thank you to the Reverend Abbeyfield and Emily had some parish magazine matters to clarify before publication.

'You did very well there, Millicent,' said the vicar when the place was empty save for Emily Bampton and her. 'Now I have the small matter of a suitable editorial for the next edition to discuss with Emily.'

'Then I shall not detain you any longer. Thank you for your support.' Millicent smiled at him. 'Now, I wonder how Montague is getting along?'

There was also a near riot at Montague's news conference. He had outlined the facts he wished them to know, he had confirmed the identity of the murder victim and explained that his officers would be making house-to-house enquiries. He had also told them about the snowdrop campaign, adding that he did not believe the word snow had any connotation with dangerous drugs so far as this investigation was concerned. But in the world of sceptical journalists a denial is often a clue to something rather more positive.

'Are you saying that Stephen Gallholme was involved in drugs, Detective Inspector?' demanded one. 'If not, why make references to snow?'

'Are you giving police protection to everyone who has received one of those letters?' called another. 'And if not, why not?'

'Have people in other parts of Britain also received similar death threats?'

'Can you give us the names of people who have received these threats?'

'Why are you maintaining such secrecy when the public have a right to know the extent of this campaign of death?'

'Have any black people received the snowdrops?'

'Will you be calling in Scotland Yard and heat-seeking helicopters?'

'Is this a drugs-related death? Have other drug dealers also received snowdrops?'

'Will drugs dogs be searching the estate and the houses around the district?'

'Is the snowdrop campaign the work of anti-drugs campaigners?'

'Did the deceased stir up any feeling against the Right to Roam campaigners and have magic mushrooms any link with this case?'

'Will your detectives be armed during this investigation?'

'Is the killer likely to strike again?'

'Is this the work of a serial killer?'

'Who stands to inherit Trippingdale Estate now that its new owner is dead?'

'Was the victim poisoned? Are snowdrops poisonous? Were they laced with poison?'

'Is witchcraft involved in this murder?'

The whole roomful of journalists was throwing questions at Pluke following his statement that the deceased had received a snowdrop through the post, which Pluke described as 'a token of death' during his address and to which he had added a comment that snow was a slang word for cocaine.

In the midst of the pandemonium Pluke held up his hands to command silence. 'We are taking every feasible step to examine every possible aspect of the posted snowdrops and we are looking into the previous life and work of Stephen Gallholme.' It was a very carefully worded statement. 'I am asking everyone in this district to let me know if they have received such a letter in the post and, of course, we are liaising with other police forces throughout the country in an attempt to determine whether the snowdrop campaign is more widespread, or even more sinister that we first thought. I must add, however, that I am not convinced the person who sent the snowdrop is the killer,' he added with an air of finality.

'And why not?' demanded a journalist.

'You may quote me as saying that my belief is based on my professional experience and the evidence already to hand. I may be able to elaborate when the results of the post-mortem are confirmed later today. That is all I have to say at this stage.'

And, perspiring heavily in his thick overcoat, Pluke walked out of the news conference. They had got their story and their photographs of one of the pressed snowdrops; he knew this murder would make headline news in both the national and regional papers.

When he walked back into the Incident Room Inspector Dick Horsley wanted to speak to him. 'I've just had Meredith on the phone,' he said. 'He's finished the post-mortem. Can you give him a ring?'

174

9

Pluke rang the direct line to the pathologist. 'I've completed my examination of Mr Gallholme and felt you should know the result straight away, since it'll take a while for my written report to reach you.'

'Thank you.' Pluke knew that early knowledge of the cause of death could benefit his enquiries.

'As we thought at the scene, he died from drowning, Mr Pluke. There is no doubt about that. And he died in that huge trough; he did not die elsewhere nor was his body transported to the scene after death. Water in his lungs is identical to the sample we secured from the trough. This confirms the place of death. You will recall that the deceased's head was held under the water not by weeds, but by some instrument. And here I have amended my earlier thoughts. Initially, I felt that two instruments had been used. To some extent that could explain why the base of his skull was broken – but that didn't kill him. There is massive bruising in that region too, in spite of the riding helmet, suggesting something like a sledgehammer. My original thoughts were that a second instrument, with a long handle, had been used to hold his head under the water long enough and firmly enough for him to drown.'

'That prognosis did seem to fit the circumstances,' agreed Pluke, recalling his own views that one tool might have been used. 'So what is your amended conclusion?'

'I favour the single implement theory,' said Meredith. 'In reaching that conclusion I had to consider the timing required and the swift actions necessary to deliver a severe and accurate blow, which would stun the victim or would unbalance him so severely that he tumbled head first into the water; added to which there would have to be a further set of timings during which he would have picked up the second implement and then used it. Furthermore, it had to hold the fellow's head beneath the surface long enough for him to drown, in spite of any struggles. The use of two weapons in those rapidly moving circumstances would be very complicated, Mr Pluke, almost impossible, I'd say. Consequently I now believe it unlikely that two weapons were used. Furthermore, it is most unlikely that two suitable tools would be so conveniently on hand for that purpose. Even if the killer had planned the murder in some detail, with two weapons he would have had great difficulty in choreographing the sequence of events so that they were guaranteed to produce the result he wanted.'

'It was an act of spontaneity, you think?'

'Or a very skilled execution, Mr Pluke. Whatever happened, the killer used the moment with terrifying speed and immense skill, wielding a tool that was so very conveniently available. For all these reasons, Mr Pluke, I think a single implement was used. You are looking for one murder weapon, not a pair.'

'I did feel it would have been a somewhat complicated and ponderous procedure to have used two instruments of death,' agreed Pluke.

'Using two, it would be virtually impossible without a lot of rehearsals and some degree of luck,' said Meredith. 'So let us now consider that single tool. What was it? I favour a farming implement of some kind. I believe it was a pitchfork, a locally made straw-fork, perhaps. I have seen these around the moorland farms; they are strongly made, they are plentiful and many are still in regular use even if they are a century or more old. Made by the local blacksmith, they have two pointed iron prongs set fairly wide apart – certainly wide enough for a prong to slide down either side of a man's neck and, of course, the prongs are arched where they are attached to the handle. That arch would fit quite snugly around a human neck, I would suggest, Mr Pluke. The handles of such tools were usually made of stout wood but they varied considerably in length. A tall farmer would order a long-handled form while a shorter man might require something not quite so long. But whatever the length of the handle, it would be capable of delivering a very powerful blow if wielded like a stave. I think the tip of such a long handle would be heavy enough to have delivered the first blow, the one which knocked Mr Gallholme off balance and into the trough. After all, Robin Hood knocked Little John off his perch with such a stave, Mr Pluke!'

'So your theory is that the attacker swung the fork so that he hit Mr Gallholme on the back of his neck with the end of the shaft. That would unbalance him and topple him face down into the water – it was powerful enough to break his skull at the base – then the attacker immediately switched his grip and turned the fork round so that he could push Gallholme's head under the water and hold it there.'

'Precisely, Mr Pluke. And to achieve all that, he must have worked very quickly with considerable skill.'

'I tend to concur, Mr Meredith, and I agree with you that those fork handles were quite capable of delivering a very powerful blow. I've known a bulldog be stunned by one.'

'There are bruises on the back of Mr Gallholme's neck; if we find such a tool, then I am sure I can match it to the marks on his body. And that applies to the marks on each side of his neck, bruises with nicks in the skin. There might even be some DNA or other evidence on the shaft. So that is how he died, Mr Pluke, forcible drowning facilitated by some kind of hand-held implement. Murder, in other words.'

'Thank you. I will inform my officers.'

'I should add, by the way, that Mr Gallholme was in every other way a very healthy person: no heart problems, no signs of drug dependency, no diseases or major operation scars. Nothing that would have caused his death. And I did examine his clothing, Mr Pluke, but that revealed nothing of interest; his belongings were merely a white handkerchief, keys to the stable and to his house, a silver-coloured Longines wristwatch but no money, credit cards or other papers. He travelled light, Mr Pluke; after all, he was merely out to ride his own horse in his own grounds. There may be useful DNA samples in his clothes. I will ensure that samples are taken.'

'Excellent, Mr Meredith.' Pluke was delighted with these results.

'Call me if you need any more information, Mr Pluke.'

And so that vital part of the investigation

was complete. All Pluke now had to do was find the murder weapon – it would help identify the killer. A local farmer or agricultural worker, perhaps?

Detective Sergeant Wayne Wain, aided by a pink-cheeked and happy Detective Constable Paula Helston and accompanied by six detectives from the Scenes of Crime department, were searching Trippingdale Hall. Built of local stone, the Hall had a comfortable and rather unpretentious appearance, probably because part of it dated to the late sixteenth century, with extensions and alterations occurring regularly during the ensuing years. Mullioned windows, large chimney breasts, gabled projections, a spacious entrance hall and stone arches in the gardens, but linked to the walls of the house, gave it a lived-in and rather rustic appearance. Inside, there was lots of oak panelling, some dating from Jacobean times, some late seventeenth-century fireplaces and chimney pieces in oak, a splendid library, an open stairwell, stone floors at ground level and lots of wonderful antique furnishings. The room immediately on the left as one entered through the huge porch was used as the Estate Office – this was Basil Broadbent's kingdom – while a smaller adjoining room was his secretary's domain. These were separated from the living quarters by a massive studded oak door. Beyond that door, the rest of the huge house was private, with six further rooms at ground-floor level, eight bedrooms and three attic rooms. Broadbent had admitted them to the private quarters, the studded door normally being kept locked when the family was in residence.

'Has anyone been into the private quarters since Mr Gallholme was found dead?' Wayne Wain had asked him.

'No, not even the cleaner. I have kept it locked,' Broadbent had told him. 'Out of respect, you understand. Till things get sorted out.'

'We have to search his rooms and personal belongings,' Wayne Wain had been firm but understanding. 'For evidence, for clues, for a motive, perhaps, addresses of contacts ... anything, really.'

'I won't try to stop you or be obstructive in any way.' Broadbent had appeared very co-operative. 'I want this bastard found.'

'A woman was seen leaving here on Thursday last, early in the morning.' Wayne had wanted to know if Broadbent had any notion of his employer's private activities. 'She had a small car, dark-green, we think, a Vauxhall Corsa or something similar. In her thirties, dark hair, smartly dressed in a white blouse and dark-green skirt. She was spotted by a holidaymaker out walking; he thought nothing of it until we began to quiz him, so he didn't get the car number. She wasn't delivering papers or milk – we've checked. Any idea who she might have been? Or why she was leaving the Hall so early in the morning?'

Broadbent had shaken his head. 'Sorry, she doesn't mean a thing to me. So far as I knew, he had no women friends in this area; he'd not been here long enough to form any kind of relationship and I know of no over-night residents. He didn't have a formal dinner or anything like that. I'd have known if he'd arranged that kind of thing.'

'Well, if you do learn anything about her we'd like to know. For elimination purposes, of course.'

'Mrs Preston, Lily, who did his cleaning and evening meals, well, she might know if the woman had stayed overnight. I suppose he could have had a guest without me knowing about it. Mrs Preston makes his bed and so on. She lives along the lane, that house with the green gate, Myrtle Cottage. The woman wasn't her, by the way, she's well into her late fifties and has grey hair.'

'We'll ask her,' Wayne had assured him.

And so they had begun their search. It was an expert search with each detective being allocated a specific task such as looking for diaries, letters, address and telephone number books, the personal computer and its link to the Internet or e-mail facilities, clothing not belonging to Stephen Gallholme, toiletries of the kind a visitor might have brought, bank accounts and statements, credit card demands, details of living expenses including that of keeping his horse, empty wine bottles and anything that might carry fingerprints not belonging to him, as well as any other indication of another person staying here or even visiting on a short-term basis.

It was true in such searches that a detective never really knew what he or she was seeking until it was found; some thing that seemed out of the ordinary: a scribbled note in the margin of a newspaper, a champagne bottle in the dustbin, discarded condoms – anything slightly unusual could be relevant. In this case it was a photograph. It was standing on Stephen's bedside cabinet close to his phone. Paula Helston drew Wayne's attention to it.

It was in colour, depicting a young woman sitting cross-legged on what looked like a park bench. She was in her thirties, estimated Paula, with light-brown hair, spectacles, a round and rather pretty face, and she was dressed in light summer clothes, a short-sleeved blouse in a neutral colour but with a rather high collar, a blue skirt and neutral sandals.

'That looks like a railway station seat,' Wayne Wain said. 'You can tell by those knobbly legs. The seat's, that is, not hers. So is she on a station or is the seat in private hands? Lots of them were sold off, you know, after Beeching's axe closed dozens of rural stations hereabouts. And Paula, what is the era of her clothes? Any idea?'

'It's hard to say, but judging by the style and length of that skirt, and the appearance of her blouse, I'd say it's late Seventies, give or take a few years either way. And her hairstyle is about right for that period. My mother looked a bit like that when I was at infant school.'

'Is there a note with the photo?' Wayne took it from her and examined the rear, but it bore nothing. Quickly, he slipped aside the metal holders and allowed the back of the frame to drop into his waiting hand. It revealed the other side of the photograph and there was a message in black ballpoint. It simply said 'To Stephen with love. Ann. xx'.

'Ann. So who is she? Take that away, Paula, we'll see if we can find Ann, whoever she is.'

Before they left, the detectives had assembled a wide variety of articles for examination. In addition to the photograph of Ann, it included Stephen's address book, some references to his previous employment, a personal list of telephone numbers, a family photograph album, a water glass found on a bedside cabinet in another bedroom, which otherwise appeared unused, some oblong white tablets discovered in an unmarked box in his bedroom, his pocket diary, wallet and contents, which were on his dressing table, and two wineglasses discovered in the library; they contained some residue from red wine in the form of small flakes of sediment. Apart from these items there was nothing in the domestic quarters that attracted the attention of the detectives; everything appeared to be absolutely normal and maintained in a tidy and clean condition.

There was no sign of unwanted visitors, domestic strife, violent lovemaking, unhealthy interests like pornographic videos or books; in fact, the house appeared to be that of a very contented and normal person. As one might have expected there were family portraits and photographs on some of the walls, including one depicting a young Stephen on horseback and others who were ancestors from several generations. Wayne Wain did, however, ensure that Scenes of Crime teams examined the entire household for fingerprints, although he realised it would be difficult to trace everyone who might have left a mark – Stephen's mother and her callers, for example. After completing his search, he left the Scenes of Crime officers to finish their work; with Paula Helston, he returned to the Estate Office. Broadbent was there; although it was a Sunday, his normal day off, he had decided to be available all day should he be required by the detectives.

'We're taking one or two items away for scientific examination,' Wayne told Broadbent, listing the objects in question. 'But we've found nothing of immediate interest, except this photograph. It was beside Stephen's bed.' He placed it on Broadbent's desk and invited him to examine it. 'So who's this, Mr Broadbent? Any idea? It's signed by somebody called Ann.'

Broadbent shook his head. 'Sorry, I've never seen her here. I've not been here all that long, though; I came in 1985. Mr Stephen was away then, working in London. I never knew his friends. Even if he brought people home for the weekend, I rarely met them – I run the estate, which meant I had little to do with his private life. I'm afraid I don't know much about him prior to his inheritance of the estate. If he did come home, it was usually a short visit, a weekend mostly, and I rarely talked to him about his own affairs.'

'So this lady could be from his previous life in London?'

'I'd say so. I don't think she's from around

here, I don't recognise her. But I could be wrong.'

'She seems to be sitting on a railway station seat, the kind you'd expect to find on a rural station.'

'Sorry, I can't help,' apologised Broadbent. 'I'm not very clued up about railway stations, used or disused. The National Railway Museum at York might help. How old is this woman? Thirty-five? And photographed when? I'd say within the last twenty years. It's not his mother, I can tell you that.'

'Thanks anyway, we'll keep asking. We have his former work address so we can have enquiries made by the local police. Or maybe the press would help trace her?'

'While you are here, Sergeant, I think I might have realised who the woman caller was, that one you mentioned earlier, with the little green car. This leaflet' – and he produced a coloured brochure from his in-tray – 'came on Thursday. I got one at home. I remembered when I found this one on my desk while you were in the house. I think that woman might have been delivering these.'

Wayne took it from him and examined it. It was advertising gardening machinery, tools, ornaments, seeds and plants, which were available from a new garden shop. A white box at the bottom of the back page contained the address of the premises in

Crickledale – along with the name of Diana and Neil Harwood, the new owners.

'Can I take it?' asked Wayne. 'We'll go and see her.'

'Sure, I've the copy which came to my house if I need to use it.'

And so, after thanking Broadbent for his co-operation and advising him that officers were still working inside the building, Wayne and Paula left the Hall.

'Right,' he said. 'First, let's visit this garden shop.'

'Won't it be shut?' asked Paula.

'Not on a Sunday in the middle of spring, the gardening season,' countered Wayne. 'Let's do that little chore before we return, then we might have something positive to report.'

Within twenty minutes, they were entering the spacious shop, which was in fact a garden centre on the outskirts of the town. The shop was merely part of the whole enterprise and it was busy. Wayne and Paula parked and entered the airy place, each enjoying its scents and sights. It was full of gardening tools of every conceivable kind from spades to edging tools, and there was machinery like lawnmowers and hedge trimmers, along with ornaments such as statues, sundials and gnomes, as well as plastic pond liners, fencing, paving slabs, rows and rows of seeds, plants in pots –

everything for the modern garden.

They went to the counter; a sign requested they press a bell for attention and after it rang somewhere in the depths of the building, a tall, powerfully built man emerged from an office. In his mid-forties, he looked like a rugger player or a shot-putter. 'Yes, how can I help you?' he asked.

'I am Detective Sergeant Wain from Crickledale and this is Detective Constable Helston.' Wayne produced his warrant card to confirm his status. 'I'd like to speak to Mr or Mrs Harwood, please, about this leaflet.'

The man's face registered his alarm. 'I'm Neil Harwood,' he told them. 'Is there something illegal about our brochure?'

'Oh, no, nothing like that.' Wayne smiled. 'But do you have a person who distributes them?'

'Well, yes, my wife and I, we both deliver them. By hand. We tour the villages and local market towns. We're just new here, you see, and can't afford to pay people to do that kind of chore, so we do it ourselves. We wanted to get those brochures distributed before the weekend.' The puzzlement was still clear on his face as he wondered why on earth the CID should be interested in his somewhat mundane business arrangements.

'And who delivered this leaflet to Trippingdale Hall?' asked Wayne.

'My wife would do that during the week.'

'What day and what time, Mr Harwood?'

'Thursday, I think. I'm sure that's the day she'd have been in the Trippingdale area. And it would be early. We've got to be in the shop all day and the only time to make that kind of delivery is very early. We set off at six or thereabouts and finish by half past eight, snatch a bit of breakfast and come here to open up. So what's all this about, Sergeant? Have we done anything wrong? Has there been a complaint about us? Waking the sleepy villagers or something?'

'Not at all, Mr Harwood. So what does your wife look like? And what kind of car does she drive?'

'She's got a little Vauxhall, a Corsa. A new one. Dark-green. And she's thirty-six, dark hair, always smartly dressed when she does those trips because she has to go straight to work after breakfast. There's no time to get ready afterwards and she likes to be smart at work. Sergeant, am I going to be enlightened about all this?'

Wayne Wain then explained about the murder inquiry based at Trippingdale Hall and told Mr Harwood that a witness had seen a woman of his wife's description leaving the vicinity of the Hall on Thursday morning. No one knew who she was and, although her presence had occurred two days prior to the murder, she had to be eliminated from the inquiry. She could have been to the Hall for all sorts of reasons, legitimate or otherwise.

'We had no idea who she was, you see, we thought Stephen Gallholme might have been entertaining a lady at the Hall overnight.'

'My wife had better hear all this,' said Harwood. 'I'll call her.'

Minutes later, a very presentable and attractive woman stood before them; with dark, well-groomed hair cut short, she was dressed in a crisp white blouse, a bottle-green skirt and smart black shoes. After listening to her husband's account of Wayne's questioning, then Wayne's version of the same event, she smiled at the detectives. 'Yes, that was me on Thursday,' she admitted. 'I've not met your Mr Gallholme but I did call at the Hall and at the houses nearby, to drop off our leaflets. I then toured the adjoining villages and got back here about eight thirty.'

'Did you see anyone while you were near the Hall?' asked Wayne.

'No, not a soul. Not even the man you said had spotted me.'

'Thanks,' said Wayne. 'You've saved us a lot of time and expense. We'd have been chasing all over the place to get you named ... but thanks. We can cross you off our list of suspects now.'

'You mean I was a murder suspect?' she cried.

'We have to follow up every sighting, which means everyone is a suspect until they've been eliminated,' he told her. 'But we know you were there for perfectly legitimate reasons and besides, it was a couple of days before Mr Gallholme died. So you're in the clear. Thanks for your co-operation.'

'I never thought my leaflet deliveries would turn me into a murder suspect!' And she managed an uncertain smile.

'Well, now you are not.' Wayne Wain smiled. 'Sorry to have troubled you.'

'I hope you find your man,' said Neil Harwood.

Minutes later, they were heading back towards Trippingdale Hall, this time to report their endeavours to Inspector Horsley, the officer in charge of the Incident Room.

'You were happy with her story, were you?' Paula said to Wayne as he drove swiftly through the lanes.

'Yes, I saw no indication of a loophole or evidence of lying, or covering her tracks or anything. And her account tallies with the one we got from the holidaymaker. Why? Did you think she was not telling the truth?'

'Yes, I think she was. But you did not question her husband, did you, Wayne? After all, that couple admit they are out and about very early. Perhaps they saw something on Saturday morning? And...' She paused.

He glanced at her, narrowly averting disaster on a sharp bend, as he said, 'Go on, Paula. Say it. Have I missed something?'

'Well, didn't Mr Pluke tell us that an agricultural tool of some kind had been used to hold Stephen under the water? That place was full of gardening tools, and ... and ... well, I think it would take someone with great strength to hold a drowning man under water for the length of time required to kill him ... and that man, Harwood, wasn't exactly a dwarf or a seven-stone weakling, was he?'

'If he did kill Stephen, what kind of motive might he have had?' asked Wayne.

'Something to do with his wife, perhaps?' Paula suggested. 'After all, she was seen leaving the Hall at six forty-five one morning, but she never said what time she got there. Was there something between her and Stephen? We don't know, do we, Wayne? And we don't know whether that place sells snowdrops, do we? In pots or however snowdrops are sold for domestic gardens.'

'So we've a lot of digging to do.' Wayne Wain chuckled, wondering if she understood his gardening joke. 'Let's put all this to Pluke, shall we?' he said. 'And I think I owe you a big bottle of champagne ... to be

193

drunk in the bath, perhaps?'

'And I will try to find out a little more about Neil Harwood,' she added, ignoring his pass. 'While you try to unearth more about Stephen Gallholme. We know virtually nothing about his past, do we? It's almost as if he didn't want anyone to know.'

'Perhaps he was hiding something,' mused Wayne.

10

Before continuing his own specialised enquiries, Pluke took Horsley to one side. 'We
must find the murder weapon as a matter of
some urgency,' he said. 'It has to be nearby,
but there must be thousands of straw-forks
in this area. Finding the right one will not
be easy. Perhaps you could ask the Task
Force to make a detailed search along the
lanes and roadsides? Hedge bottoms. Barns.
Stables. Fields even. Anywhere that an implement of that kind might have been
concealed.'

'It's already in hand, Montague,' said
Horsley. 'But we will redouble our efforts.'

'And I think we should check the back-
grounds of the estate staff and workers, and
the people who live nearby. Do any of them
have convictions, for example, or have they
come to the notice of the police in any way?'

'We're doing those checks as each witness
is interviewed, Montague. So far, though,
we've found nothing incriminating against
anyone.'

'Gallholme himself had no record, then?'

'No, we've found nothing so far but the
local police are making enquiries in his

former home area and around his work-place. And his estate manager, Broadbent, is clean too – we've checked him.'

'We mustn't forget our gatekeeping friend,' said Pluke, 'Aaron Pinder. He seems rather volatile at times.'

'I can put him through a CRO check now, if you like, although he's not been formally interviewed yet.'

'Yes, do that. Forewarned is forearmed. Now, Mr Horsley, there is one other matter to consider – this is not the first drowning in Trippingdale.'

'Really? I haven't heard about another, Montague.'

'It was a long time ago,' said Pluke. 'Before I joined the Force, in fact. In 1966, if my memory serves me correctly. A child, a small boy, was drowned in the stream near the dale head. I remember my parents talking about it. It was big news at the time but I cannot remember the details. I was a young man working in London then, you see, with little interest in Crickledale as I began to spread my wings. For a brief time I lost close contact with events in this area.'

'London, Montague? I had no idea you had seen the world!'

'I got a job in a bank, Mr Horsley, banking was to be my career and I thought it would broaden my experience if I worked in the capital, but I soon changed my mind. I hated city life so returned to Crickledale and joined the police service, a far more rewarding and satisfying life.'

'Goodness me! You learn something every day. You a bank clerk! But that drowning. Murder, was it?'

'No, an accident I believe. I wonder if you could discover more about the case?'

'Our records will have been destroyed, won't they? The ten-year clear-out?'

'Probably,' said Pluke. 'But there must be some account of it somewhere – a newspaper file, perhaps, or the coroner's office, or even our own records. Not every organisation destroys files after ten years and we don't destroy everything.'

'If it was an accident, how could it be relevant to our enquiries? Do we really need to spend valuable time hunting down old records of a case that sure has no bearing on this one?'

'I shall not know whether it has any bearing on this case until I learn the facts, Mr Horsley. In my opinion it needs to be researched. Two drownings in a fairly small area of private parkland might not be a coincidence, even if they are separated by more than thirty years.'

'Then it will be done,' confirmed Horsley. 'I'll get a team to start searching.'

Having dealt with the routine elements of the inquiry, Pluke's mission during the remainder of that Sunday was to interview those people who had complained about receiving pressed snowdrops. It might not be possible to visit all in the time available today and he also realised that, being a Sunday, some might be enjoying outings in the splendid Yorkshire countryside. But there was always tomorrow.

Fired with a missionary zeal, therefore, he asked a detective to drive him into Crickledale and, having been deposited in the market square, Pluke told the fellow he would continue his duties on foot. The detective returned to the Incident Room leaving Pluke standing in solitary splendour, looking remarkably like an abandoned scarecrow in his huge, dirty, ragged all-enveloping and ancient coaching coat, his dicky bow, spats and his blue-ribboned panama.

He had the file of complaints beneath his arm and, thankful that the wind was not very brisk, opened it to study the contents. From the list of names and his knowledge of the geography of their addresses, he would determine the most suitable sequence of interviews; he would adopt a route that allowed him to visit each of the interviewees with the minimum of walking and without any necessity to catch buses or hail taxis. Not that there were many taxis in Crickledale – or buses, for that matter. And, he told himself, he must not forget any additional recipients who might have declared themselves to Millicent at church. He hoped her assistance would have proved beneficial – he would discuss things with her at lunchtime.

First along Pluke's route was Elias Hosegood who, for many years, had been a prominent member of Crickledale District Council. It was Hosegood's persistence that had resulted in double yellow lines being imposed upon the roads in Little Leverton, a pretty riverside village some eight miles from Crickledale. The place was popular with tourists, hence the need for some kind of parking restrictions, but that action had earned him the nickname of Nogood Hosegood. Although the residents did not like tourists and day-trippers, they liked the yellow lines even less and Hosegood had lost the subsequent election.

Hosegood, now in his late sixties, had retired from both his profession as a salesman of paper cups for drinks vending machines and from his council duties, but he continued to regard himself as a person of some importance in the locality. Pluke, as a local detective with his knowledge of Crickledale and its many people, was aware of those landmarks in the career of Elias Hosegood.

So far as Pluke knew, Hosegood had never been involved in any shady deals, corruption scandals or vote-rigging allegations, so why would anyone send him a token of death in the form of a pressed snowdrop? Was it some delayed reaction following his yellow-line campaign for Little Leverton? Was it someone expressing suppressed anger at such a drastic response to the village car-parking problem which, after all, was merely seasonal? Or had Hosegood crossed someone during his council duties or, indeed, had he offended someone in more recent times? If so, why had all those other people been sent snowdrops? They weren't councillors or ex-councillors and had probably had little or nothing to do with yellow lines.

Furthermore, Stephen Gallholme hadn't been living locally when the yellow lines were imposed and he had come off worst among Pluke's people of interest. So had the phantom snowdrop-posting person been offended by some other matter, something common to all the recipients? If so, what? Pluke felt that Mrs Mayweed had very little in common with Elias Hosegood and the deceased Stephen Gallholme seemed to have nothing in common with either of them. Verily, it was all very vexatious for Montague Pluke.

When Pluke knocked on his door. Elias answered. 'Mr Pluke! Good heavens, fancy seeing you here on a good Sunday morning!'

He was a tall, stooping man with a mop of grey hair that looked like a magpie's nest, eyebrows like hairy caterpillars and large, yellow, gap-ridden teeth, which reminded Pluke of Stonehenge.

He wore a grey cardigan, which swamped his ageing and pensionable frame, grey trousers that had never been pressed since Adam was a lad, and a pair of carpet slippers that looked pre-war. It was the sort of clothing a household man would wear on a Sunday morning, unless he was going to church, of course, or had been cajoled into an outing of some kind.

'It is a very good day for setting one's best clocker upon the eggs,' responded Pluke. 'But Sunday is not very good for turning the sheets on one's bed. However, I am here on police business, Mr Hosegood, the matter of your pressed-snowdrop mail.'

'Good heavens, you *are* taking it seriously, Mr Pluke. I just thought I should mention it in passing. I never expected a full-scale investigation by our leading detective. You'd better come in. Martha will see to some coffee for us.'

As Hosegood was not a murder suspect, the free gift of a cup of coffee could hardly be construed as a bribe, so Pluke stepped across the threshold, using his right foot first, and thanked Elias for the offer. He had missed his morning coffee in the Incident

Room, such was his desire to tackle this inquiry. As Elias led his guest into the sitting room of their semi-detached house with its conservatory, patio and gravel drive, he called to Martha, 'We have a guest, Martha, it's Mr Pluke. Could we have some coffee please? Two cups.'

'Right,' called a voice from the kitchen from which emanated the strong smells of roasting beef, onion gravy and Yorkshire puddings.

'So, Mr Pluke.' Elias indicated an easy chair into which Pluke lowered himself after removing his hat. 'I have a sherry before Sunday lunch. Can I tempt you?'

'Thank you, but no, Mr Hosegood. I do not drink on duty. The coffee will be sufficient.'

'As you wish. I'm going to have one anyway. So how can I help?' he asked as he went to his drinks cabinet to pour himself a generous schooner full of a sweet variety.

'I am visiting all the people who notified the police about the pressed snowdrops,' began Pluke.

'It's not all that important, surely? I wouldn't have bothered you chaps, you know, if it hadn't been a token of death, Mr Pluke. But you said there were others? Were there many others?'

'More than a dozen.' Pluke did not wish to divulge official police secrets by giving the precise total; besides, he did not know how many other people had actually received the flowers. 'But before I proceed, have you heard about Stephen Gallholme?'

'From Trippingdale Hall? I've never met him, but has he received one?' Hosegood returned and settled on a chair opposite Pluke.

'Without wishing to alarm you, Mr Hosegood,' Pluke said, 'Mr Gallholme has been murdered. And he received a pressed snowdrop before he died.'

'Oh, my God...' Hosegood spilt his sherry on the floor and hastily rubbed the carpet with his foot to hide it. 'Mr Pluke, you do give people some nasty shocks...'

'However, I am of the firm belief, Mr Hosegood, that the sender of the flowers is not the killer of Mr Gallholme. Due to the overriding need for police confidentiality, I cannot give the reasons for such a conclusion but I do need to trace the sender of those flowers. For elimination purposes, you understand. I am here to see if you can shed any light on a possible suspect.'

'You're sure about that, are you? That the sender is not the killer...' Hosegood had left his seat and, with shaking hands, was now pouring himself a large glassful of whisky. The sherry had vanished down his throat; the whisky would, before long, follow the same route.

'No one can be absolutely sure of such things,' Pluke ploughed on in his session of serious alarm. 'But I am reasonably confident. So, Mr Hosegood, have you given further thought to the identity of the snow-drop sender?'

'Well, when I got it, I did wonder about it but couldn't think why I had been sent such a thing. I thought it was some kind of advertising stunt, which would be followed up by something else and then happened to mention it to my neighbour and he said his wife had got one. Anyway, I began to talk about it to other people and discovered what it meant – and that's when I decided to mention it to your chaps.'

'Your neighbour's wife? Who is that?'

'Well, not exactly a neighbour, they live five doors away. The Plodgers. Gabrielle and Stanley.'

Pluke checked his list; Gabrielle Plodger was one of those who had referred the matter to the police. 'Mrs Plodger is on my list,' he confirmed. 'I shall be talking to her very shortly.'

'When I mentioned it to Stan, he said Gabrielle had got one and when I mentioned it to her she said she'd heard that Jeremy Dramjoy had got one. He's the treasurer of the Crickledonian Society, you know. Well, we all got talking and when someone said they were tokens of death, we thought we'd better inform the police. We didn't think it was serious until then and now you mention a murder...'

'So, within your own experience, several people acknowledged receipt of these flowers, Mr Hosegood,' Pluke interrupted him. 'Did you sense any common factor?'

'No, we didn't, Mr Pluke. We're all from Crickledale, of course, and when we talked about the letters, they all appeared to be from the same source. Same kind of envelopes, same handwriting, same style of flowers, same postmark.'

'That is our opinion too, Mr Hosegood. And I can add another factor.' Mrs Hosegood entered with a tray of coffee cups and biscuits, and placed it on a table between Pluke and his host. She smiled and began to pour his coffee as he continued, 'It is my view that all the recipients are prominent within our community in some way.'

'It's funny you should say that, Mr Pluke. I said that to Martha, didn't I, love? That all of us who'd got snowdrops were people of some standing in the community.'

'Yes, dear, you did say that.' She smiled. 'There you are, Mr Pluke. Please help yourself to biscuits and there's more coffee in the pot if you need it. Milk and sugar on the tray.'

'You are most kind, Mrs Hosegood.' And she left.

'So in addition to the Plodgers and Jeremy Dramjoy, with whom did you discuss the matter?' was Pluke's next question.

'It's hard to say, it was more than a week ago,' admitted Hosegood, taking large sips from his whisky glass. 'Jennifer Morlix, yes, I discussed it with her, she'd got one too, and Molly Mayweed, Wally Whimbrel, and Agatha Teem...'

Pluke was checking the names on his list and nodded. 'Yes, they're all on the list.'

'Oh, and Ken Kenyon. The Rotary Club president.'

'Right, he's here, he referred the matter to us too.'

'You can see the quality of those people, Mr Pluke,' said Hosegood. 'I am surprised, though, that you didn't get one, being so eminent in our society.'

'It is a factor to consider.' Pluke smiled. 'Certainly, I should have recognised it for what it was, unlike some of the recipients.'

'It seems rather pointless sending such things to people when they do not know what they are, or what they imply.' Hosegood was enjoying his whisky now. He had almost consumed the glassful. 'And the more we discussed it, the more people we discovered who said they'd received them. A plague of snowdrops, Mr Pluke.'

'A veritable scourge, Mr Hosegood. So it was only when talking about it that you

206

discovered its message and only when you mentioned it to others that you decided to involve the police?'

'Right, Mr Pluke. Most of us had kept the snowdrops thinking something else would follow, like they do with those advance notices telling us about Reader's Digest mailshots or competitions, but once we discovered their meaning, we felt a crackpot was behind the mailings, so we decided to tell the police.'

'A joint decision and one that might not have been made without knowing the meaning of the flowers. Well, Mr Hosegood, you have been most helpful, but I have one final question – in your opinion, have any or all of these people got something to hide or have they done something in the course of their public work that could be considered either wrong, sinful, illegal or even against the principles of decent people? Some form of misbehaviour, perhaps? Secret or otherwise?'

'No, Mr Pluke, nothing.'

'There *is* a common factor, Mr Hosegood. I need to find it.'

'Well, like me, those people have just done their best for the community, that's all. They're not criminals or nasty pieces of work. They're people who want to help others in all kinds of ways. But what about Stephen Gallholme? He didn't hold any

207

public office, did he? He wasn't involved with the community, was he? He'd just returned to his family home.'

'He was prominent in his own way, Mr Hosegood, and it might be said he helped the community by providing jobs for them,' said Pluke, standing up and placing his panama on his head. 'But so far as the murder is concerned, don't have nightmares. Now I must leave. I shall speak to the Plodgers next.'

The Plodgers had an elderberry growing in their front garden, an odd sort of plant for a suburban household but Pluke knew its presence protected the house against all manner of ill-boden things, especially lightning strikes and warts, and it also kept flies away. He wondered if they knew the significance of the elderberry tree or whether it had been planted in the garden before they occupied the property. But its presence pleased him. He rang the bell.

Stanley Plodger was younger than most of the Stanleys known to Pluke and his wife was even younger than her husband; Gabrielle was a vivacious thirty-something with long blond hair, a fresh and pinkish face, blue eyes and beautiful white teeth, which made even Pluke's heart beat faster when she smiled. With a stunningly slim figure, she wore faded blue denims and sandals, and her husband did likewise; he was in his forties, balding on top but with a luxurious growth of long dark hair reaching down to his shoulders.

Rather slender in build, he was about six feet tall but had a look of power within, rather like a panther, thought Pluke. In a past age they might have been described as hippies. Gabrielle led him into the rear garden, which seemed to be full of bamboo fences and ferns, and settled him on a garden seat made of bamboo. Stanley Plodger approached Pluke with interest upon his face, offered him a drink of natural apple juice, which Pluke refused on the ground he'd just had coffee and that it was getting on for lunchtime.

'So, Mr Pluke. What can we do for you?' asked Stanley, sitting opposite on a bamboo stool.

Pluke explained his renewed interest in the mailed snowdrops and they listened carefully, then Gabrielle said, 'I had no idea of the awful message until Molly Mayweed told me.'

'You mentioned it to her?'

'Yes, she came to one of our meetings.'

'Your meetings?' queried Pluke before proceeding.

'Yes,' said Stanley. 'We have meetings here, at our house. I am secretary of the Crickledale Moth Plotting Society and Gabrielle is the chair.'

'Chair?' asked Pluke.

'You might say chairlady or chairperson or chairman, but we say chair.'

'Ah,' said Pluke. 'So what does a Moth Plotting Society do?'

'We plot moths.' Gabrielle smiled. 'By that I mean that we make records of all moths seen in the area, especially the rarer ones, and we plot their presence on a map.'

'Ah. Most interesting, I am sure.' Pluke sighed.

'It is important work. We supply our findings to the British Moth Plotting Society; they take readings from the whole of Britain and can then calculate the relative rarity or otherwise of moths and their distribution. It helps to identify moth-friendly habitats.'

'I am sure it is most valuable work,' agreed Pluke, who wondered if they believed that the souls of unbaptised children sometimes turned into moths. 'So why did Mrs Mayweed come to your meeting?'

'She saw me in the street one day and casually mentioned she'd seen a Blair's Shoulder Knot in Crickledale...' continued Gabrielle.

'Blair's Shoulder Knot?'

'It's a species of moth, Mr Pluke, fairly new to this country, not uncommon in the south where it depends on Monterey cypress trees, but rare this far north. I invited her along – we are always keen to recruit new members – and when she saw our elderberry tree she told me all about its effect of keeping witches at bay and preventing lightning, so I told her about the snowdrop I'd received. And that's when I learnt about the implications of a single snowdrop in the house. Later, I was talking to Elias Hosegood. His garden fence adjoins ours at the very top of our garden even though he's five doors away...'

'I've just come from him,' said Pluke.

'I see. Well, after we'd discussed the pressed snowdrops, he said we should inform the police. He thought a crank was sending them to us.'

'So who is responsible, Mr and Mrs Plodger? Have you any idea?'

'Not a clue, Mr Pluke,' Stanley Plodger replied. 'I must admit I never took the business very seriously and neither did Gabrielle, although Elias did make us think it could be someone with a grudge. Then Mrs Mayweed told us about the significance of the flowers and now you tell us about Mr Gallholme...'

'I doubt if the sender of the letters is the killer.' Pluke felt he should convey that impression to them. 'But I would welcome any suggestions as to the identity of the sender, or the motive behind the letters.'

'We'll help all we can.' Stanley assured him.

'In this case, the letter came to you, Mrs Plodger, did it not? Not your husband?'

'Yes. I have no idea why anyone would pick on me.' Gabrielle smiled. 'I have no problems at work – I do part-time waitressing in a coffee shop in York and part-time waiting in a restaurant on the Leverton Road, but apart from my moth work I don't have much contact with the public. Stanley and I keep ourselves to ourselves, don't we darling?'

'Home birds, that's us,' agreed Stanley. 'Not ones for clubbing or pubbing. We much prefer mothing.'

'And your work, Mr Plodger?'

'I'm in organic foods, Mr Pluke. I run a small shop in York, in Micklegate. That keeps me busy during the week and on Saturdays.'

'Your own business, is it?'

'Yes. I rent the premises but the business is mine.'

'Have any of your customers reason to resent something you have done?' Pluke asked, thinking of the York postmark on the envelopes.

'I don't think so. There's been nothing in recent months to suggest any of them is angry with me, certainly not to the extent of sending death threats. We do get our disgruntled customers, of course, but usually it's some minor matter that is dealt with

212

there and then. Besides, I doubt if any of my customers know where I live.'

'The letter came to your home address?'

'It did, Mr Pluke.'

'And Mrs Plodger's role in the business? What is that?'

'She is a partner, she helps out in the shop and does the book-keeping; she took those part-time jobs when we started. We needed the extra cash and she's kept them on. They give her a break from me and from the business.'

'If you do think of anyone who might have sent the letters, please call me,' asked Pluke, rising to leave their comfortable garden. 'In your discussions with other recipients something significant might emerge.'

'We will do our best, Mr Pluke.' Stanley Plodger smiled.

'I do hope you find the person responsible, Mr Pluke,' oozed Gabrielle. 'Such people have no idea of the anxiety they create.'

'On the contrary,' said Pluke as he took his leave, 'I think they know very well the effects of what they are doing.'

As it was around lunchtime, Pluke walked home for his midday meal; he had forgotten that he had said he might have a bar snack with his colleagues, but that did not unsettle Millicent. She had prepared enough for two because she knew he might forget his earlier plan; he always came home for lunch and she did like to have him with her. He hung his hat and coat in the hall, pecked Millicent on the cheek and sat down at the table, which was already prepared. She gave him a glass of water and then placed a succulent gravy-adorned Yorkshire pudding before him, saying, 'It's so nice that you can come home for lunch, dearest, when you are so busy.'

'It is one of the major pleasures of my life, Millicent.' He smiled. 'I would far rather dine with you in the comfort of our own home than sit among forty detectives and dozens of Sunday trippers in a noisy bar of a public house eating food prepared in a micro-wave oven.'

'You say the nicest things, Montague.' Truly, he had forgotten his earlier plans.

As they were enjoying their Yorkshire puddings, served on their own in the traditional way with onion gravy, Montague asked if she had achieved any success in her discussions after church.

'Yes, my dear,' she said with pride. 'The vicar has received a pressed snowdrop and so have Miss Bampton – she's the editor of the parish magazine – and Mrs Keysmith, a member of the congregation. There was another lady, too, but she ran out of the church hall before I could halt her. I do believe my revelations alarmed her. I have no idea who she is, by the way, I think she must live out of town and come here to church for some reason. However, Hortensia – that's Mrs Keysmith – thinks she still has hers behind the mantelpiece clock but the others disposed of theirs. And Mrs Mayweed was there and she was most distressed when she heard about the death of Mr Gallholme. She thought everyone was under sentence of death. I did manage to calm them down by telling them you did not think the killer had sent them.'

'You did very well, my dear. Now, did they realise the implications of the snowdrops?' he asked.

'Not until I told them – except for Mrs Mayweed, of course, but she hadn't said anything to the others. When I did tell them, I must admit there was pandemonium, Montague.'

'Pandemonium? What sort of pandemonium?'

'They all panicked somewhat when I said that Mr Gallholme had been murdered after receiving a snowdrop. Poor Mrs Mayweed almost passed out. I do think they are now all very frightened, Montague; the town could be in turmoil if you don't do something. You really must catch the person responsible.'

'The fact that people at church have received them does suggest that other

215

people in Crickledale might also have done so, Millicent. The Catholics and the chapel-goers, for example, and even the Free-masons and people like the Samaritans and the ladies of the Women's Institute ... who knows where else he or she has struck?'

'Montague,' she said. 'Forgive me for asking such an impertinent question, but if you do not think the killer of Mr Gallholme sent the snowdrops, why are you spending so much of your own valuable time making enquiries about them? You are the officer in charge of the investigation. Surely, matters of lesser importance, like this and other routine enquiries, could have been under-taken by someone of lower rank?'

He coughed discreetly behind his hand and answered, 'Millicent, I am the only de-tective, certainly the only one in Crickle-dale, who fully understands the implications of single snowdrops in the household; the murdered man received such a token, as well as several other citizens. I am convinced the murderer did not send the snowdrops – but I must prove that to be so and I must do it before I can eliminate the snowdrop sender from our enquiries. There is a motive for sending those flowers, Millicent, and I must determine what it is. It might be that the same motive has caused the death of Mr Gallholme, even if the snowdrop sender is not the killer.'

'It is all very complicated, Montague.'

'And that is why I cannot allow this vital part of my investigation to be conducted by someone with less knowledge and less detective experience than I,' he said.

'I understand, Montague. Now, it is time for your roast beef, mashed potato and carrots.'

'Most welcome, I assure you. And this afternoon I might have words with the vicar before I proceed to others on my list,' he said, wiping some gravy from his chin.

After an abortive visit to the vicarage and then the church, Pluke toured the graveyard in search of the vicar. During his tour he glanced with reverence at the array of Pluke dynasty tombstones, then noted a vase of fresh flowers on a grave in an older part of the cemetery. Not knowing of any recent death in the town, he went to examine it; it marked the grave of a child called Stanley Bilston aged eight who, as the inscription said, had 'died tragically' on 7 May 1966. The epitaph bore the words 'Died in innocence, loved in life'.

The flowers would be for his anniversary, Pluke decided. Today was Sunday 7 May 2000. So could this be the child who had died in Trippingdale? A child who was still remembered? In his wanderings and musings, Pluke then located the Reverend

217

Hywel Abbeyfield at the far end of the churchyard where he was making an assessment of the spaces available for future generations.

'Good afternoon, Mr Pluke,' he greeted the detective. 'I am wondering if there will be enough space for me when I pass from this world and of course for others who may wish to spend eternity here.'

'Planning for the future, eh?' Pluke smiled. 'And one must not disturb existing graves; the deceased within any graves that are disturbed might return to haunt the vicinity. And of course, bad luck will follow.'

'And even I, as a Christian, know that it is considered unlucky to walk or tread upon a grave, Mr Pluke. Not that I believe such things, of course. But I am sure you are not here to discuss churchyard lore. Might I hazard a guess that your visit follows the panic caused by your Millicent this morning?'

'Panic, vicar?'

'Panic is the word I would use, Mr Pluke.'

'I am sorry if her comments provoked such a response, but it was a means of learning something of value to my enquiries into Mr Gallholme's murder. She told you about that, I know. I asked her to ascertain whether any of your flock had received snowdrops in the post, Mr Abbeyfield, and I understand some have – including you.'

Abbeyfield repeated and expanded the story he had given, somewhat briefly, to Millicent, after which Pluke asked, 'I need to find the person who sent the snowdrops, Mr Abbeyfield. It is most important.'

'I should write it off as the actions of a crank, Mr Pluke. I cannot see how it can be linked to a murder investigation.'

'It is linked by the fact that the murder victim also received such a flower, Mr Abbeyfield. That makes it relevant to our enquiries and it is necessary to eliminate the sender of the flowers. I need to find the person and to talk to her.'

'Her?'

'I am sure it is a woman,' said Pluke. 'Undertaking that kind of action has all the hallmarks of feminine behaviour: flowers; anonymity; no direct action; no open violence ... all feminine traits, Vicar.'

'So women criminals behave different from men?'

'They do, Mr Abbeyfield, even if I am not allowed to say so for politically correct reasons. The death of Mr Gallholme, however, has all the hallmarks of being committed by a man, chiefly because of the strength required. And the accompanying brutality of watching a man fight for his life, then die. I am not sure a woman could endure that. So, Mr Abbeyfield, if the sender of the flowers is a woman, why would she send one to you?'

'I haven't the faintest idea, Mr Pluke.'

'Four members of your congregation have also received them, I am told. Your magazine editor, Miss Bampton, a Mrs Keysmith, Mrs Mayweed and another lady.'

'Miss Codling. Anne. She is new here, Mr Pluke. She has come to live in one of those new bungalows along Meadowfield Way. A retired bank clerk from Wimbledon and a very nervous lady. She's had treatment for her nerves, stress or something similar. She ran out. I do hope Millicent's good intentions have not sent her into recession.'

'How long has she been here?' was Pluke's obvious question.

'A few weeks, six maybe. She's just finding her way around the place, getting to know people, and then this ... it could devastate her.'

'It is all very odd,' said Pluke. 'Let us consider your Mrs Keysmith and the new lady, Miss Codling. Neither is known to me as being a prominent member of Crickledale society. Are they? The other recipients of the snowdrops are all key people within the community of this small town.'

'Oh, well, so are those two ladies, Mr Pluke. Mrs Keysmith is descended from a long line of aristocrats – her family have been in the Yorkshire Dales since Norman times and they built several castles, took part in the government of this country, held high office and were leaders of the nation, not merely the local community.'

'I had no idea!' admitted Pluke. 'But of course I specialise in horse trough history, not matters of national history.'

'And Miss Codling, well, her grandfather founded a hospital for sick children in Southampton and pioneered treatment for children with bone diseases. A wonderful man, Mr Pluke; Miss Codling is very proud of him.'

'So they are also people of some stature, Mr Abbeyfield. One must wonder who would send them – and you – a death token.'

'Someone with a sick mind, Mr Pluke.'

'As I suggest – a woman, Mr Abbeyfield. One of your congregation, perhaps?'

'Why pick on my congregation, Mr Pluke?'

'I was considering a woman who felt such people might not be living up to the standards set by their position in society, Mr Abbeyfield, like a vicar who falls short of the high standards of his office, or a married lady who does not meet the high standards of behaviour expected of her. That sort of thing.'

'None of us lives up to the high standards of our calling, Mr Pluke. Not even you, I would venture to say. We are all sinners, are we not?'

'I did accept coffee from an interviewee this morning, Mr Abbeyfield, and I have been known to take a sherry while on duty. So you are right. None of us is perfect.' And for some reason Pluke saw a vision of Mrs Plumpton bending over his desk to clear his out-tray.

'But you have not received a snowdrop, Mr Pluke, so quite clearly your sins have not been found out.'

'Then if my surmise is correct, who would know all about the sins and shortcomings of all those people who have been targeted?'

'I think that is something for you to find out, Mr Pluke. But if I do have a flash of inspiration I shall certainly contact you. It was not me, I can assure you of that. We want no more pressed snowdrops in this town and no more murders.'

'Well spoken, Mr Abbeyfield. Now, on my way I chanced upon the grave of a child, Stanley Bilston according to the inscription. Aged eight. It bears a vase of fresh flowers, unusual in that the death occurred in 1966.'

'Yes indeed. I know the grave, but he was buried before my arrival here, Mr Pluke. I do not know the details of his death but the family do tend the grave with care and put fresh flowers there very regularly, especially at this time of the year.'

'His family?' queried Pluke.

'Well, a woman, to be precise. His mother,

I am given to understand. She always comes alone and never enters the church. I've never spoke to her. She's not a member of my congregation, you see, and I don't like to trespass upon her grief. I do not want her to think I am canvassing to increase my congregation.'

'Most honourable, Mr Abbeyfield. I am sure she would make contact if she needed your help. Well, I must press on. I have others to visit.'

11

While Pluke was continuing his highly specialised enquiries, Detective Sergeant Wayne Wain and Detective Constable Paula Helston were struggling to learn more about the life of Stephen Gallholme. Their search at Trippingdale Hall had revealed surprisingly little of his earlier life but it had produced snippets of personal information. They had learnt that his home had been in Haywards Heath and that he had not worked in London, as the Yorkshire people had thought; his office had been in Horsham. Wain had therefore contacted West Sussex police with a request that they provide him with as much information about Gallholme as they could muster, particularly whether or not he had ever come to their notice. He was able to provide them with the basics for their enquiries, especially his date and place of birth – Trippingdale Hall on 13 July 1958 – starting points that were vital to such enquiries.

There were many avenues the police could explore, ranging from his former workmates to their own crime intelligence and collator files, via a range of agencies such as those covering public utilities, credit rating, National Insurance and others. If it was possible to find out anything about Stephen Gallholme, the detectives of West Sussex would do so – and they would pass it to Wayne Wain.

Wayne's local enquiries were, for the time being, concentrated upon Trippingdale Estate and its immediate surrounds, where he began a more in-depth interview of Basil Broadbent. Wayne and Paula were invited into his rather plain office and offered seats.

Being a Sunday, his secretary was absent – she would be interviewed in due course – but he did offer to prepare coffee and biscuits. As he worked, Wayne Wain observed him closely – he was a large man in his fifties with thick, curly and rather gingery red hair bearing just a hint of grey, dark-brown eyes and the ruddy complexion of a countryman. About six feet tall, he wore a countryman's clothes – greenish tweed trousers, a thick shirt with a woollen tie, a green-based tweed jacket and brogue shoes. He looked physically and mentally powerful but exuded a welcome air of calm. Wain told him about the enquiries into Stephen's past, with due emphasis upon the West Sussex link, and then, when the coffee appeared, he began to quiz Broadbent, first asking about the general condition of the estate.

'Thanks to an efficient staff, it's in a very

healthy state,' he told Wayne Wain. 'The Hall is expensive to maintain. We've lots of outgoings and heavy expenses but we are making an annual profit in spite of that. In addition to Trippingdale Hall and the parkland, we have eight farms scattered over a wide area. Some are a considerable distance from here, they were acquired over the years. Closer, we have Home Farm with a herd of pedigree Friesians, about five hundred sheep, as well as agricultural land where we produce potatoes, turnips, barley and oil seed rape. We own a few thousand acres of moorland with shooting rights and the public house down the road. There is no village of Trippingdale, as I'm sure you have realised, but most of the scattered cottages and houses belong to the estate. We've recently built a block of holiday cottages and a caravan site on one of our distant farms too. Now, of course, thanks to Mr Stephen, we hope to develop the parkland previously closed to the public. We're about to produce a feasibility study; he did not want the place closed and unproductive; he saw its potential both as farm land and as a tourist attraction. As I said, Sergeant, Trippingdale Estate is very healthy.'

'A good acquisition for an ambitious person?' Wayne smiled.

'Very,' agreed Broadbent. 'But it's not for sale.'

'Your success makes a change from hearing all about doom and gloom in the rural economy.'

'We are very positive and very professional in our forward planning,' Broadbent continued. 'But I must stress we would never want to get rid of the Hall even if we did get tempting offers – from time to time we have been approached to sell it, with proposals from hotel groups who have recognised its potential and big businesses wanting to convert it into a conference centre or some such thing.'

'I thought big houses like this were difficult to dispose of?' asked Paula.

'I'm sure some are, but this one is in a beautiful setting and we have taken care to maintain it and to bring it up to modern standards of interior decor with new fittings, plumbing and so on. It will remain a private house for the foreseeable future, although the possibility of opening it to the public has not been ruled out. It had some wonderful antiques and a nationally acclaimed family portrait gallery.'

'That could happen soon, now the last occupant is dead,' suggested Paula.

'It is something we shall have to consider seriously,' admitted Broadbent. 'There are other family members in Australia who could inherit. Our solicitors will advise us about that.'

'It's not straightforward, then?'

'Far from it. Inheritance can be very complex at times, particularly when there is no direct heir. At this stage, I have no idea who will become the new owner.'

'Has there ever been a battle over the inheritance?' was Wayne's next question. 'I'm thinking of a motive for the murder.'

'No, that's never caused problems in the past. It's always been accepted that direct descendants of the resident Gallholme family would inherit the estate. We did recognise the problem if Mr Stephen did not produce an heir – his divorce without issue set things back a little. We thought he'd remarry and have a family. He was young enough. That's all changed now. I shall be discussing the future with our young solicitors as soon as I can make an appointment – next week, all being well.'

'Why did he get divorced, Mr Broadbent?'

'I don't know. It has never been discussed with the staff.'

'And he has no brothers or sisters?'

'None, but he does have those Australian cousins or half-cousins. I think the Australian branch is very remotely connected. Probably they have no idea they are in line to inherit the estate. There is no title with it, though. One of my urgent tasks is to get things sorted out very quickly.'

'I'll need the names and addresses of the

Australian cousins,' said Wayne Wain. 'We'll have to talk to them, for elimination purposes. I'll get the Australian police to do that. And we'll need to speak to your solicitors and accountants.'

'Of course. I realise that. I'll provide what help I can to pave the way for you.'

'Thanks. My priority at the moment,' said Wayne Wain, 'is to learn something of Stephen's life, friends, enemies, contacts and his movements in the time he's been here. I need to find out what he did with himself locally, whom he might have upset, who might have borne a deep grudge against him, that sort of thing. So far, I've found out nothing. He seems to have led a very quiet and very clean life. It's almost the "all work and no play" syndrome. I wonder if his wife found him boring? Is that why they were divorced?'

'Your guess is as good as mine, but I've been thinking about his quietness since I learnt of his death,' mused Broadbent. 'It's made me realise how little any of us knew about him. He wasn't one for talking about himself. We did have discussions when he came into the office. He was always very pleasant and amiable, and seemed very keen to become thoroughly *au fait* with all aspects of the estate. He was full of ideas, good ones, too. His mother didn't want to be bothered with expansion, but he was very enthusiastic. I know I speak for all the staff when I say we were looking forward to working with him. But so far as his private life is concerned, he rode out very early each morning, alone as far as I am aware, and that's all he seemed to do. That appeared to be his chief relaxation. We – the estate staff, I mean – all knew he went riding at six; otherwise he didn't leave the house very often.'

'Had he renewed any earlier friendships?' Wayne asked. 'Joined anything like a sports club or society? The local hunt? Had people to stay overnight or come in for a meal?'

'I can't say with absolute conviction, but my gut feeling is that he did not; he'd only been here three weeks, Sergeant. Most of his time away from estate work involved getting his domestic arrangements straight-ened out and dealing with his mother's personal affairs. I doubt if he'd had time to make friends or join things.'

'Point taken. And the big question: enemies. Had he any enemies?'

'I'd say not, Sergeant. Certainly so far as the estate staff members are concerned; they saw his outlook as refreshing and very welcome.'

'His idea to open the dale to the public, did that cause friction?'

'Not to my knowledge. Most of us thought it was long overdue and very sensible. He couldn't see any reason to keep the parkland closed and neither could we.'

'Would Mr Stephen know about the other drowning tragedy?' asked Paula. 'Was that the reason for keeping the dale private?'

'Other drowning?' Broadbent seemed puzzled by this reference.

'A child was drowned in the stream, Mr Broadbent, in 1966 – an accident, we are told. Mr Pluke asked us to bear it in mind during our enquiries.'

'That was long before I arrived,' said Broadbent. 'I've never heard it mentioned by anyone. I don't think it would have any bearing on the decision to keep the parkland closed but I can check. There might be something in our files. Do you have any more details?'

'Sorry, no, we're trying to find out more,' admitted Wayne Wain. 'In the meantime, you've got that fearsome gatekeeper to keep people out.'

'I don't know how we'd manage without Aaron. He takes his duties very seriously.'

'Nothing and no one can get past him.' Wayne Wain laughed.

'He's fierce all right! He'll have to learn to admit strangers, although we'll issue permits first, to people like your Mr Pluke. We'll admit them for serious research or natural history study, that sort of thing, then consider allowing the general public in.

We've always said the staff can take their families and friends into the parkland, though, so it's never been totally out of bounds.'

'Even so, it's a twenty-four-hours-a-day job for Aaron?'

'We're not too strict about it, even if he is. The job was created specially for him by Mr Gallholme senior, when Aaron became unfit for labouring work. There was no gate-keeper before that time and we didn't have any real problems with people wanting access. Now, though, his wife stands in for him if he wants a haircut or needs to visit the doctor or something. He likes watching local cricket and football on Saturday or Sunday afternoons, so she takes over for him them. If the pair of them want to be away for a longer period, either we leave the gate open and risk the consequences, or we install one of our other workers on a temporary basis.'

'Our Detective Inspector Pluke had the necessary permission,' said Wayne Wain. 'But Pinder didn't welcome Mrs Pluke.'

'But you didn't have permission.' Broadbent grinned. 'When you rushed through, he rang me. Nothing and no one gets past old Pinder, mark my words!'

'We'll have to talk to him next.' Wayne Wain sighed. 'And his wife. The gate would be closed and locked at six yesterday morning? When Stephen set off for his ride?'

'It would, but Stephen wouldn't use that route. He'd go through the Hall grounds to the castle and beyond.'

'I was thinking of his attacker,' said Wayne. 'He must have gained access somehow – and left the scene fairly quickly, without being noticed.'

'Let's face it, Sergeant, if someone were really determined they could get into the parkland by all sorts of routes on foot. They could come down the dale from the top or across the moor and we'd not know they were there. They'd never get in by vehicle, though, except through Pinder's gate or, of course, they could come through the Hall grounds if they knew about that route.'

'You'll be reviewing all that when you admit the public?'

'Right. We'll need new signs painting, new instructions for the staff, precise advice from our lawyers about the responsibilities of having members of the public on our land, that sort of thing.'

'So if my geography is correct,' ventured Paula, 'the killer is most likely to have used the route through the Hall grounds. That's possible without being seen by anyone, even when using a motor vehicle?'

'Yes, that's true. Home Farm is a mile from the Hall and even if the milking was under way, none of the workers would have a view of the Hall grounds or the castle. It seems to me, Sergeant, that only someone with a knowledge of the estate's roads would have known about that route. It suggests the killer is someone connected with the estate, either now or in the past, or someone living locally.'

'That's not a very pleasant thought, Mr Broadbent, but it is inescapable,' said Wayne Wain. 'Our teams are talking to all your staff, past and present. You have a list I can use, as a double-check?'

'Yes, I'll get one for you. But I'll be honest – I can't think of anyone who would have done this to Mr Stephen.'

'Some of the staff have been here a long time, I believe?' Wayne asked.

'They have. Pinder for one,' replied Broadbent. 'He's been here all his working life. And Mrs Pinder, she was a shepherdess on the estate. There's Mrs Preston, too, Stephen's housekeeper. Her late husband spent his entire working life on the estate. And they'll know others who've retired.'

'We'll talk to the Pinders next,' Wayne Wain reminded himself. 'Well, it's time to go. Come along, Paula, we'll need your feminine charms to get Pinder in a mood to talk.'

As they walked away from the Estate Office, Wayne said to Paula, 'For all his helpfulness, we didn't get much out of

Broadbent, did we?'

'I think he was being as honest and helpful as he could. He can't tell us what he doesn't know,' Paula replied. 'Three weeks in a working environment isn't long to get really acquainted with someone, especially one's rather private new boss.'

'Are we looking for a killer who's come in from afar, I wonder? Followed him up from West Sussex, perhaps?'

'It's something we have to consider,' agreed Paula.

'Right, I'll suggest it to Pluke. But even those who knew him as a child or young man in this locality might not know him as an adult.'

'Perhaps you're right. Come on. I wonder if Pinder will recognise me from yesterday's gate-crashing?'

Meanwhile, Montague Pluke was not having much success. The fact that a black cat had galloped across his path and that another column of travelling gypsies with a piebald horse had met him face to face did not seem to be producing the necessary element of luck. During that Sunday afternoon he trudged around Crickledale, knocking on doors and speaking to people who'd rather have been watching some old black-and-white film on television than speak about pressed snowdrops to a funny

235

long-haired detective dressed in a coat that had seen better days and a hat that would not have been out of place on a yacht in a Mediterranean seaside resort.

Feeling that he might have overlooked a vital piece of information, he noticed that the Cosy Café, on the corner of the market square, was open. All the tables were empty and the prospect of complete silence coupled with an opportunity to study his file in comfort would be beneficial. He could rest his tired feet with the added bonus of tea and a scone with butter and jam on it, so he entered, selected a table and ordered his snack from Miss Millie Miller, the owner. He opened his file and put aside one of the envelopes containing a pressed snowdrop, arranging it so that the flower was visible in the hope that it might give him the inspiration he needed.

Then he began to study his notes, at which point Millie Miller, like a ship in full sail, hove to with a tray of tea, cups, milk, sugar and scones.

'I had almost given up hope of any customers this afternoon, Mr Pluke – not that it's a bad day, it's not, but it's rather cool – and then you came in. And if passers-by can see you at the table in the window, they will come in too. There's nothing like an empty café for making people stay away, that's what I say, so you can see how pleased

I am to see you. A scone with jam and butter, tea with milk, you said? I do hope you enjoy it because my mother always said there's nothing like a good scone with real butter and homemade jam on a Sunday afternoon, a proper "tea on Sunday" person, she was, you know, all laid out properly with no crumbs on the cloth and polished cutlery, a real stickler, she was...'

'Thank you.' He tried to stem the flow of words but she was having none of it; he began to wish for another customer to occupy her. How did one conjure up extra customers? There must be some formula ... catch sight of three magpies, perhaps? Three for a girl ... if he could see three magpies during the next few seconds, would it make a young female customer enter for a snack? There weren't many magpies in the town centre, though.

'Good heavens, Mr Pluke, don't say you got one of those snowdrops as well? Now I am surprised. I thought it was only those folks who had been having a bit on the side, if you know what I mean, and I never thought you were that sort of person so there must be some other reason because my cousin Penny got one. Penny Knee-halter, you know, at that charity shop in Church Street, the one that raises money for old folks homes, she runs it. Nice lady but a bit of a one for men younger than herself;

not that her husband worries, he's past it anyway...'

'You know other people who received one?' he managed to invade one of her rare pauses between breaths.

'They were talking in here, not very long ago, Jeremy Dramjoy from the Crickle-donians and Wally Whimbrel – isn't he something to do with raising money for blind cats? Well, they'd both got one and had no idea what it was all about until I told them and that shut them up...'

'What did you tell them?'

'Well, Mr Pluke, I'm surprised you don't know about these things but snowdrops like that, on their own, well, they're tokens of death, you know, not to be taken into the house and Jeremy got really upset when I told him that, and so he tried to laugh it off and said it was all poppycock and old wives' tales, and it had been sent as a joke or an advert of some kind from Reader's Digest...'

'Did they mention other people who'd been sent one?'

'Well, I'm not one for eavesdropping on other folk's conversations, especially in this business – you've got to be discreet, you know, a bit like a priest in confession or a doctor or a hairdresser, or a taxi driver – but I did hear that snooty Mrs Mayweed had got one and Mr Hosegood, and Jenny Morlix and the Plodgers, and that chap from Rotary, Kenyon I think his name is ... they'd all got them and had no idea what they meant, and I think it was Mrs Mayweed who told them. She came in here one day with a friend when some of them were talking about it and she told them, well, Jenny Morlix I think it was, what the snowdrops meant. I mean, no one had any idea ... but I never imagined all those folks had been at it, Mr Pluke, having bits on the side, some of them seemed far too old, you know, but they do say there's always a good wine in old bottles or something similar...'

'I did not receive this snowdrop in that manner,' said Pluke. 'And most certainly I have not been having anything on the side, as you put it. My Millicent would be most alarmed at the notion ... the very thought of it!'

And then he was saved. Two ladies in Sunday hats came in, selected a table near the window and settled at it.

'I really must go, Mr Pluke, I mustn't keep my customers waiting. But it was lovely talking to you. Be with you in just one second, ladies. Afternoon tea as usual, is it?'

And then Pluke realised the second significant point of the snowdrop. It was the symbol of purity. Is that why it had been sent to all those people? Had each of them done something the sender had regarded as impure? Like having an affair or a flirtation,

239

committing adultery or fiddling expenses? In thinking about the people who had received the snowdrops, and in considering their position in local society, it was quite likely. If they fell short of the high standards they had set themselves, and which they paraded before the public, then they might receive a jolt from someone who felt they should be reminded of the fact they were not living up to those high ideals. As he regarded the lonely flower on his table, he realised that this had opened up a whole new line of enquiry.

What had each of these people done to attract a pressed snowdrop from someone who considered himself or herself as holier than the rest of them? Herself, almost certainly, he thought. Surely the sender was a woman? Men did not resort to that kind of secretive and sneaky tactic. And, quite clearly, it was someone who knew the secrets of all those snowdrop recipients. It was also someone who knew where they all lived. So what had Stephen Gallholme done to attract this kind of attention? That was a most important matter to unravel because his indiscretion might be the motive for his murder.

Luck had been on Pluke's side after all.

When he'd drunk his tea and eaten his scone, he would return to the Incident Room.

12

As Wayne Wain approached the impressive Trippingdale Gate with Paula Helston at his side in the unmarked police car, he reduced his speed so that his arrival was far more sedate than yesterday. Even as he drew to a halt in a parking space beside the left-hand tower, Pinder emerged from its open door and shouted, 'You can't park there!'

Quite slowly and with exaggerated deliberation, Wayne put on the handbrake, switched off the engine and emerged to greet the red-faced gatekeeper.

'I said you can't park there.' By now, Pinder had reached the offending vehicle; Paula remained in her seat, awaiting developments. 'We don't allow visitors to the dale, not without permission.'

'I am parked here and I shall stay parked here until I have concluded my business.' Wayne spoke softly, without any sign of anger.

'We'll see about that!' Pinder's face was beginning to develop a rich plum colour, which started to creep on to his pale scalp. Clearly he hadn't recognised Wayne and Paula from yesterday's drama. 'This is private property and no one parks there without my permission, no one, certainly not Sunday ramblers, picnickers and litter droppers. Now clear off before I call the police. And if you think I can't call them, I can, they're just along the road.'

'I am the police,' said Wayne Wain, producing his warrant card and showing it to Pinder. 'And my partner is a detective also.'

'Well, you should have said, they're all at the castle. I'll open up, then.'

'We don't want to go to the castle, Mr Pinder, not yet. I am Detective Sergeant Wain and this is Detective Constable Helston. We are here to talk to you about the murder of Stephen Gallholme.'

'I know nothing about that, I've nothing to say.' His reaction immediately became one of caution.

'I am sure you can help us with our enquiries, Mr Pinder. We can deal with this in a very civilised way, which is what we would prefer. Alternatively, we can ask you to accompany us to Crickledale Police Station and if you are not willing to co-operate in either of those ways we can arrest you on suspicion and interview you when you've calmed down after a few hours in the cells.'

Pinder did not respond; he glared at the offending car and at Wayne, then peered into the car to glare at Paula.

After a moment of silence he said, 'All right, then, but it is Sunday afternoon, which is our busy time and we get shoals of visitors trying to get into the estate. Hordes of them, they seem to think they can ramble where they like. I'll give them right to roam ... right to vandalise and disturb crops more like. It's my job to stop that sort of tripper, I've got responsibilities. I could have been watching cricket today – Sunday league, I'll have you know – but with all this carry-on at the castle I thought I'd better stay. I don't want all and sundry messing up our parkland.'

'Then we shall talk here, Mr Pinder, and you can keep an eye on your gate.'

'I said I have nothing to say. There's nothing I can tell you about what happened. I don't know anything about it, so what's the point of talking?'

'We'll see, shall we? Now, your wife? Can she look after the gate while we talk?'

'She usually does. I'll tell her.' And, with a huge sigh of resignation, he stomped away towards his house.

'You handled that very well.' Paula emerged from the car as Pinder disappeared into his tiny home. 'He's a proper little Hitler, isn't he? I wonder if he's always like this?'

'He must be worth his weight in gold to

the estate. I wonder what he'd be like on a football stadium's gate or as a bouncer on the door of a London club? But say what you like, I wouldn't like to meet him on a dark night when he's in a bad mood and upset with me. Hello, here he comes.'

Pinder returned, his florid complexion now a more reasonable pinkish hue and his initial anger greatly subdued. 'The wife says she'll see to the gate while we talk. We can go into the house and would you like a cup of tea?'

'That is most civilised of you, Mr Pinder,' oozed Wayne Wain. 'Yes, I think we would like that.'

'You'd better come in, then.'

The sitting room was the tiniest Wayne Wain had ever seen. Without even room for a settee, there were three small and very cheap upholstered chairs around the fireplace, with a television set squeezed into one corner. Even that looked second-hand. There was no room for anything else. The fire was burning and it filled the room with a sticky heat.

Wayne and Paula entered and saw that the window looked directly on to the road, which passed within inches of the outer wall. Mrs Pinder, almost as large and threatening as her husband, hovered in the doorway, so Paula smiled and said, 'It's good of you to ask us in.'

'Being neighbourly costs nothing,' affirmed the stout, iron-haired lady. 'Tea, is it? Milk and sugar?'

'No sugar, thanks,' said Wayne. 'Neither of us takes sugar.'

'I'll be a minute or two, so sit yourselves down. There's not much room but it's big enough for the two of us.' As she spoke, her husband appeared in the doorway behind her. She departed when he came in; Wayne and Paula then settled down on the rather battered chairs. The hearthrug was threadbare too, and the whole place had an air of poverty and cheap furnishings. Money seemed to be in short supply; this couple were probably living on a pittance.

'So what is it you want to ask me?' Pinder sat in one of the chairs and began to wring his hands rather nervously. His earlier anger had changed to genuine worry. 'I want to help, we all do, we thought a lot of Mr Stephen, but I know nothing, Sergeant.' And he spread his hands as if to emphasise his words.

'Lots of witnesses think they know nothing until we begin to put our questions,' Wayne told him. 'It's the little things that count in this kind of inquiry. So, Mr Pinder, let's get this over as soon as we can, then you can return to your duties. It's Aaron, isn't it? And your job is described as gatekeeper to Trippingdale Estate?'

'Yes, that's right.'

'Mr Broadbent has described some of your duties to me, so there's no need for me to go over all that again. Let's go straight to yesterday morning, Saturday.'

'Right you are.'

'What time did you start work?' was Wayne's opening question.

'There's no special time for starting, but I'm usually up at half six. Before I have breakfast, I unlock the gate so the estate workers can get through without waiting for me to open up for them. That's if they need to. They don't always want to go into the parkland or over to the castle fields that way.'

'And yesterday? Saturday? You did that?'

'Yes, I was up and about as usual, unlocked the gate at half six or thereabouts.'

'Then what?'

'I had breakfast.'

'Would that be in this side of the gatehouse or the other? Your house spans the road, doesn't it?'

'It was this side, in the kitchen, at the back of where we are now.'

'So you couldn't see the road or the gate while having breakfast?'

'No, from there I can look into the estate, quite a way up the dale.'

'A nice view?'

'Very pleasant, Sergeant, open countryside.'

'You talk of the dale and the parkland. Is there a difference?'

'No. Because the dale is private we call it the parkland. It's the same, really, dale, parkland, call it what you like.'

'But if anyone did come through the gate, you might see them after they had gone through, walking or driving up the dale?'

'Aye, I suppose so. I can see part of the road as it goes into the parkland but it's only estate workers who'd want to come through at that time of day. They open the gate themselves, you see, once it's unlocked. It's locked overnight. I have to unlock it first thing for them, then they can come and go as they want.'

'And if one of the estate workers happened to come very early, before you'd unlocked the gate, what would he do?'

'There's a bell-push on the wall, for emergencies. He'd press it, then me or the wife would go and see to things, unlock it and let him through.'

'So, Mr Pinder, while you were having breakfast at the back of the house, anyone could come through the gate, after half past six or so, without you knowing? Or between half past six and whatever time you finish your meal.'

'Well, yes, I suppose they could now you mention it, and I couldn't always guarantee I'd see them from the kitchen once they'd

247

got deep into the parkland. But we never get tourists at that time of morning. I've never known a tourist or rambler try to get into the parkland before about half ten.'

'It's not tourists and ramblers I'm worried about, Mr Pinder, and I'm not trying to determine whether or not you were doing your job properly. I know you were; I know you're the finest gatekeeper for miles around. What I am suggesting is that someone could have entered the estate property without you knowing while you were having your breakfast, after half past six or so.'

'I'm usually pretty good at spotting trespassers, Sergeant.'

'I'm sure you are. But you see, that's about the time that Mr Stephen went riding; he usually set off just after six, so we are told. He'd be riding somewhere in the dale's parkland while you were having your breakfast.'

'Yes, but he never came this way; he always went through the Hall grounds and out the back, up past the castle. That's summat I can't see from our kitchen window, not as far as the castle. He'd not want to be through this gate, though.'

'So the only people likely to come through this gate between, say, half past six and half past ten, on a normal day, would be estate workers? What would they be doing, Mr Pinder?'

'None came through yesterday, Sergeant, not on a Saturday. But on a weekday, there's the maintenance teams, walls, fences and things, them who see to the sheep, mebbe the estate carpenter or stone mason if summat needs fixing, that's the sort of people who come through early. But not every day.'

'So we are agreed that if the person who killed Mr Stephen came through your gate while you were doing something in the house, you might not have seen him?'

'That's what's been bothering me. It's just possible, I suppose, although I think I would have seen him ... I really do, Sergeant.'

'Bothering you, you said? In what way?'

'Well, I mean, my job is to keep trouble-makers out but it looks as if somebody got past me to kill Mr Stephen. It makes me look as if I've not been doing my job properly.'

At that point Mrs Pinder arrived with a tray of tea and biscuits.

Paula was quick to take it from her and place it on the floor, the only available space, as Mrs Pinder said, 'Help yourselves and Aaron, see to your guests.'

'Mrs Pinder.' Paula halted the big lady as she was about to leave. 'When Mr Pinder is having his breakfast, what are you doing?'

'I'm at work, miss, in the supermarket in Crickledale. I've a cleaning job each morning, half six to eight o'clock.'

'On Saturdays too?'

'Oh, yes, six days a week.'

'And how do you get to Crickledale?'

'We have a little car, a Fiesta, an old one. We keep it in the Hall buildings. I can drive, you see, so I take myself in to work every morning. I set off about quarter past six and get back about half eight as a rule. It helps, the extra cash, I mean. Aaron's not on a big wage and we can use all the extra money we can get.'

'So around quarter past six each morning,' said Wayne, 'you drive from here into Crickledale. It's a long, narrow road, isn't it? With no junctions until you get close to the edge of the town?'

'That's right.'

'How long does it take you?'

'Not long, ten minutes mebbe.'

'So if someone were coming out of town, along that road in this direction, either on foot or by transport like a bike or car, you'd see them?'

'You couldn't miss them, Sergeant.'

'So yesterday, Saturday, was there anyone on that road?'

She shook her head. 'Me and Aaron have been going over that time and time again ever since we heard about Mr Stephen. There was nobody, Sergeant, not a soul. Whoever it was must have got to the castle by going through the Hall grounds, that's all

250

I can say. Mind you, it's only a ten-minute run for me, so somebody could have come along the lane after I'd got to work. After half six onwards. I leave just after eight to come home, except some days when I stay later to do my own shopping. We get concessions, you see, working there. I did a bit of shopping in Crickledale market place on Saturday, then took some flowers to the graveyard, a family grave, so I got home later, just after nine. But even then there's not many people using that road at that time of day. Most times I never see a soul. Mrs Broadbent goes into Crickledale as well, but later than me.'

'For work?'

'Yes, at the newsagent's.'

'Thanks, we'll have a chat with her later. Thanks for telling us that,' said Wayne. 'And thanks for the tea.'

'You're welcome.' And she vanished, to leave her husband alone with the detectives.

'So, Mr Pinder, yesterday morning, when your wife went to work, what did you do?'

'Well, with Margot working I do jobs in the house early on: make the bed, clear the breakfast things, clean the hearth and lay the fire, hoover this side of the house and dust, sweep around the house outside, leaves and things, generally keep the place neat and tidy.'

'A modern man, eh?' Paula smiled.

251

'My old mates would have had a field day if they'd known, me making the bed and the like!' He blushed.

'Your wife can be very proud of you,' Paula praised him. 'So, what time do you think you'd completed those chores?'

'Dunno, half seven mebbe, eight o'clock even. It takes quite a time to do things properly.'

'Then what do you do? Or what did you do yesterday?'

'Well, once I get everything settled I come in here to look out for folks wanting to get through the gate. The wife fetches the *Daily Mirror* and mebbe another paper or a magazine, and I do a bit of reading while I'm gatekeeping.'

'And while she was out, you were in the house the whole time?'

'I was. I had to be handy for the gate. I can't leave. It's like being a lighthouse keeper, but the wife does stand in for me sometimes. Saturday afternoons, mainly, when I watch cricket or football, and some Sunday afternoons if there's a match.'

'But not mornings?'

'No, I'm usually here of a morning.'

'So who came through your gate yesterday morning?' asked Wayne.

'Just that funny little chap in the long coat. I thought he was a professor or something, but he had a permit so I let him through. I didn't know he was a policeman then. I didn't know he was coming to look at the old trough. The office never tells me when it's issued a permit. I wish they would, Sergeant, it would make life easier for me, knowing when to expect strangers with permission to go into the parkland.'

'You could have words with the office,' offered Paula. 'Why don't you suggest that to the secretary or someone?'

'Oh, no, they'd think I was complaining or making a fuss about nothing. I don't want to make a fuss about things.'

'So the first person you saw was Detective Inspector Pluke?'

'He was looking for the Giant's Trough. I could have told him about it, Sergeant. We all knew it was there, those of us who work here, but we never thought it was important. But he found the master, didn't he? Very funny if you ask me. He was quite shirty with me, that little chap, but I sometimes wonder if he and Mr Stephen had had a bit of barney about something...'

'It was ten o'clock when he arrived, or thereabouts. He'd not had any kind of hard words with your master,' stated Wayne Wain. 'He found Mr Stephen dead in the trough and tried to save his life. It is murder, by the way, in case you thought Mr Stephen might have died accidentally.'

'Yes, we've heard all about it. A dreadful

thing. Me and the wife were devastated, Sergeant. He was such a nice chap, was Mr Stephen.'

'Do you visit the castle at all, Mr Pinder?'

'Not very often, I never have time. It's a long walk from here, a good mile away I'd say. Besides, having worked on the estate all my life, I've seen enough of the castle.'

'How long do you think it would take to walk there?' asked Paula. 'From here, I mean.'

'Thick end of half an hour I should think. Mebbe twenty-five minutes, it depends, really, on whether you're just strolling or rushing along.'

'And how long from the Hall, using the back route you mentioned earlier?'

'Not quite so long, quarter of an hour mebbe, going across country on estate lanes.'

'So the Hall is somewhat closer to the castle than you are?'

'Oh yes, we're in a sort of rough triangle, with this gate and the castle being near the longest edge, if you understand.'

'The hypotenuse,' said Wayne Wain. 'With the Hall at the right angle, opposite the hypotenuse. I've seen the map.'

'That's all double-Dutch to me,' admitted Pinder.

'Now tell me about your master. Did anyone hate him? Do you know of anyone who might have borne him a grudge of any kind?'

'Not in these parts, Sergeant, we all thought the world of him. Very quiet chap, he was. Liked his own company. Most of us knew him as a lad, you see, and we were really pleased when he took over. We thought he would breathe new life into this place, it needed it. His dad spent too much time chasing women instead of looking after things although he had a good estate manager. Then, when he died, his old mother went a bit stale. A bit funny, really, not quite right in the head, although mebbe I shouldn't say that. Things were just ticking over. She wasn't one for changing things at her age or pushing for new ideas and schemes. Mr Stephen had all sorts of fresh ideas.'

'Like opening up the parkland to the public? And the old village and castle?'

'They were part of his scheme, yes.'

'It would have made more work for you, Mr Pinder, more opening and shutting of your gate, and more people coming through.'

'Well, yes, but he did talk of making this gatehouse into a ticket office and charging an entrance fee with full-time staff to see to things, like they do in other big houses open to the public. It would have meant giving me and the wife another cottage on the estate. There is an empty one not far from the Hall, a nice place with proper bathroom and water closet. He said he'd find me another light job, not so tying as this one. I'd have loved that, a bit of freedom as I'm getting older, and I know the wife was looking forward to it.'

'A new life for you, then?'

'Yes, it would have been. We were pleased to see him take over, Sergeant. Now he's gone we're not sure what will happen. I get my old age pension in two years' time. I've no pension from the estate although they'll look after me when I do retire. I would like to be settled and not be tied to opening and shutting this gate all day.'

'You used to work on the Home Farm, according to Mr Broadbent?'

'I did, looking after the milking herd and doing other things, labouring mainly, turning my hand to anything: haymaking, harvesting, hoeing turnips, hedging, ditching, walling, sheep clipping and whatever. Then I collapsed one day and the doctor said I had to take things easy.'

'A problem in your profession.'

'It was. He said my heart was a bit dicky and wouldn't stand a lot of strain, so Mr Gallholme, Stephen's dad that was, gave me this job. It was good of him, he could have paid me off. In spite of his reputation, he was good to me, a very good boss.'

'Reputation?'

'Chasing women, Mr Wain. Catching servants in the bedroom, that sort of thing. They reckoned no woman was safe when he was in one of his moods. He had a job keeping staff.'

'A common failing among some of the gentry, Mr Pinder. So you had a different house before living in the gatehouse?'

'I had. They got another man to do my work and he got that place. It was a tied house, you see, it went with the job. I moved in here, not ideal but it could be worse. It's not a bad job even if the pay isn't as good as being a labourer. There's no overtime, either, and no perks. At least working with the cows I got free milk. It's a bit tying as well, but I don't mind that. I don't want to go far, not at my age, so long as I've got my cricket and football on a weekend.'

'Mrs Pinder used to work for the estate, I believe?'

'As a young lass, she was a shepherdess, the best for miles. Then they reduced their flocks. She got bits of general work then on the estate, sometimes in the house and sometimes with cattle or poultry along with some bits of shepherding from time to time. We got married and she gave up work. Then I became unfit for heavy work and because she fancied more money she got her little job cleaning at the supermarket. She likes it, it gives her a bit of pocket money.'

'The job here isn't well paid, then?'

'Not enough to run a car on, Sergeant, but we can manage thanks to the wife. There's nowt to spare, mind. But old Mr Gallholme was very good to us, making sure we had somewhere to live and a light job for me, but his old lady couldn't have cared less. She never gave us a pay rise even when we asked and she wouldn't see to repairs on the house. She was an old bitch sometimes, Sergeant, if you'll pardon my French.'

During their chat, Wayne and Paula had consumed the tea and biscuits, but Pinder had left his; now, as they ended their interrogation, Wayne turned to Paula. 'Is there anything else we have to ask Mr or Mrs Pinder at this stage?'

'Yes. Mr Pinder.' Paula smiled. 'I believe there was another tragedy in the dale some years ago. A small boy drowned.'

'There was, miss, a terrible accident, but nobody talks about it. I can't say anything about it if that's what you are asking. I was away on holiday when it happened but you'll find folks around here don't like being reminded about things like that.'

'People must have talked about it, surely?' responded Paula.

'Mebbe they did, but working up here, alone, you never hear much gossip. Besides, I never listen to tittle-tattle and I never repeat stuff like that. It upsets folks, reviving old memories best forgotten.'

'Thank you,' said Paula. 'You have been most helpful, Mr Pinder, and you see, you did have something to offer us.'

'Well, I suppose so, but you never think you know anything, do you, in this kind of case. I just hope you find the chap who did it.'

'I'm sure we will,' Wayne Wain told him, rising from his chair.

'Did you want to get through the gate now?' Pinder asked. 'To go up the dale or to the castle? I'm sorry I was rude out there ... but I do get a lot of stick from tourists who think they've a right to go through. Some don't take no for an answer, they seem to think that road is open for them all. I lose my temper with them, you know, the bolshy ones.'

'Don't let it worry you, Mr Pinder, life's too short to bother about people who are rude. But we don't want to go through the gate, not on this occasion.'

'I might recognise you next time.'

'I'm sure you will and please thank your wife for the tea.'

'Right, I will.' And they left.

'So what do you make of him?' asked Wayne Wain as they drove the short distance to the Incident Room.

'I think he does know something about the

boy's drowning, he must. If he worked on the estate, everybody would be talking about it for months afterwards. I think he's like the locals, they'll say nothing if they don't want to.'

'So we've more enquiries to do about that. And what about his guilt or otherwise? Of the murder, I mean.'

'He can't prove he didn't go out of the house yesterday morning, can he?' she said. 'His wife was out of the way, there was no one else around. He could have sneaked out of the house without anyone seeing him at that time of the day and gone up the dale to confront his boss about something. We don't know exactly what transpired between them, do we?'

'So you'd mark him down as a suspect?' suggested Wayne.

'He's not been eliminated, has he?' countered Paula. 'He has no witness to confirm his alibi, has he?'

'Right,' said Wayne Wain. 'I'll have words with Pluke. Pinder goes into the frame. Suspect Number One, is he? I wonder if we have any other names in the frame?'

13

Montague Pluke, Wayne Wain and Paula
Helston all returned to the Incident Room
around the same time, Pluke having persuaded Millicent to drive him from the
town. As Pluke was divesting himself of his
greatcoat and hat, he asked Wayne to update
him on his enquiries into the background of
Stephen Gallholme. Wayne obliged with due
emphasis upon the role being played by
West Sussex police and he ended with full
details of his chat with Aaron and Mrs
Pinder.

'And you consider Pinder to be a suspect?'
Pluke concluded from Wayne's delivery.

'He has no provable alibi, sir.'

'But he has no motive, has he? He was
looking forward to Stephen's improve-
ments.'

'He's very volatile, sir, and he cannot
prove where he was on Saturday morning at
the material time. His wife was away for
nearly three hours. She's a cleaner at the
supermarket. That's time enough for Pinder
to walk up to the castle, lose his temper for
some reason, knock Stephen unconscious
and hold him under the water until he

drowns. It even allows time for him to walk home to make things appear normal at the gatehouse.'

'I accept that, Wayne. And Pinder would know Stephen's morning routine, it was known to all the staff. But that doesn't supply us with a motive and a motive is important. We must ask ourselves why Pinder would kill the man who promised a better future for the estate – and maybe better times for Pinder himself.'

'There must be a reason, sir, even if we can't find it just yet. Gallholme would not be killed without a reason so it's our job to find out why Pinder killed his boss – and that means digging deeper into Pinder's life.'

'You are making too many assumptions, Wayne, dangerous assumptions. We have absolutely no evidence against Pinder. I accept that he is the sort to lose control, that he has a temper and I might even believe he could kill on the spur of the moment, but none of that is evidence of his guilt. And in addition to Pinder's background, we do need to know more about the victim. Perhaps the motive lies in his background, not Pinder's.'

'I am working on that, sir,' added Wayne Wain.

'Good, and I'd like to know more about Aaron Pinder too. I have asked Inspector

Horsley to obtain any criminal record he might have. So far as Stephen Gallholme is concerned, people don't pass through his life without someone knowing something about them. Even the most reclusive person does not escape the interest of others. Whatever happened to Stephen Gallholme in that castle must have been sparked off by some kind of enmity, some very powerful emotion, and it is that which makes me believe we must delve deep into his past, back to his childhood if possible. This might be connected in some way to those snow-drops letters. I have concluded that each recipient has something to hide, a guilty secret of some kind – one which is known to the sender of the mail. The fact that Stephen Gallholme received a snowdrop would suggest he had something to hide too, that he had a guilty secret.'

'What led you to that conclusion, sir?'

'The snowdrop is an emblem of purity, Wayne, and its opposite, impurity, is gener-ally – but not exclusively – associated with sexual misconduct. Adultery, perhaps, or some other sexual irregularity. I am going to ask Inspector Horsley to put teams on to each of the recipients in an attempt to dis-cover their impure secrets – and I want you to do likewise as far as Stephen Gallholme is concerned. Search for his secret, Wayne. Is it something to do with that woman, Ann, the one in the photograph at his bedside? You see, the fact that he did receive the snowdrop means that someone *does* know something about him. That makes it all the more important to find the person who sent the snowdrops because she knows Stephen's secret.'

'What on earth could he have done, sir, to bring about his death?'

'Something impure, perhaps? Was he committing adultery? Or was he deviant in some other way? Did any of his unknown activities provide a motive for murder? Is Broadbent being open with us? Does he know something about Stephen's past, something he is not revealing for reasons of misplaced loyalty, maybe? These are the kinds of questions we must answer.'

'I don't think he was impure with Aaron Pinder's wife, sir, if that's what you are thinking. She's old enough to be his mother and is built like a battleship. Having an affair with Pinder's wife doesn't seem likely, even if Pinder is our chief suspect.'

'That's not the way to speak about a lady, Sergeant.' And Pluke's eye twinkled in mild rebuke, even if he did respect Wayne's views. 'But the point I am making is that the person who knows Stephen Gallholme's secret also knows the secrets of all the others who received a snowdrop in their mail.'

'Could Pinder be the phantom snowdrop

poster, sir? Or Mrs Pinder?'

'It is very possible, Sergeant. Why not get a sample of their handwriting? Ask them to write out someone's address, someone who has already received a snowdrop. On the other hand, I think I should talk to them so I shall ask them to do that. If I am honest with you, I would like to meet Mr Pinder in my official capacity.'

'And you still believe the snowdrop poster is not the killer?'

'I still believe the snowdrop sender is a woman. It is the sort of thing a woman would do. To kill Mr Gallholme, however, required strength and skill – and a lot of both.'

'I tend to agree with you.'

'You may disagree if you wish, Sergeant. I am not infallible like Her Majesty.'

'I respect your opinions, sir, and can now understand that your time following the snowdrop line of enquiry has not been wasted.'

'Would I waste my valuable time on something that is not of any value to our investigation, Sergeant? You know me better than that. But I must not take up any more of your time for looking into Stephen Gallholme's past.'

'Very good, sir.'

'Meanwhile, I shall contemplate further about the snowdrops in the hope I can identify the sender. But first I am going to visit the deserted village in the parkland.'

'But there's nothing there, sir!'

'It is located in a part of the parkland not accessible to the public, Sergeant, like the castle. I want to see where that earlier drowning occurred, although I am not sure of the precise site at this stage. But a stream does run close to the deserted village, the map tells me that, and I want to have a look at it. After what you have told me about Mr Pinder working on the estate as a labourer it is important that I should have a full knowledge of the entire private dale. I need to understand the layout of it all; and I need to know what he could or could not see from every room and every corner of the gatehouse.'

'I hope Pinder lets you through his gate, sir.'

'I can deal with him if he's very objectionable.' Pluke smiled. 'And I shall use this opportunity to visit him and his wife officially to obtain samples of their handwriting. Now, did you ask him about the earlier drowning?'

'I did, sir. He knew about it but claimed he wasn't familiar with the details. He said he was away at the time.'

'Was he telling the truth?'

'I think he was being rather devious, sir. He's lived and worked here all his life and I'm sure the accident would be a talking point among the local people, so he must have learnt something about it from local gossip, especially if the child belonged to a local family.'

'Then let us hope we can find out more about the accident. Now, off you go to complete your enquiries. Don't forget to talk to Mrs Preston, Stephen's housekeeper. It's amazing what such ladies either know or think they know.'

'Yes, sir. Now, you said you were going to the deserted village. Are you going by car?' asked Wayne, wondering if he was to be the driver.

'Yes, but I shall seek the services of a detective who is not as busy as you are. You have work to do, have you not?'

After dismissing Wayne Wain, Pluke went across to Dick Horsley who was working on his computer keyboard. 'Has anything of interest come in yet, Mr Horsley?'

'Not a thing, Montague.'

'We have a good suspect for you, one without an alibi: Aaron Pinder. Detective Sergeant Wain will provide the details. So I am now going to the deserted village, Mr Horsley, for a brief reconnaissance of the landscape and to examine the probable scene of that 1966 drowning. I need a car and a driver; is there anyone who needs to know more about this remote dale?'

'Anita, that's Detective Constable Newton over there. She's just come to hand in a statement from the post lady who delivers in this area. Anita, a moment please,' he called to her.

'Sir?' Anita Newton was a tall, slender woman of around thirty. With a delightfully feline face, dark hair cut short, dark eyes and bodily movements that would make a panther look clumsy, she flowed across the floor towards Horsley.

'Mr Pluke requires a driver, Anita. Can you spare half an hour or so?'

'Yes, sir, it will be a pleasure. It will be a help, too, to let me appreciate the layout of the area when I'm talking to witnesses.'

'Like the post lady?'

'She told me she had been up to the deserted village, sir, about six months ago, just for a look around. The gatekeeper let her through, when she was off duty.'

'Did he really? Then it seems he succumbs to feminine charms!' Horsley smiled. 'Right. Montague! I have a driver for you.'

'Excellent!' Pluke beamed, reaching for his hat and coat.

Minutes later, Pluke was being shown to a small tan-coloured Ford, an unmarked official car, but he felt like a Lord Mayor being escorted to a state limousine. 'Are you enjoying your work with us?' he asked Anita as they approached the car, with Pluke wondering why Millicent did not walk like this.

'Very much, sir, thank you. It's my first time on a murder inquiry.'

'There is a first time for us all,' proffered Pluke. 'It's a case of learning from every experience. So what have you learnt so far?'

'Not a lot, sir, apart from the information we've all been given.'

'I saw you were filing a statement, Detective Constable Newton. Someone you have interviewed?'

'Yes, sir. She couldn't help, though. She knows nothing and saw nothing yesterday morning. She's the post lady, sir. Patricia Lucas. I caught her at home, it being Sunday.'

'Post Lady Patricia.' Pluke smiled, thinking he had heard the term Postman Pat somewhere. 'She delivers this area, does she? Including Trippingdale Hall?'

'Yes, sir, early on a morning. She gets here about seven and finishes her round about eight thirty. There's lots of isolated farms and houses hereabouts.'

'And I suppose she saw no one in this area yesterday? Not even Mr Stephen on his horse?'

'No, sir, no one. She didn't go up the dale, though. There are no houses or farms up there, nothing beyond the gatehouse. There is never any mail to deliver beyond the gatehouse.'

'How very true.' Pluke had now arrived at the car. Anita opened the door and he settled in, removing his panama because it brushed the roof of the little vehicle. 'Have you seen this old village and the castle?'

'I saw the castle, sir. We had a look around that as part of our briefing, just to set the scene in our minds, but we did not go to the village. Patricia Lucas had been, though, she was telling me about it.'

'Has she really?' Now the car was easing away from its parking area close to the Incident Room. 'I understand members of the public are not allowed through that gate?'

'They're not, sir. The gatekeeper told her she could go through one day when she wasn't working, to have a look at the castle and the old village. She went about six months ago, she told me.'

'That was long before the murder and long before Mr Stephen returned to the estate,' said Pluke. 'So it seems Mr Pinder *does* allow people through from time to time. Do you know whether she got permission from the Estate Office?'

'She didn't, sir, she told me. She said Mr Pinder said it would be all right if he gave permission. He was allowed to let friends through, he said. The estate did not mind that.'

'And did she pass comment on her visit?'

'No, sir, she said there was very little to

see. No houses, nothing really, just a few bumps and hollows in the ground where the old buildings used to be and a lovely little stream. The village is right at the head of the dale, sir, very remote.'

'I was of the opinion that some persons were allowed through, Detective Constable Newton, because the castle field did bear indications that people were using its paths. You have confirmed my suspicions. So well done. And from this, you will have learnt that even the most insignificant and apparently valueless pieces of information are of value to an investigating officer.'

'You mean it is important that Patricia Lucas visited the old village, all that time ago?'

'It might have some bearing on my enquiries, Detective Constable Newton. Now, let us see if we can get safely through Trippingdale Gate without being ambushed by that gatekeeper. I will obtain a sample of his handwriting and that of his wife during our return trip.'

Anita eased the unmarked car to a halt before the gate and seconds later the imposing figure of Aaron Pinder emerged from the house. It seemed he was now exercising rather more caution than hitherto because he approached the car in a courteous manner.

Anita wound down her window and

smiled. 'Police,' she said, showing her warrant card. Pinder stooped and peered at Pluke, then nodded his consent. It was clear he recognised Pluke but he made no comment on the matter.

'We are going to the deserted village,' Pluke called to him through the open window. 'We shall be about half a hour.'

'There's nothing there, Mr Pluke.' Pinder addressed him by his name. 'Not even a standing wall or the floor of a house.'

'There is always something for him who knows what he is seeking.' Pluke beamed.

Pinder did not reply, but merely shook his head as he wondered about the sanity of some detectives. Why go to look at nothing? There was no one at the old village today, he could have told them that, but he opened the gate and allowed the car to pass through. As Anita drove Pluke up the winding road, which meandered along the floor of the dale between tall drystone walls, he expressed a view that the Task Force should have completed their search of the castle grounds and interior. Nonetheless, there was still a knot of police vehicles around the castle, some having used the Hall route and others the one he was now being driven along.

But he did not stop there.

He asked Anita to continue to the deserted village and as they drove, Pluke admired the scenery while pointing out some rural delights to Anita – a kestrel hovering above a field, a flock of peewits feeding in the same field, the heathery heights of the moors, the windswept gorse and broom bushes with an occasional hawthorn braving the robust landscape, a clump of buttercups brightening a verge, the dry-stone walls, a tiny remote barn used as a shelter for man and beast, a skylark singing ahead of them as it bounced up and down upon an invisible strand of elastic and an unremarkable horse trough built into the side of a small mound. He stopped just long enough to record its presence and take a photograph.

'It's a very remote and wild place.' She smiled at Pluke, recognising his enthusiasm for the untamed expanses of Yorkshire. At each side of the road there were green fields, some of which contained sheep while the others were empty of livestock, perhaps being allowed to lie fallow for a year. One or two had been ploughed, she noted, and new crops were sprouting. It was probably wheat or barley, perhaps, the work of the estate. And behind the fields on both sides were the rising moors, bleak and uninviting; they formed three sides of the dale, effectively closing it from the world. Pluke could understand the Gallholmes wishing to keep it private. As they climbed higher, the fields gave way to open moorland, which extended to the sides of the carriageway. Huge granite boulders could be seen protruding from the nearby spread of deep heather; patches of bracken interrupted the clean sweep of the heather and as they drove, a brace of grouse clattered from their heathery shelter beside the road, shouting, 'Go-back, go-back, go-back...'

'Unspoilt is the word,' Pluke told her. 'Unspoilt by developers, builders, tourists, day trippers, caravans and cars. It is in this kind of place that you find nature at its best, undisturbed by human beings and the cast-off evidence of their presence. This is adder country, Detective Constable Newton'

'Adders!' she cried. 'I hate snakes!'

'They will not harm you if you leave them alone,' he said. 'But in the past people would kill adders on sight because they believed they brought bad fortune or even death. They would draw a circle in the ground around the adder, believing it would not cross the line to escape, and then they would beat it to death with a stick made from ash. Adders were supposed to fear the wood of the ash. If an adder appeared on the doorstep of a moorland home, it was thought an occupant of the house was doomed to die ... rubbish of course. But it resulted in the death of many unfortunate snakes.'

'They're poisonous, aren't they? If they bite you?' she asked.

'The adder is Britain's only poisonous snake,' Pluke confirmed. 'But its mouth is rather too small to inflict harm upon a human, although if you stood on an adder or frightened it while sporting bare feet or toes poking through a sandal, then it might manage to nip a toe. And if it did, you'd be wise to seek hospital treatment...'

'Ugh ... I hope we don't find any at the deserted village.'

'I think the noise of our approach will send them racing for safety, although it is a bit early in the year for them anyway. They prefer the very warm days of summer, and did you know that it was believed the markings on the belly of an adder could be translated as "If I could hear as well as see, no mortal man should master me"? That is because it has long been thought that the adder is deaf ... ah, here we are. It seems we are approaching the site of the abandoned village of Trippingdale.'

He pulled a crumpled map from his pocket and began to check its features against the surrounding landscape. At the head of the dale, the metalled road came to an end and degenerated into an unmade track; at each side of the carriageway at that point there were what appeared to be turning circles or even a parking area, although there were no notices to indicate this. Like an oasis in the heathery surrounds was a large open patch of smooth green grass, the grass having been shorn by the moorland sheep which even now dotted the landscape around them.

'Let's park here,' said Pluke, putting away the map and indicating a smooth patch. As they eased the car to a halt, they noticed a small beck, which ran from the hills and wound its way through the green grassy area, passing a disused sheep-dipping trough that had clearly been abandoned years ago. The smooth patch was little more than an area of uneven ground about the size of two football pitches; around its eastern edge ran the little beck. It was narrow, with low banks and full of rounded rocks; its bed was stony, too, and it was very shallow throughout its length. He peered into the water as he walked along. 'I see no fish,' he said on one occasion. 'Much too shallow for trout and even grayling, I'd say.'

'May I ask what we are looking for, sir?' Anita asked as she followed at his heels. In her opinion, the expanse looked like a picnic site, albeit with no rustic benches or tables.

But, with the open aspect, the lovely smooth grass, the clear, rippling stream and the tang of the brisk moorland breeze, it was precisely the kind of place that motor tourists would love. Few would come to look at the remains of the former village simply because there was nothing to see, no standing walls, floors, former gardens – nothing save this beautiful and peaceful beckside site. Only the presence of uneven areas of ground suggested something had once stood here, a tempting proposition for archaeologists.

'We shall not know until we find it,' was his answer. 'Let us explore this ancient place with care. Let me know if you find anything of interest. You go over there, towards that standing stone, and continue until you meet the stream, then come along the banks towards me. I shall head the opposite way, to that mound of boulders, then I shall walk along the stream towards you, examining the grassy remains as I progress. I want to see as much of the stream as possible. I shall take a look at the old sheep-dipping trough, too; the whole exercise should take little more than fifteen or twenty minutes, Detective Constable Newton.'

As Pluke wandered away, he pulled a plastic bag from his coat pocket; Anita noticed, shook her head in puzzlement and walked on as directed. Pluke made for one extremity of the green patch while the baffled Anita went to the other. Several minutes later they regrouped. By now, Pluke's plastic bag contained several bits and pieces, all items of human litter by the look of it. Was he tidying the place?

'Well?' He smiled as if challenging her.

'Nothing, sir,' she said. 'Just grass and heather, and that pretty little beck. But it's awful, isn't it, the way people throw their litter away.'

'I have a bag full here.' He lifted it to show her. 'Three beer cans, two plastic drinks bottles, a plastic sandwich wrapper, the remains of a sliced bread wrapper, the shreds of the wrapper from a bar of chocolate complete with silver foil, a yoghurt carton, some orange peel that hasn't decomposed and a wine bottle.'

'Well, I saw some litter, sir, in the beck, but didn't think you would be interested in that.'

'Then show me, Detective Constable Newton. That is precisely what does interest me.'

She led him to a beer bottle in the stream; he could reach it by standing on a rock in the centre of the narrow waterway and popped it into another plastic bag; she showed him several more plastic bags and wrappers, two more Coca-Cola cans and a piece of greaseproof paper, which had been stuffed into a hole in the banks of the stream. She'd also found a golf ball on the green.

'So.' He smiled. 'A lot of rubbish, eh, Detective Constable Newton.'

'People are so selfish aren't they, Mr Pluke, leaving this kind of litter behind

278

when they could easily take it home.'

'People like this are impossible to educate into mending their ways, Detective Constable Newton. But I am sure you are wondering why I have collected this rubbish, so what else does it tell you?'

'That a litter bin is necessary, sir, and there isn't one.'

'Right, but I doubt if such people would use it. So what does the need for a litter bin indicate?'

'I'm not with you, sir. I don't understand what you are asking.'

'The need for a litter bin, as shown by the presence of this rubbish, suggests to me, Detective Constable Newton, that people are in the habit of coming here.'

'Yes, sir, I would agree with that,' she said in a puzzled voice.

'But we have been led to believe that no member of the public is allowed into this dale or to visit the castle or the deserted village. So who are all these people, Detective Constable Newton? Members of the public? Friends of the estate owner? Would such friends be so ungracious as to leave litter behind? In my view, the presence of this litter suggests that considerable numbers of members of the public *do* come here on a fairly regular basis.'

'Oh, I see. Yes, of course, sir. I agree with you. It's just like another public place, isn't it? Now you mention it, I can see where cars have parked. It looks fairly well used. It's not what you'd expect for a private piece of parkland.'

'Exactly, Detective Constable Newton, which reinforces my belief that even the most insignificant piece of evidence is of value during a murder investigation. Now let us return – and we shall present Inspector Horsley with our bags of litter.'

'Will you ask him to examine it, sir? Forensically, I mean?'

'I don't think that is necessary or of any particular value,' he said. 'It is merely the presence of the litter that is important in my opinion, not who left it there. So come along, let us make our way back to the Incident Room. And I am delighted I have seen that lovely stream, rippling over its shallow, rocky bed. Quite charming. I will stop at the castle *en route* to check on progress there and then I shall ask Mr and Mrs Pinder for a sample of their handwriting.'

Anita parked where Millicent had disgorged Pluke on his first visit – it seemed an age ago but it was only yesterday – and together they negotiated the kissing gate and climbed the short pathway to the castle.

The uniformed constable on guard duties outside the main gate recognised the detective inspector. He said, 'They've just about finished, sir, searching the place, I mean.'

'Is Detective Sergeant Tabler here?' Pluke asked.

'In the far corner, sir, near those small rooms.'

'We can go in, can we?' Pluke had no wish to tread upon parts of the scene not yet examined.

'Yes, sir, there's only the draining of the trough to complete.'

Pluke, with Anita at his side, entered the huge roofless castle to find that since his arrival yesterday the scene had changed completely. Almost every scrap of vegetation had been cleared from around the trough. Only its centre remained covered with briars and rubbish, including the horse-shoe-topped tower. That could be cleared only when the water had been drained. Even so, it looked as if a gardener had clipped away generations of briars, weeds and assorted undergrowth to reveal the giant stone trough in all its splendour. Pluke almost gasped in admiration of the wondrous sight before him.

Here it was for all to admire, the largest horse trough in Britain. And it was still in one magnificent piece and functioning as efficiently as it had been on the day it was created. And how had it been created? There was a puzzle for archaeologists – had a veritable army of stone workers carved it from a giant piece of rock, or was it a natural phenomenon? And if it had been man-made, how on earth had it been transported to this site? And how long had it taken to excavate the centre of this huge piece of stone? Surely a thing of this size was impossible to move so it must have been made here, yet it did not have the appearance of being carved from a solid piece of rock, which had stood here for countless ages. It was too symmetrical, too carefully produced, rather than a conventional trough that had been magnified many times.

In Pluke's opinion the puzzle of the trough's origins was even more intriguing than the mystery of the creation of Stonehenge. Pluke noticed the inlet pipe – water was fed into the trough from what appeared to be a single pipe, which relied on gravity and the fall of water from the surrounding moors, while the exit pipe, of the same size and built high into a wall, ensured that the trough never overflowed. It was a masterpiece, Pluke felt. Making an effort to drag himself away from this jewel of the horse trough world, he found Detective Sergeant Tabler working in one of the small buildings, which had been utilised as a makeshift office.

'Oh, hello, sir. And Anita. We're just finishing here.'

'You've cleared the tangle of briars and

undergrowth that covered the trough, Sergeant. What a tremendous achievement.'

Pluke found himself thinking this act alone had saved him countless man-hours of intensive labour; he'd have had to undertake the task himself, had he wished to reveal the trough in all its magnificence.

'It wasn't too difficult, sir, not with a dozen men working hard. We've still got the centre areas to finish. The rubbish is outside, behind the castle. There's roofing timbers, too, and all sorts of junk. We'll have a glorious bonfire when we're sure we've finished with it all.'

'So what did you find, Sergeant? Anything of consequence to the inquiry? Murder weapon, perhaps?'

'It is not bottomless, sir, I can confirm that, although it does have some very deep sections. It seems to be sitting on a huge rock with deep holes in it, like very deep wells. We haven't found anything that might be the murder weapon, sir. We have located quite a lot of litter, though, the sort that tourists leave around: drinks cans, food wrapping paper, that sort of thing. We've retained it all, just in case. Some of the wrappers had been thrown about by the wind and they were caught in the tangle of briars. There'll be more when the water's drained out.'

'And we have found more litter in the

deserted village, Sergeant.'

'So it appears the place is used, sir, by the public?'

'Our conclusion precisely, Sergeant. This place is visited by the sort of people who drop litter.' Pluke smiled, realising that Anita was absorbing everything said by Sergeant Tabler. 'But is there anything that might be linked directly to the death of Stephen Gallholme?'

'Not so far, sir, but as you can see, we haven't drained the trough yet. That's being done later today by the Fire Brigade. I'm expecting them within half an hour.'

'It will be most interesting to see what is revealed. I would expect parts of the bottom to be covered by a thick layer of silt,' Pluke reminded Tabler. 'That might be capable of hiding a good deal – as, indeed, the deeper sections might.'

'We'll bear that in mind, sir.'

'Parts are more than three feet deep, Sergeant? Those old wells?'

'Yes, sir, they are. They'll need a more careful search. I think we might have seen the handle during our operation if it had been resting on a shallow section, but we saw nothing. It could be in the deeper parts. We'll know very soon.'

'And the horse has been returned to the Hall, Sergeant?' was Pluke's next question. 'And examined by Scenes of Crime?'

'Yes, sir. I believe nothing useful was found upon it, no evidence of other people handling it. Before we moved it, it did appear quite content to remain in one of those small buildings. It had a store of hay and straw, straw bales and hay in a rack on the wall. I think those places have been used recently as stables.'

'Hay and straw, eh? But no fork to carry it with?'

'That's what we thought, sir. We looked. We wondered if the fork had been kept in that stable specifically for use with the hay and straw we found there, for that horse, or for horses belonging to friends of the estate owners.'

'Or visitors?' Pluke wondered.

'Possibly, sir. Friends of the resident family, perhaps, horsy types?'

'It would make sense, Sergeant. From the scenario you have provided it would seem that the castle was visited regularly, even before Stephen returned to take up his duties. I think we can count horse riders among the visitors too.'

'I'd say so, sir, and I'd say that Stephen decided to make use of it to rest his horse from time to time. It seems he came here and dismounted, but I doubt if he intended staying long, the Hall is only a mile or so away. Anyway, sir, the horse is now back at the Hall, in its usual stable and one of the farmworkers has offered to look after it.'

'You've searched the stables there?'

'We have, sir. Nothing.'

'No hay-forks or straw-forks?'

'Several, sir. We've taken possession of them for analysis.'

'Good. But none here. It is feasible that the killer found a weapon here, that he did not fetch it from the Hall to the castle. It was conveniently on hand for his task and it was disposed of.'

'That seems to be the case, sir. Even if the fork was very old, it might have been kept in one of these castle stables for use by modern riders. It makes you think the killer knew it was there.'

'We had better check among the horse riders of the locality, Sergeant, to see whether any ventured this way, with or without permission. One of them might have noticed a fork here at some stage. Well, I must be going. Come along Detective Constable Newton, back to the gatehouse for words with the Pinders.'

Anita eased the car to a halt before reaching the gate and Pluke disembarked, asking the policewoman to accompany him. The sturdy Mrs Pinder, in the kitchen preparing a cup of tea, had noticed their arrival and had alerted her husband; he was preparing to open the gate when he saw them heading towards him on foot.

'Ah, Mr Pluke.' Pinder appeared to be slightly puzzled by this double approach and said, 'Is there a problem?'

'Good heavens no!' Pluke smiled. 'It's just that we are gathering evidence in respect of one aspect of our enquiries and I have to seek your co-operation. And that of Mrs Pinder.'

'Well yes, of course, anything to help, but one of your sergeants was here earlier.'

'He was dealing with one line of enquiry, I am dealing with another,' Pluke told him. 'Did you know that Mr Stephen received a pressed snowdrop in his mail? And that other people in Crickledale have also received them?'

Pinder shook his head. 'No, no idea.'

'If you did receive one yourself what would it mean to you?'

'You mean a real snowdrop flattened?'

'Yes, in a manner of speaking.'

'Well, it wouldn't mean a thing to me, nor to my missus. Why? Should it?'

'I suppose the answer to that depends upon who sent it and who received it,' said Pluke. 'But to rule you out of the inquiry, I would like a sample of your handwriting, Mr Pinder, and that of your wife.'

'Would you?'

'We can then compare your writing with that of the sender and I am sure we would be able to prove it was not you.'

'Well, I've never sent flat snowdrops or any kind of snowdrops to anybody, so I'll be pleased to oblige. And I'm sure the missus will.'

Mrs Pinder, when the matter was explained to her, said she had no idea of the meaning behind the mailed snowdrops. She wasn't superstitious, she told them. Like her husband, she was pleased to write in capital letters on a piece of paper provided by Pluke, the name and address of one of the recipients. Pluke chose Mrs Molly Mayweed because he could remember her address and, without showing any kind of recognition of her name, each of the Pinders wrote the necessary words.

Pluke then asked them to sign the envelope with their full name, to prove authorship. 'Excellent!' He beamed. 'Thank you, both of you. You'll be happy to know that your writing is nothing like that which has been used on the offending mail. It means I can eliminate both of you from these enquiries.' Nonetheless, he tucked the samples into his file for future reference as Mrs Pinder slipped out of the room.

'Will that be all, Mr Pluke?' asked Pinder as they prepared to leave.

'Just one more thing, Mr Pinder. Are there just you and Mrs Pinder here? Living here, I mean?'

'Oh, yes, just the two of us. The place is hardly big enough to swing a cat anyway, Mr Pluke. We couldn't cope with lodgers or anything like that. If the estate wants to house its staff, there's plenty of spare cottages and rooms.'

'You've no family?' Pluke asked gently.

'No, we've never managed to have children, Mr Pluke. It's something the wife has always regretted, but it wasn't to be.'

'You've been married a while, then?'

'Thirty-two years this June, Mr Pluke. And very happy we've been as well, Margot and me. Mebbe we're not rich, but we've had a good life together.'

'You've worked on the estate all your lives, both of you?'

'Oh, yes,' said Aaron. 'Since I was a lad and Margot for a long time after she left school. Then she got her cleaning job. Old Mr Gallholme was very good to us, giving me a job when the doctor said I was unfit to work. He could have sacked me, but he didn't. I don't think the old lady would have been so thoughtful.'

'My sergeant asked you about the accident in the dale, the child who drowned?'

'Yes, he did, but we couldn't help. It was a long time ago; folks don't talk about it. They don't want to renew old memories. Some things are best forgotten.'

'Thank you.' Pluke smiled. 'But let me

recap on yesterday's awful events. There were just yourself and Mrs Pinder in the house yesterday morning?'

'Yes, nobody else.' There was a slight look of puzzlement on Pinder's heavy face. 'You think somebody might have got through this gate somehow, yesterday morning? The sergeant did quiz us about that as well.'

'It's something I have to consider,' said Pluke. 'Clearly someone did manage to gain access to the parkland by one way or another.'

'That's what we thought. But it wasn't through this gate, not while we were here. So is that all, Mr Pluke?'

'For the time being.' Pluke nodded. 'And thank you for your co-operation.'

'Did you find anything up at the old village?' asked Pinder.

'A deserted sheep-dipping trough, but it's horse troughs that interest me, away from my police duties, that is.'

'Margot, that's the missus, would have used that old trough, Mr Pluke, years ago. In those days sheep had to be dipped regularly. It was quite a performance, making sure every one of them was done properly. Shepherds had to be on top of their job, then. Maybe that trough should be kept as a museum piece, Mr Pluke?'

'A nice thought, Mr Pinder. Some use for the future, perhaps, when the estate is made more accessible? Now, there is just one more thing, Mr Pinder. When we parked on the site of the deserted village, we found quite a lot of rubbish, the kind that disfigures the countryside,' Pluke told him. 'Maybe a litter bin would be a good idea? And one at the castle?'

'I've no idea where the rubbish comes from, but you'd better have words with Mr Broadbent,' Pinder advised him.

'Goodbye, then,' said Pluke and they left the curious gatehouse. Anita drove them away.

'To the Incident Room next, I think,' Pluke instructed her.

'Sir,' she said as the car gathered speed. 'You told Mr Pinder you could rule him out of the inquiry if his handwriting was negative?'

'I was referring only to the snowdrop inquiry, Detective Constable Newton,' Pluke replied, 'not the murder investigation.'

14

Shortly after Pluke and his attractive chauffeuse returned to the Incident Room the
Fire Brigade arrived at the castle, eager to
begin their draining programme. Discovery
of the murder weapon, if it was hidden in
the trough, would regenerate the inquiry.
Meanwhile, house-to-house enquiries conducted locally had not produced any useful
leads – many of the occupiers of the
scattered houses and farms were estate
workers, although there were some holiday
cottages, currently empty, and of course the
Hall itself was empty too, save for the Estate
Office in the east wing. The Incident Room
staff were still awaiting the result of investigations being carried out further afield,
such as those delving into Gallholme's life
away from Trippingdale. Surprisingly for
the police service, weekends sometimes
caused administrative delays of this kind. In
spite of the work of the detectives, much of
the accrued information was negative rather
than positive.

No one had seen any strangers or indeed
anyone local in or around the Hall or parkland in the early hours of yesterday morn-

ing. The cowman was the only person up and about before half past six; he'd been at work before seven and had walked the cows into their byre at Home Farm, using a short section of the winding back lane, which led from the Hall to the castle. He'd not seen anyone around the premises or in the parkland, not even Mr Stephen. In fact, the first person to be noticed was Pluke himself and his arrival had been observed by the Pinders around ten o'clock. Among those interviewed was Lily Preston, the lady who had housekept and cooked occasionally for Stephen Gallholme.

Her contribution was useful in the sense that it provided nothing to suggest that Stephen had antagonised anyone since his return to Trippingdale but it failed to produce evidence of any romantic connection in his life since returning to the Hall. In Pluke's mind, an illicit romance did not appear to be a motive for his death. Most certainly he'd not become involved with Diana Harwood, the woman from the garden centre – checks on her movements and those of her husband had eliminated both from the inquiry. Their garden centre did not sell snowdrops either, neither did they sell hay- and straw-forks of the kind thought to have been used to kill Stephen. The identity of Ann, the girl in the photo at Stephen's bedside, had not yet been established and Lily Preston had not been able to help with that. She knew the photograph – she'd seen it when cleaning Stephen's bedroom – but he'd never commented upon the picture nor given any hint as to the identity of its subject. Lily was adamant she had not seen the woman at the Hall.

A plain woman in her early fifties, Lily had spent some time in the big house, seeing to Stephen's laundry, ironing, general cleaning of the house and making some of his meals, in particular his evening meal during the week. Mr Stephen took care of himself on Saturday and Sunday, she said; that suited her because she often had her own family and grandchildren to visit her over the weekend. She had not been anywhere near the Hall on Saturday morning – she hadn't risen from her bed until half past eight and that was confirmed by her husband. She did say that Stephen had spent much of his time in the house, sorting out his mother's effects, rearranging his own accommodation and generally settling into his new routine.

She'd been asked for her memories of the 1966 drowning; she remembered it but could not recall any of the details. 'People don't talk about it,' she had told the team of detectives who had interviewed her. 'I was very young at the time, a teenager living in Crickledale, so I never really knew what had happened, except a little lad had drowned in the stream. I don't know who he was or how he came to be there. It was a long time ago, you know, memories fade.'

A similar uninformative picture emerged from the others who had been interviewed. The outcome strengthened the fact that Stephen led a very quiet and almost introverted life at Trippingdale. Although he could not be described as a recluse, it appeared he never socialised in the locality. Pluke regarded that as rather odd, but it might explain why he had made no real friends or social contacts since his arrival. He did own a car, however, a rather modest two-year-old Ford Mondeo, but did not appear to use it a great deal. If he chose to tour his estate, he tended to use one of the company's vehicles, a two-year-old Range Rover in which he travelled to the outlying parts to meet those who worked for him. It seemed his only interest was to study his new responsibilities and to do his best for Trippingdale Estate and its staff. In doing that, he had offended no one.

After Pluke had been updated on these developments, or lack of them, he said quite unexpectedly to Horsley, 'Do you realise, Mr Horsley, that I have not yet looked around the Hall?'

'Wayne Wain and Paula did that search, Montague. They did a thorough job. We haven't done a forensic search of it yet, though. It's not been thought necessary at this stage.'

'Nonetheless, I think a tour would be of benefit to me. It will complete my picture of Trippingdale Estate and its characters, and it will provide me with the necessary atmosphere,' he said. 'So where is the key?'

'I have one here.' Horsley produced it from his desk drawer.

'I think a woman's presence might be advisable. They tend to notice matters of family interest that escape mere males,' said Pluke. 'I shall take Detective Constable Newton with me... and is Mr Broadbent available?'

'I can ring him for you,' offered Horsley.

Broadbent had remained in his office and was anxious to help in any way, so Pluke said he would collect him within a few minutes. Perhaps Mr Broadbent would act as a guide for his tour of the Hall? Broadbent readily agreed.

'So what's this all about, Montague?' asked Horsley before Pluke departed. 'You are being deep and mysterious, aren't you?'

'To date, Detective Inspector Horsley, our enquiries have produced nothing of positive value. No sightings of suspects, no motive, no murder weapon, no positive leads. So if the answer to our enquiries is not in the parkland or castle ruins, then it might be *inside* the big house. I consider a look around might be useful. There is nothing mysterious in that, is there? It is common sense in my opinion.'

'When you put it like that, yes, it does make sense,' admitted Horsley.

'Now before I go, have you learnt anything about the earlier drowning in the dale? That child who died in 1966? It's possibly Stanley Bilston who is buried in Crickledale church-yard and still remembered. No one appears willing to talk about it, they're all claiming they know nothing and such convenient loss of memory makes me more anxious to find out precisely what did happen.'

'There's nothing in our files. We've been through all the old records that still exist so it was obviously not a murder. As you know, we clear out the files every ten years. I have a team in the local newspaper offices right now, Montague. The *Crickledale Gazette*. I'll let you know when we get their results.'

'Good. I'd like to know precisely where the child was drowned. Now I must go. Ready, Detective Constable Newton?' he called to her.

'Yes, sir.' She smiled and at the sight of her his heart pounded rather more loudly than it should in a man of his age. She followed him from the room as he made for the Estate Office.

Pluke, as an active member of the National Trust, had visited many stately homes. Trippingdale Hall, a splendid mansion and family home, was ripe for inclusion upon their lists and Broadbent was well informed about its history and that of the resident family. He told Pluke that the first Hall dated from 1572; this had been demolished and rebuilt about a century later but was destroyed by fire in 1769. It had been rebuilt a second time and parts of that structure formed the central portions of the current mansion. Since that time the Hall had been regularly improved and extended, the exterior work always being in local stone.

In addition to the family coat of arms, with its triple horseshoes, Pluke was fascinated by the wealth of good luck symbols carved in stone or growing around the premises. They included a weatherworn ABRACADABRA triangle on the west wall, a harp to the left of the main door, a hawthorn bush and an elderberry in the front garden, a large horn of plenty carved on the patio, lots of figures of horses and horseshoes, a sailing ship on the end of the outbuildings and a carving of Pegasus on the front wall of one wing. On a chimney breast he noticed a lyre, which was supposedly the emblem of success and ambition – and there was much more. Clearly, the owner wanted as much good fortune as the fates could muster.

The house itself was beautifully furnished with antiques, many coming from French chateaux even in recent times, and Pluke discovered that the original owners of the estate had been titled, but the title had expired. There were no more Lords of Trippingdale, but the family name of Gallholme had lived on through recent owners who were distant relatives.

Broadbent highlighted what he called the Rogues Gallery, the family portraits and photographs, which lined the upper and lower corridors. The collection, some in oils by artists known and unknown, was comprehensive and, according to Broadbent, was known throughout the land to connoisseurs and art collectors. It depicted every owner of Trippingdale and the family of every owner – except Stephen Gallholme in his adult phase. There was a picture of him as a child, however. He was riding a horse in a local gymkhana. Now, in view of his inheritance, it would have to be complemented by an up-to-date picture of some kind.

That could be a portrait in oils, perhaps, or a recent photograph if one was available. Photographs and oil paintings of the weddings of past family members, all featuring the ornate front porch with the coat of arms and horseshoes conspicuous in the background, were prominent, along with commemorations of all births, deaths and family occasions. Pluke noted they included coming-out parties, coming-of-age celebrations, confirmations in church and successes in the world of country sports, commerce and the arts. It was a very complete and most unusual family gallery.

'We'll have to find a recent photograph of Stephen,' Broadbent said. 'So far as I know he's never had his portrait done in oils, and I'm not sure there are any good photographs around. But that's a job for the future. We must maintain this family gallery; it's a famous feature and is part of the history of the Hall.'

'So which of these are his parents?' asked Pluke.

Broadbent led them to a pair of portraits, both in oils. They were hanging side by side in gilt frames and each displayed a background that Broadbent said was the drawing room at that time, 1955. It had since been redecorated. The picture showed a formidable lady in her prime, a tall, well-made beauty in her early forties with striking dark eyes and hair, a peach-like complexion with a hint of a Mona Lisa smile and a figure that must have captivated any man. She was shown standing close to the mantelpiece in a long formal dress of deep blue and white, and there was a vase of white lilies in the background. Pluke knew that the lily was the emblem of innocence and purity. The caption said 'Laura Gallholme, 1955'.

Her husband was also a striking man, very tall and slender like his deceased son, but with broad shoulders, a strong face with blue eyes, a dark clipped moustache and short dark hair. He was in a formal dark-grey suit with a golden retriever at his feet, and he was also shown standing before the mantelpiece. In his case, there was no floral adornment. The caption said, 'Constantine Gallholme, 1955'.

With Broadbent and Anita Newton at his side, Pluke contemplated the portraits for a moment, then said, 'A handsome couple, Mr Broadbent.'

'Indeed they were, Mr Pluke. I never knew Mr Gallholme, though. He died in 1980, before I took up my appointment and, when I arrived, Mrs Gallholme was – how can I put it politely – past her prime. I never knew them as their portraits depict them. I find that rather sad, actually, they did indeed make a handsome couple.'

'So where is their wedding picture?' asked Detective Constable Newton with just a hint of romance in her eyes.

'There isn't one – they were never married. I've heard Mr Gallholme wasn't the marrying sort,' said Broadbent with the blunt honesty of a Yorkshireman. 'He did like the ladies, so the older folks tell me, he had a job keeping female staff. But not many people notice that omission, Miss Newton. And I might add that beyond these four walls, the fact has never been mentioned to anyone. The estate staff and local people have always been led to believe they were married, there was no reason to think otherwise. I discovered the truth from Mrs Gallholme while discussing the inheritance problems that might have followed Stephen's divorce, particularly as he was without issue. She told me how things were because she thought I should be aware of possible difficulties, although the question of inheritance had in fact been settled in her husband's very carefully worded will. Due to her state of mind at the time, I did wonder whether she was telling me the truth or not, so I did some research – it's true all right. The family managed to create the myth that they'd had a quiet wedding on some tropical island, quite a romantic notion so soon after the war, but in view of these unusual circumstances I think you should know the actual situation.'

'The power of a woman's observation, Mr Broadbent! Well done, Detective Constable Newton. So was there a reason for them not marrying? Living together out of wedlock was very much against the conventions of that time, particularly in families of this kind.'

'They did everything to make it appear correct – apart from staging a fake wedding photograph. Mrs Gallholme adopted the Gallholme name. She changed it by deed poll. Her previous name was Dowber, Laura Dowber, *Mrs* Laura Dowber. Her husband was a staunch member of the Church of England, one of those who thought he was a Catholic, and he would not divorce her when she began her affair with Constantine Gallholme. Her husband did not make a fuss about it. He just told her to go and live with Gallholme if she wanted, but that he would never divorce her.'

'And did he?' asked Pluke.

'No never. He died in 1970 but in spite of the freedom his death offered, the couple decided not to undergo a marriage ceremony; by then, of course, everyone thought they were married. They had a son, too, so marriage seemed unnecessary. All the other legalities had been attended to – Constantine's will had seen to that – things like the inheritance of this estate and so on. As I said, Constantine was a ladies' man but apart from that a wedding at that late stage of their lives would have caused a good deal of unnecessary scandal. Let sleeping dogs lie was the policy of the time.'

'So if Stephen was born in 1958, he would be illegitimate?' Pluke observed. 'His mother was then married to a man who was not his father.'

'Yes, but no one knew that. His mother bore the name of Gallholme by that time, everyone knew her as Mrs Gallholme and Constantine Gallholme's will made sure of his son's inheritance. He was, after all, the natural son of his father with Gallholme blood in his veins and there were no other children of the union. If people did know or suspect the truth, no one ever commented on it, least of all the staff. In spite of all their precautions, I doubt if it could have remained a total secret. I'm sure some older estate workers must have known or at least guessed the truth. But it never got into the public domain. I must admit I had no idea until Mrs Gallholme gave me the facts. I do know she worried about the estate after Stephen's divorce.'

'Could this mean there is a claimant somewhere on Mrs Gallholme's side?' asked Pluke, trying to think of a motive for Stephen's murder.

'No, we went into all that,' said Broadbent. 'Her first – and well, only – husband is dead and there was no issue from that marriage. And after all, Stephen does carry the Gallholme blood. But over and above that, Mr Gallholme's carefully laid plans, enforced by his will, foresaw every kind of problem in that respect; his will is abundantly clear. Stephen was the heir to everything, and if he himself had produced an heir that child, male or female, would have inherited the estate.'

'But now Stephen is dead without issue. The Australian cousins will inherit; that is quite clear, is it?' Pluke asked.

'I'm sure they will, Mr Pluke. There is no one else. Stephen himself knew that but I don't think it put pressure on him to re-marry. He never commented on it, though.'

'So what does Stephen's birth certificate say as far as his mother is concerned?'

'It gives the name of Laura Gallholme as the mother and Constantine Gallholme's name as the father. Quite legitimate, on paper.' Broadbent smiled.

'You have the certificate?'

'Yes, I had to take possession of it during the transfer of the estate to Stephen. It's in my office. You'd like to see it?'

'Please,' said Pluke. 'Right, let's continue our tour, shall we?'

The internal tour produced no further excitements for Pluke, although he enjoyed the exterior of the Hall. He loved the gardens with their array of colourful spring flowers, the conservatory with its vines and the former stables containing two old horse-drawn coaches, a twinge of nostalgia for Pluke. He wondered if the first owner of his famous overcoat had driven, or come into contact with, either of those coaches. And then he saw the wonderful horse trough behind the stable. A splendidly ornate structure featuring two deep, stone-built troughs, back to back, with a hand-operated pump standing proud between them. The long curved nozzle of that pump could be turned so that it would fill either of the troughs and everything was in full working order.

Within seconds he had found the camera he always carried, taken several pictures, entered details of the trough (c. 1775) in his notebook and got provisional approval from Broadbent to include this masterpiece in his forthcoming publication, *Manorial Horse Troughs of Yorkshire*.

Later, in Broadbent's office he inspected Stephen Gallholme's birth certificate in the full realisation that history was never quite like reality and made a note of the details in his pocketbook. In the confines of the office, he did enquire whether Broadbent knew anything about the accidental drowning of the child in 1966, but Broadbent repeated that he knew nothing. Wayne Wain had asked the same question, he told Pluke; it had happened before his appointment as estate manager and no one had talked to him about the incident. In fact, he had no idea it had occurred until Wayne Wain had raised the matter and he could not see that it had any connection, however remote, with the death of Stephen Gallholme.

'The family was clearly very superstitious, Mr Broadbent. The horseshoes on the coat of arms, for example, and at the Giant's Trough, then those emblems all over the house. The buildings are replete with good luck symbols.'

'The Gallholmes were indeed noted as being very superstitious, Mr Pluke, and when Mrs Gallholme joined the family she became entranced with the notion. She adopted all their beliefs and in fact extended them; she was like a convert to a new religion. She became almost fanatical, Stephen told me that.'

'And Stephen himself?'

'I think he tried to shake off those old ideas. He was a modern man, Mr Pluke, he didn't believe in things like unlucky thirteens or carrying a rabbit's foot around, but, to be honest, I don't think he ever totally succeeded. His mother's influence during his formative years was too strong; I once saw him cross himself when a solitary magpie flew in front of him and that was only a few days ago.'

'Centuries of indoctrination cannot be eliminated overnight, Mr Broadbent,' said Pluke. 'Now, before we leave, have our teams interviewed you about your own movements yesterday morning?'

'I have spoken to your Detective Sergeant

Wain and his partner, that lady detective.'

'Good, then I need not trouble you too greatly, but I would like to hear your version of the events of yesterday morning. Your own movements in particular.'

'Of course. I got to the office around nine o'clock, expecting Mr Stephen to come in for a chat.'

'And prior to that?'

'Nothing, really, Mr Pluke. I got up at eight, washed and shaved, got dressed, had my breakfast and walked over to the office. I live in Trippingdale Cottage beyond the Hall; it's about a fifteen-minute walk from here. I enjoy the morning exercise.'

'So did you see anyone around the place?'

'No, no one. I've gone over that in my mind countless times, Mr Pluke, but I saw nothing and no one.'

'You could confirm your presence in your home if we asked?'

'My wife was with me, she was there until just after half past eight. You could ask her.'

'And what did she do after half past eight?' enquired Pluke.

'She works in Headley's, in Crickledale. Part-time. Mondays, Tuesdays, Fridays and Saturdays. She went to work. She has to be there before nine and she does a full day on a Saturday.'

'That stationer and newsagents?'

'That's the one, Mr Pluke.'

'Thanks, we might have to speak to her, although our teams might have interviewed her already in the course of their enquiries. All in the process of elimination, you understand.'

'Yes, I know you have to ask all these questions. As I've told you, I'm always pleased to help.'

Pluke thanked Broadbent for his time and for providing such a useful and honest background about the Gallholme family, then left the office. He did suggest that Broadbent might care to go home – they could always reach him there if necessary – but the estate manager said he was happy to remain in his office for the time being. It enabled him to straighten out a lot of outstanding work and his wife would be busy catching up with her own household chores; she'd be glad to have him out of the way. As they left, Pluke asked Anita Newton, 'What is your opinion of Mr Broadbent?'

'He seems to be a very down-to-earth man, sir. Helpful and willing to spend time assisting us.'

'Not a suspect, you think?'

'He can't be totally ruled out, can he, sir? He could have had time to murder Stephen after his wife went out to work, I suppose. And he would know how to find his way around the place without being seen. But he smacks of honesty and besides, he said he

309

welcomed the arrival of Stephen Gallholme. I'm certain he's being truthful about that.'

'We'll have to check his alibi, but I'm sure it will stand up,' Pluke agreed. 'We must talk to his wife because one cannot take any chances. Now, I think it is time I paid another visit to the castle. I would think drainage of the trough will be well under way and I'd like to see what progress is being made. Perhaps you would drive me there, Detective Constable Newton? We'll go through the Hall grounds this time, I'd like to view that route to the castle.'

'It will be a pleasure, sir.' She smiled.

With Pluke noting points *en route*, Anita drove slowly through the Hall grounds and along the mud-based lane to the castle. There was nothing of particular interest, Pluke told her, although the views were beautiful from the slightly elevated drive. When Pluke's car eased to a halt in front of the edifice, he walked in and saw that the giant trough was almost empty. Two fire appliances and their crews were working around it, although a lot of vegetation remained in the central area. It continued to surround the horseshoe tower, for its dressing of briars could only be removed when the trough was empty. The scene was one of determined activity, with the noise of the appliance engines and pumping machinery dominating the ruins to the accompaniment of shouts and instructions from the fire officers.

With Anita at his side, he made his way through the throng until he spotted the senior fire officer. Pluke knew him through the course of his work in Crickledale. 'Good afternoon, Mr Andrews. It is good of you to help us in this way.' Pluke raised his voice to make himself heard about the noise.

'Our pleasure, Mr Pluke,' answered the officer, a powerful-looking man in his late thirties. He raised his voice too, but was clearly accustomed to carrying on a conversation against such a background. 'An exercise of this kind is the ideal way of keeping our crews occupied on a good Sunday afternoon. It's all valuable training. Now, we've sealed off the supply pipe – the water entering the trough is gravity fed and comes from the moors behind us – and we've diverted that inflow down the slope beside the castle. It's using the route of an old beck to reach the stream in the foot of the dale. No problems with that. We're pumping the standing water out, as you can hear and see, and it's going into the same drainage system.'

'Any problems so far?'

'Nothing to worry us. There's a lot of sediment at the bottom and a good deal of rotting vegetation like branches and briars, and lots of debris from the roof and castle itself. Then there's that central clump of stuff, but we can cope even if it takes a while. It's quite a fascinating trough, Mr Pluke, as I am sure you appreciate.'

Pluke then provided his own glowing testimonial to the trough but learnt something new about it when Andrews told him, 'I'd heard it was bottomless, too, but it's not, Mr Pluke. The bottom is uneven, very much so, and most of it is solid rock. It's fairly shallow in places but very deep elsewhere. Parts of the surrounding wall are man-made, but some sections make use of natural shapes in the rock. Whoever created this trough has made it strong enough and waterproof enough to contain the weight of the rising water. You can see that wall now – it looks fairly symmetrical from the outside – three feet or so high with level tops and bottoms. But inside, there are some very deep pools, eight, nine, ten feet, and then some very deep shafts like mines or wells. They're natural features, I'd say, whose depth we can only guess at. They do look bottomless, I must admit, so perhaps these gave rise to the legend. We'll try to pump those dry too, but they might have inlet supplies below ground level, which we can't close off. If that's the case we might not make much impression on them.'

'So really, the trough is a type of artesian well or series of wells, harnessed to make one large unit?' asked Pluke. 'In addition to the inlet source, it seems water rises from underground and the whole thing has been surrounded by a wall to make it safe, probably, to stop people and animals from falling into those very deep shafts? A natural trough, I suppose, with an outlet to drain off surplus top water?'

'Or a very early medieval swimming pool! But whatever its origins, your Sergeant Tabler tells me you are seeking a murder weapon here?'

'It's not been found elsewhere, Mr Andrews, and there is a fair chance it was disposed of in the trough. It's a straw-fork, we think, with two prongs and a long handle.'

'I know the sort of thing, Mr Pluke, a type of pitchfork. I used one as a child on my grandfather's farm. Wouldn't a wooden handle make it float?'

'That is something I have considered. If you throw such an implement into this depth of water – say the three-foot-deep areas or thereabouts – then I think the metal prongs would sink to the bottom, leaving the handle to float in the near upright position as the prongs rested on the bottom. The thing would stand almost vertical in the deep water.'

'I'd agree with that, Mr Pluke, but if the shaft were all metal...'

313

'That would make it very heavy, Mr Andrews. Too heavy for the average person to use, I would suggest. I've never come across a metal-shafted pitchfork.'

'Right. But a wholly metal tool would sink to the bottom and could even be lying in the sludge. We've found nothing standing upright – the water level's low enough for us to have seen that kind of fork – but if it were an all-metal tool, there's still time to locate it. We'll use grappling irons on the really deep places. It could be down one of those.'

'If the murderer knew the trough very well, he might have been able to locate one of those deep holes in which to hide the weapon.'

'People living a long time in this area might know about them,' agreed Andrews. 'But I didn't know they were there until we began to draw off the water.'

'Right,' said Pluke. 'Now suppose a fork with a metal head but with a wooden handle were guided into one of those very deep pools. Would it sink out of sight, or would the handle cause it to float, to hang suspended upright in the water, perhaps?'

'That would depend on the weight of the metal parts, I would say,' Andrews pondered. 'If they were very heavy, they would drag the fork deep into the water. The whole thing would sink. Or, of course, a truly determined person could add weight to the fork, tie a stone to the prongs for example. There's plenty of big stones lying around here. That would drag it down, and if you pushed that combination into one of those deep wells, it would disappear in spite of the wooden shaft. We could always attempt to drag those deep shafts with grappling irons. Who knows what we might pull out!'

'If it has been disposed of in this trough, we must find it,' said Pluke with determination.

'Then we shall,' stated Andrews. 'But it will take some time. It's a slow job, as you can see.'

'Now, one other question. Do you object to the press taking photographs of the search? I have no objections and it will make a good photo opportunity for them.'

'No, that's fine; it's good PR for the Fire Service, Mr Pluke.'

'Thanks, I'll offer that at our next news conference. Now I must leave you to continue the good work.' And Pluke thanked him anew, saying Sergeant Tabler would be remaining at the scene until completion of this task. Any messages for Pluke could be relayed through him.

Pluke then returned to the Incident Room, bearing in mind it was almost time for the afternoon news conference; also, numbers of his teams would be returning to feed into the system the results of their investigations. Cups of tea would be brewed and enjoyed, after which the teams would resume their enquiries before ending the day at nine this evening. Those impromptu conferences very often produced snippets of valuable information, thus they were encouraged.

'Has anything happened, Mr Horsley?' asked Pluke as he strode in and began to remove his huge coat and cumbersome hat.

'Yes, two things of interest, both important,' was the response.

'One interesting factor emerged during our visit to the Hall, Mr Horsley, but let me hear your news first.' Pluke smiled.

Horsley came towards Pluke's desk with some messages in his hand. 'First, our man Pinder. He has convictions, Montague. several over the years. All for violence. Some are more than ten years old so they have been expunged from his official record. We do have them in our collator's file, though. They were things like punch-ups outside dance halls when he was young and only five years ago he was involved in a fracas in York. For some unexplained reason he punched a passer-by. His file says he tends to blow up without warning, lashing out with his fists.'

'Right, that keeps him firmly in the frame.' Pluke nodded. 'We will have to re-interview him, I fear. If Stephen upset him in some

316

way yesterday he might have lashed out with whatever happened to be available. But go on. You've more?'

'Some gen from West Sussex about Stephen Gallholme, Montague. And he was not as pure as everyone thought he was. He served a prison sentence, would you believe, for manslaughter.'

'Good heavens! When?'

'Eleven years ago. He was involved in a traffic accident, a piece of foolish driving by all accounts, in a sports car. He ran off the road and careered down an embankment into a river, drowning his passenger, a woman. Initially he was going to be charged with causing death by dangerous driving, but on legal advice, in view of the unusual circumstances, he was charged with man-slaughter. He served two years, Montague. Convicted at Lewes Crown Court in 1989, he came out in 1991. The case didn't make the newspaper up here because he had an address in that area. No one connected him with Trippingdale Hall.'

'Our earlier research showed he had a clear record,' commented Pluke.

'Convictions are expunged after ten years, Montague, they can't be given in court if there is a successful subsequent prosecu-tion; we got this from the collator's records in West Sussex. It wouldn't show up in our files.'

'Thank goodness for local records,' said Pluke. 'So who was the dead woman? Anyone connected with this part of the world?'

'No, a business colleague, older than him. I've had words with an officer who worked on the case, he was a traffic constable at the time and he thought Stephen was having an affair with the woman who died, although that was never proved. Stephen was devastated by her death. They said he never fully recovered.'

'Was her name Ann?' asked Pluke.

'You're on the ball, Montague! Yes, she was the woman in the picture at his bedside. I've had an e-mail of her picture sent by West Sussex police, there was a photo in their file. It's here, all right. She was married, a Mrs Ann Wilson. I've asked West Sussex to do a check on her husband's whereabouts for Saturday, but I've no reason to think he came all this way for revenge, not after all this time.'

'Was any reason given for going ahead with a manslaughter charge rather than dangerous driving?' asked Pluke, not without reason.

'He made no attempt to rescue her from the car, it seems. He was thrown out and injured only slightly, and could have saved her if he'd made the effort. He didn't. Quite literally, according to my contact, he let her drown. The car sank into the water – it was

318

deep at that point. He never tried to rescue her. You can imagine what the press made of that! He was despised for his cowardice.'

'Nasty,' said Pluke.

'Very cowardly,' Horsley agreed.

'So cruel, so pathetic...' added Anita Newton.

'But extremely interesting,' said Montague Pluke. 'He'd be married at that time, wouldn't he?'

'Yes, his divorce was later. His wife stood by him. He claimed the woman was a business colleague and their relationship was platonic. My contact did say, though, that his divorce might have resulted from another relationship outside marriage.'

'He was a man for the ladies, then? Like his father?'

'So it would seem, Montague, although perhaps not so ruthless.'

'All this is extremely interesting. It makes it even more important that I find out as much as possible about the child who drowned in Trippingdale, Mr Horsley.'

'You still think there is a connection?'

'I will be in a better position to answer that when I have the details,' Montague Pluke told him.

'I'll contact you the minute my teams return from the newspaper office.'

'Good. Now, what can we tell the press about today's developments?'

15

Prior to the news conference, the team who had been searching the newspaper office library returned to the Incident Room and reported to Horsley. He hailed Pluke, who was sitting at his desk, once again perusing his file of snowdrop mail complaints. 'Montague, you'd better hear this.'

So Pluke went across to Horsley's desk.

'Detective Sergeant Agar and Detective Constable Collins have returned from the newspaper office.'

'Ah, good. Any luck?'

'Yes, sir,' said the sergeant, a slender man with neat hair who dressed in a dapper grey suit. 'It took a long time because we didn't have an actual date, so we had to plough through all the cuttings for 1966.'

'But you found what I wanted?'

'Yes.' The detective constable showed Pluke a thick file. 'We took photocopies of all the relevant cuttings; the case made quite a stir at the time.'

DS Agar began, 'The boy was called Stanley Bilston...'

'Bilston, you say?' Pluke interrupted.

'You know the name, sir?'

'A child of that name is buried in Crickle-dale churchyard, Sergeant, a child who died in 1966. I saw his grave only a little while ago. With fresh flowers upon it.'

'Really, sir?'

'The boy's mother tends it but the vicar doesn't know the full story behind that child's death. But go on.'

'Well, sir, Stanley was only eight years old and lived with his family at Moorend Cottage in Crickledale. We checked the address, sir, the cottage has gone now. It was demolished about twenty years ago, having become disused after the tragedy. The family left the area and the estate had no one else to put into the property. It became derelict due to exposure to the weather. Those facts are given in this file, sir, the local newspaper keeps tables on such changes.'

'So where was the cottage, do we know?' asked Pluke.

'Close to the deserted village, sir, there's a sheep-dip trough there now, the cottage was very close to that.'

'It would be lacking modern amenities in a lonely place like that, I am sure, but go on, Sergeant.'

'The boy was found face down in the stream, sir, the one that runs past the deserted village site. Margot Bilston, that was his mother, said he'd gone off on his bike to the Hall but when he didn't come home she went to look and found him, fully clothed in the water. She lifted him out and tried artificial respiration but it was no good. She needed a doctor but there was no phone in the cottage so she had to leave him and rush down to the Hall on her son's bike. She was on her own, but Mr Gallholme senior called a doctor and then drove the mother back to her son. Like she had done, he tried to revive him, but could do nothing. It was too late. A doctor from Crickledale did attend very quickly, but pronounced life extinct.'

'Any suspicious circumstances?' asked Pluke.

'Not suspicious as in a suspect murder, sir, but according to the inquest report there were several unanswered questions. More of a puzzle than a suspicious death, sir, but it was enough for the coroner to record an open verdict. The post-mortem confirmed he had drowned, by the way.'

'There must have been something in the background of the incident to compel him not to bring in an accidental death verdict,' Horsley added. 'Do those reports give any clues?'

'They're fairly comprehensive, sir, as they were in those days. It seems there were marks on the boy's body that were never explained: bruises, scratches and cuts, and thorns in his clothes. But the odd thing was that his clothes were completely soaked, even though he was found in only three or four inches of water.'

'That stream is very shallow,' Pluke said. 'I went to have a look at it. There are no deep or dangerous pools. It seems hardly feasible that a boy of eight could drown there unless he was forcibly held with his nose and mouth under the surface. Was there a hint the bruises or cuts might have been due to an attack? That he had been forcibly held until he drowned?'

'No, but we've got to remember that forensic science and medical matters were not so advanced then. The pathologist expressed an opinion that some, if not all, of the marks had occurred after death. The cuts and scratches had not bled, you see, and he added that bruising can occur after death in some cases.'

'And the wet clothing? Was any comment made about that?' asked Pluke.

'The coroner did wonder if the body had rolled in the water, either in life or death, because the shallowness of the stream meant the back of his clothes should have been dry if he'd fallen in face down. But the current was very slow and weak there, not enough to carry the body downstream or even roll it over. His mother said she'd found him face down and had not rolled him over. She'd lifted him straight out and carried him to the bank where she'd started respiration.'

'So the conclusion was that he had been elsewhere, in some other area of water, prior to being found dead in the stream?'

'Yes, sir, it's all here,' the sergeant replied. 'But, as the coroner said, boys will be boys, they are always seeking adventure and he might have tumbled into a deeper patch of water elsewhere when he was playing around, somewhere deep enough to have soaked him through while skylarking. And that could explain the thorns and stuff in his clothes: a boy's adventure. If that had happened, there was nothing to indicate anyone else had been involved, or that it had been anything but an accident.'

'The old trough?' asked Pluke. 'Could the boy have fallen into the Giant's Trough? Playing about, perhaps, being brave, walking along the rim of the wall, climbing on to the canopy of thorns, doing silly things, which any sensible parent would have forbidden. They'd have been there then, those thorns; they're the result of decades of growth. And there is no other area of deep water anywhere remotely close to that vicinity, not even a duck pond.'

'The trough is not mentioned in the reports, sir,' said the sergeant.

'Maybe the investigating officers and the

coroner did not know of its existence,' Pluke suggested.

'What are you saying, Montague?' Horsley was puzzled.

'Suppose, gentlemen, young Stanley had fallen into that trough, the one in which Stephen Gallholme died? Suppose he'd been playing about, as lads do, being silly or careless or brave or whatever. He could have fallen in and drowned. And suppose he was found by someone who did not want a scandal about the discovery...'

'You mean the body might have been taken out of the trough and dumped in the stream to make it look as if he had drowned there?'

'It is one possibility,' said Pluke very quietly. 'It fits the facts.'

'But why would anyone do a thing like that?' asked Horsley.

'To conceal the truth behind the death,' Pluke answered.

'Well, I can't see how there is any difference between drowning in that trough or in the stream; the simple fact is that the child drowned. If it was an accident, why cover up the truth?'

'There were social conventions to consider in those days, but it was almost certainly an accident,' said Pluke. 'Those marks, the cuts and bruises, and the thorns in the clothing, they could have resulted from the body's presence and subsequent removal from the old trough. It can't have been easy, extricating the child's body, it was bound to be knocked about and damaged to some extent, and cut by the briars.'

'And the trough is deep enough to saturate all his clothing.' Horsley nodded.

'It is indeed. Well, Detective Sergeant Agar, this is most interesting. I want to read the report myself, but when did all this occur?'

'The child's body was found on Saturday morning, sir, the seventh of May 1966.'

'So this weekend is the anniversary of his death?' commented Pluke. 'An anniversary remembered all this time later by flowers on the grave. Stephen was found on Saturday the sixth of May this year, exactly thirty-four years later to the day, if not the date.'

'A coincidence,' said Horsley. 'Surely you are not suggesting the two deaths are connected? Especially not after all this time?'

'I don't think we can rule out the possibility.' Pluke sounded emphatic. 'Two drownings, both in Trippingdale on private land, both with elements of mystery, both possibly linked to the Giant's Trough, both with Stephen Gallholme involved either directly or indirectly. And one upon the anniversary of the other.'

'As I said, coincidences do happen,' murmured Horsley. 'So you want the teams to ask about it during their enquiries?'

'Not any more,' Pluke decided. 'I think it would be wise to keep this information to myself for the time being. I have a theory, which I would like to test, but there is more to learn about that drowning. How did Margot get the boy's bike on which to raise the alarm? I thought he'd ridden to the Hall on it? If so, how had it got back to the house? Had he ridden it back? If he had died in the trough that is unlikely; someone else may have taken the bike back to his home. If so, who? And why? There are mysteries here, gentlemen, unanswered questions, sloppy police work. It means I must read those reports in considerable depth. I may uncover more coincidences. It does prove, does it not, the futility of disposing of old files. I would have welcomed an opportunity to examine our own records, flawed though they might have been.'

'The coroner's office might still have its files, Montague,' said Horsley. 'I understand your Crickledale coroner's office is like a museum, full of ancient local cases. Or we might have words with the undertaker, some of his staff might remember the details.'

'A brilliant suggestion, Mr Horsley. I shall visit the coroner's office immediately our news conference is over and, if that fails, I shall try the undertaker. Now, Detective

Sergeant Agar, in your dealings with the local paper, do you believe they intend to publish the fact that we searched their files?'

'No, sir, we did not tell the editor what we were looking for and besides, he was most co-operative, saying he would not inform his journalists of our interest. But he did say that if there is a story he'd like to have the exclusive.'

'I will keep him informed,' promised Pluke. 'Thank you for a good job done. Maybe, with the knowledge you have acquired from these cuttings, you would like to accompany me to the coroner's office? I think I know where I can find him at this time on a Sunday afternoon and feel sure he would open for us today instead of on Monday.'

'Yes, sir, thank you.'

'And you come too, Detective Constable Collins. And please treat this as confidential at this stage. But first, I must greet the gentlemen and ladies of the press.'

At his news conference, Pluke confirmed that Stephen had died from drowning, but did not mention the injury to his skull. Serious though it was, it had not killed him. He told the gathering of journalists about the activity at the castle too, saying they were welcome to take photographs of the pumping operation and adding that the purpose was to seek a murder weapon. He

328

knew it would make a good photo story for tomorrow's newspapers. Several of the reporters pressed him for more information about the recipients of the snowdrops, one journalist adding that his own enquiries in Crickledale had revealed some panic among certain people due to rumours that had begun after church, but Pluke said he had not completed that line of enquiry.

He added that he would be happy to update them in due course – with today being Sunday, that story had not yet been printed. It had been too late for the morning editions and there were no evening papers or regional TV programmes on a Sunday. Thus the snowdrop story had yet to make its full impact on the public. There was little he could add, save that enquiries were continuing and that no arrests had been made, nor was one imminent.

Then it was time to visit the coroner. Pluke said they would use the car allocated to Agar and Collins.

Collins would be the driver. 'Where to, sir?' he asked as Pluke struggled into his massive old overcoat and panama hat.

'Crickledale Golf Club,' he answered, 'to persuade the coroner to leave the nineteenth.'

Augustus Hockday Esq., HM Coroner for Crickledale and District, was a solicitor by profession, a partner in the firm of Heathcock, Hockday and Haydock. He had been coroner since the retirement of his partner, Royston Heathcock, and always appeared to enjoy the drama of the coroner's court. One of his nicer practices was to commend police officers who produced clear sketches of the scenes of fatal traffic accidents, sudden deaths and that other host of tragedies with which the police and the coroner had to deal. He always said such clarity of presentation of the evidence made the coroner's work that much easier. Thus police officers who were not very good at their jobs could record a commendation or two during their careers by virtue of the fact that they were clever with drawing instruments. Augustus was a very keen golfer and socialiser, hence his regular trips to the golf club.

Pluke entered and found him at the bar, as expected, among a group of friends.

'Ah, Pluke, my old friend,' boomed Augustus as he detached himself from his pals. He was dressed in a thick brown jacket, plus-fours with thick green socks, brown brogue shoes with white portions and he sported a yellow waistcoat beneath a red silk tie. In his early sixties, he was an impressive man, thickset and jolly, with a shock of greying hair, once dark-brown. 'To what do we owe this honour? You'll have a swift noggin with me?'

'Not so, Mr Hockday,' said Pluke. 'I'm here on police business.'

'Not another death, surely?' His voice filled the bar, rising above the chatter of the nineteenth hole golfers. 'And have you got that drowning sorted out? The chap from Trippingdale Hall? You'll be wanting me to open that inquest, is that it? Get the fellow formally identified and all that.'

'We shall need that in due course, but that is not why I am here,' Pluke told him. 'I would like to know how long you retain your case files of inquests.'

'For ever, old boy, for ever,' boomed Augustus. 'You never know when somebody might want an old case reopened. You want one reopened, is that what you are trying to tell me?'

'Yes, I would like to examine an old case,' said Pluke.

'Now?' asked Augustus.

'Preferably; it is very important.'

'Then I must not delay the process of the law. Take me to my office, Pluke, old chap, and tell me what you want on the way, and I'll get it for you. I can return here to see off that double malt. Can't let whisky go un-drunk, can one?' But just in case he did not return, he raised the glass to his lips and sank his drink in one swallow.

'I could have waited for you to finish that in less rushed circumstances.' Pluke grinned.

'I'll get another when I come back.' And he called to his colleagues at the bar: 'Mine's a double Macallan, for when I return, Harold. Give me half an hour.'

The detectives invited Augustus to join them in the police car for the journey, a considerate thought as he had clearly had rather too many whiskies for safe driving.

As he settled in the front passenger seat, he asked, 'So, Pluke, my old friend, what's your problem?'

Pluke reminded the coroner of Stephen Gallholme's death, then explained about the drowning of Stanley Bilston in 1966, saying he'd like to see the coroner's file because the police record had been destroyed.

'No problem,' confirmed Augustus. 'I can find it even without my secretary. I did not adjudicate on that case, though, it was before my time. Old Mr Heathcock was coroner then. I was fairly new to the office, learning the profession. He made me deputy coroner after a time, that's how I know a little of that case. He told me some of his concerns, teaching me the sort of thing to look for, gaps in evidence and so on. Even after all this time I can recall he had reservations about that case. He said it was like having an unsolved murder on our books.'

'It wasn't murder, was it?' asked Pluke.

'He brought in an open verdict,' said

Hockday. 'That meant he did not have the evidence to prove it was murder, yet there was sufficient imponderables to make an accident seem somewhat unlikely.'

'And what were his reservations?' asked Pluke. 'Can you remember?'

'I can indeed. One never forgets things like that. There were no witnesses, no one had seen the child after he'd left home that morning. No one could say how he had actually got into the water. Royston Heathcock thought it all very odd, even in a place as remote as the higher reaches of Trippingdale. And the second problem was the state of the body and clothing. Bruises, cuts, scratches, clothing wet all over and not just where he was lying in the water. It was shallow water, Pluke, very shallow, not much more than a trickle. How on earth could that healthy child have drowned in that? That was the question we asked, but we got no answers. There were no witnesses, you see. That was the problem.'

'I've seen the stream, there are no deep pools,' said Pluke. 'I know we're talking of more than thirty years ago, but rivers and streams don't alter much in that time.'

'It is obvious to me, Pluke old son, that you are also concerned about the boy's death, even after all this time. Are you linking it to Stephen Gallholme's?'

'I need to know more about it before I can

do that with confidence,' admitted Pluke. 'But I am investigating both; there are co-incidental matters and I think there might be a connection, however remote.'

'A wise move, Pluke, a very wise move.'

'I might add that I need to treat my suspicions with great care at this stage of my enquiries.'

'Caution is the hallmark of professionalism, Pluke. But you'd be doing me a favour if you settled the problem of that child's death. It's been niggling at me all these years. It would be nice to have the thing rounded off in one's mind, eh, even if we can't change the verdict.'

'I'll keep you informed.'

When they reached Heathcock, Hockday and Haydock's offices, they had no difficulty parking on the postage-stamp-sized forecourt and Augustus led the way.

Pluke and his companions followed him up the stone steps to the outer door, a heavy wooden edifice painted royal blue, with a brass knob and a huge letter box. Augustus produced a jangle of keys, one of which fitted the door. It opened into a large, clean and airy hall containing a receptionist's desk, three chairs for waiting customers and a newspaper rack on the wall. 'My office,' he said, indicating a door on the right, which bore his name. 'But we're going into the basement.'

The basement was at the rear of the building, down a long flight of steps and Augustus flooded it with lights as they progressed. When they reached the bottom, they found themselves in a huge, low-ceilinged cellar containing rows and rows of dusty old files. In the gloom, the rows seemed endless, but soon Augustus was striding along them, calling out the dates of the years.

'It must be down this end,' he said, shooting off at a tangent. Then he found the year in question. 'Bilston,' he reminded himself of the name of the subject they were seeking. 'Stanley Bilston, born 23.2.58; deceased 7.5.66.' After checking several files, he came to a thick, string-tied bundle wrapped in brown paper with the name Bilston written on the end. He withdrew it, untied the string to confirm the contents and passed it to Pluke.

'This child is buried in Crickledale churchyard,' Pluke said. 'His grave is still tended.'

'It was an emotional funeral, Pluke, lots of people attended. Local people take the sad loss of a child very seriously,' said Augustus.

'Enough to take revenge much later?' asked Pluke.

'Don't ask me that!' replied Augustus. 'That's one for a psychiatrist, not a simple rural solicitor-cum-coroner. Anyway, here's your file. I have to sign it out, otherwise our system falls down and our secretaries play holy hell. But you can't take it away. You don't work here, so I'll book it out to myself, Pluke. Then I can give it to you to take away, on the understanding you'll return it as soon as it has served its purpose.'

'Yes, of course. I'll study it immediately.'

'No hurry, Pluke, take your time. I know where it is if anyone wants it.' He found a ledger in the drawer of a desk near the doorway, signed out the file to himself and returned the ledger to the drawer, slamming it shut. 'Right, that's it, Pluke. Mission accomplished. Now you can take me back to the club where my whisky will be wondering where I am.'

After returning Augustus to the golf club, Pluke said, 'I thought we would all be required so we could scan this file while it was still in his office, but it seems golf is more important to him right now. I suggest we adjourn to the police station; it is closed on Sundays, so we can have a few minutes of peace to study the contents of this file. And perhaps brew ourselves a cup of tea from Mrs Plumpton's stock.'

'Thanks, sir, I'm parched,' said Agar, a sentiment echoed by Collins.

Collins offered to make the tea while Pluke and Agar began to separate out the file. It consisted of several sections.

There were the initial investigation by the police, the pathologist's report, statements from people living nearby and from the family, a set of photographs and an account of the inquest itself.

'Would you examine the inquest evidence?' Pluke asked Agar. 'I'll check through the initial actions at the scene.'

'Sir,' acknowledged Agar as Pluke handed him the relevant section of papers.

'And your colleague might care to cast his eyes over these photographs. They show the body as it was, the scene, the bruises...'

The arrival of tea did not break Pluke's concentration and he was pleased to see that his colleague sat down quietly to examine every section of the file. When each man had completed his reading, he passed his section to his neighbour for another perusal, so that each of them saw every portion of the old file. It took some time, with all making notes at Pluke's request and drinking several cups of tea. When they had finished, Pluke said, 'Well, gentlemen, what do you think of this? Detective Sergeant Agar?'

'It was treated seriously, sir, you can tell by the number of statements. Clearly, the police weren't happy about the discrepancies, but weren't about to correct them. There's a distinct lack of positive statements. I think we'd have looked at things differently, especially with more sophisticated scientific aids. But everyone living on the estate and in other parts of Trippingdale was interviewed, including his family. It was a very thorough investigation at the time, even if no one could help.'

'Rather like the current crime, DC Collins?'

'Today, we'd have had the water analysed, sir. From the stream and from his clothing, to see if it was different. And in his lungs. The pathologist said he drowned, there was water in the lad's lungs. Samples should have been retained and compared with the stream's water and with some from that old trough, that's if such technology was available. From what I've seen of the scene during our investigation, the only other place he could have drowned is that old trough.'

'Any views on the injuries to the body?' asked Pluke. 'Those photographs are very clear, even if they are in black and white.'

'Once, I saw a child who had been drowned in a fast-flowing river, sir, and he had similar injuries. He'd been dashed on rocks and scratched by underwater growths, roots and things. I'd say this lad drowned among thorny weeds and suchlike.'

'And the bruises? Could they have been done trying to rescue him?' asked Pluke.

'Not from that stream, sir, no. It's a straight lift – the mother lifted him out, the police made sure about her actions. According to these photos of the place where he was found, there were no weeds or undergrowth or obstructions in the stream. It's got a shallow pebbly bed, but that's all. It's not the sort of terrain that would cause those injuries. If he had been in the trough, though, he might have been knocked about in a rescue attempt, bumped against the sides or even against that horseshoe tower, and maybe it was unsuccessful to begin with. The scratches and marks would be compatible with a rescuer struggling to get hold of him while he was moving about in the water among those thorns.'

'I agree, sir,' said Collins. 'Does this mean you are suggesting he might have been murdered? Held with his face under the water like Gallholme? It would be easier with a lad this size than with a tall and powerful man.'

'I'm not going to go quite so far as to suggest the boy was murdered, gentlemen, but – having seen the photographs – I do agree that his body did not sustain those injuries in that stream. I think the boy was drowned in the horse trough and that those marks resulted from clumsy and perhaps frantic efforts to recover his body. I know that whoever removed him from the trough wouldn't find it an easy task; there'd be some minor injuries to the body, I am sure.'

'But why was he found in the stream, sir,

more than a mile away? And how did he get there?' asked Agar.

'There is the question of his cycle, which has not been resolved in these pages, gentlemen,' mused Pluke. 'The file does add to that puzzle. According to his mother, he rode away on his bike to visit the Hall, to play with Stephen Gallholme, and yet there is no further mention of the bike, until his mother used it to raise the alarm. She said she used his bike. So how did it get back to the house if the boy was dead? Did he ride his own bike home? If so, did he die soon afterwards, or did someone take him back to the castle, to die in the trough? How he got into the stream is a mystery to which I may have the answer soon. Now, consider the people who were interviewed about his death. Stephen Gallholme was among them.'

'Yes, sir, he was only seven at the time, a few months younger than the deceased. Hardly a credible witness, unfortunately, due to his youth.'

'I imagine he'd be tall for his age,' said Pluke. 'He was over six foot when he died and he comes from a tall family. We know from the measurements of the deceased Stanley's body that he was rather small for his age.'

'Did the dead boy actually play with Stephen the day he died?' asked Collins. 'I mean, here we have two boys about the same age living in a very remote area, some distance apart admittedly, but two lonely lads nonetheless. Surely they would play together, in spite of the class difference?'

Agar responded, 'According to his mother, sir, he went out to play with Stephen on the morning of his death, leaving home just before nine on his bike, a two-wheeler. It confirms Stephen was at home that morning. Margot Bilston is described as an estate employee and she had to work that Saturday morning. She'd agreed that Stanley could ride his bike to the Hall to meet up with Stephen so they could play together while she was working. Her parents were out, being a Saturday, so they couldn't look after him. They had gone shopping to York, catching a bus from the road end at half past eight. That was their regular routine, a Saturday outing to York.'

'Is there mention of a husband?' asked Pluke.

'No, sir. Margot lived with her parents in that cottage that's now vanished. They worked for the estate as well. There's no mention in any of the statements of a husband, or a father for the child,' said Collins.

'A very important factor.' Pluke nodded.

'According to Margot, the boy's mother,' said Detective Sergeant Agar, 'she worked until about eleven, then returned home to prepare dinner. They have dinner in the middle of the day on these moors. She expected Stanley to come in about twelve, but he didn't and when it got to half past one she thought she should go and find him. She did not look inside the castle. He had been told never to play there because it was dangerous. There's no reference to the trough in her statement. Anyway, she started her search close to home and found him in the water.'

'Poor woman,' said Pluke. 'What a dilemma for her, so alone in those dreadful circumstances. It must have had a profound effect upon her – she must have blamed herself. Now, consider Stephen's statement. It would be by question and answer – he was only seven – and taken in the presence of his father. Stephen says he did not ride his bike with Stanley, he did not go up to the stream, did not visit the deserted village or go to Stanley's house. That is all it says, there is no reference to the castle because he wouldn't be asked about it; it was not relevant to that inquiry.'

'Did he attend the coroner's court?' asked Agar.

'Not according to this file. The coroner said that, due to the witness's tender years, he would accept the statement as evidence. However, Stephen's father was summoned to give his account of events; he stressed that Stanley had not arrived at the Hall that morning, nor had the lad been seen anywhere around the buildings. Stephen had spent time indoors, playing with a Hornby train, then he'd gone to see some new lambs at Home Farm. He'd not been anywhere near the stream.'

'No word of Mrs Gallholme in all this?' asked Agar.

'No,' said Pluke. 'Not a word. Perhaps she was away that weekend?'

'So there's a lot of unanswered questions, sir,' agreed Agar. 'You would not have allowed us to be quite so lax about it.'

'I would not indeed. But the CID was not involved, Detective Sergeant Agar. It was treated as a sudden death, not a suspicious one, and investigated by a uniformed constable from Crickledale. The conclusion was that young Stanley had drowned where he was found, the stream was recorded as the scene of his death. No one pursued the possibility that he might have died elsewhere and the trough is never mentioned in the file, although the boy's mother did refer to the castle, saying her son had been told never to play there.'

'So what happens next, sir? Clearly, you believe the boy died in the trough and that his body was moved to the stream to make it appear he had drowned there. That's a very strange thing for anyone to do.'

'I do believe that was the case and I'd like the pair of you to read all those cuttings to see whether any hint of this was given in the news coverage of the inquest. Was there any suggestion, in the eyes of the public, that the boy's death might not be all it seemed? Or was the entire thing neatly wrapped up as an unfortunate accident? You may continue your reading back in the Incident Room. I wish old Mr Heathcock, the coroner at that time, were still alive so that I could question him, but I don't think we need trouble the undertaker over this.'

And then he remembered Mrs Mayweed.

16

Pluke recollected that Mrs Mayweed was the daughter of old Royston Heathcock, the former coroner. Police officers in small country towns necessarily enjoyed a close relationship with the coroner and his staff and Heathcock had worked well with the young Pluke. In his many official visits to the practice Pluke had become acquainted with all three partners, Augustus Hockday, Royston Heathcock and Agathos Haydock. Mrs Mayweed had worked there too, as a young girl, prior to her marriage. She had been secretary to one of the partners, he recalled.

Memories of those days as a patrolling constable began to trickle back as Pluke struggled to recall events that had happened more than quarter of a century ago. As a young constable on foot patrol he'd often had to cope with a sudden death inquiry. Such work was routine for uniformed constables in rural areas, many of the deaths not being regarded as suspicious in any way but merely unexplained for a time. Often they were the result of unexpected heart attacks or fatal accidents of various kinds.

Nonetheless, the task of dealing with them included all manner of skills, including the arrangement of post-mortems and preparation for any subsequent inquest.

The young Pluke had enjoyed the challenge of such investigative work and it was his visits to the coroner's office that had allowed him to become acquainted with Molly Heathcock, later Mrs Mayweed. She'd not been particularly attractive, he recalled, certainly not enough to appeal to the younger Pluke in any kind of romantic way, but he did remember her as a young woman intent on bettering herself.

As the only daughter of Royston Heathcock, it had been hoped she might be encouraged to study law, even as a mature student, and then join the business as a solicitor. She'd always been ambitious and had met that man who made kettles. He'd convinced her he would be a millionaire before he was forty and so she had joined his enterprise as his secretary, and then she'd married him. It was Pluke's recollection of those days that Mrs Mayweed would have been working in that solicitor's office while the death of young Stanley Bilston was being investigated by the coroner in the same office.

If Augustus Hockday's reaction was any guide, then the case had clearly been discussed in the office, with Royston Heathcock regaling his future deputy coroner, the same Augustus Hockday, with his views and cautionary advice about the investigation of puzzling deaths. No doubt others had listened in or even been invited to contribute their views. Haydock, a partner at that time, would have been included too and certainly the secretaries would be aware of the talk especially if something like the suspected murder of a child was under discussion. It was those memories that persuaded Pluke to believe that Mrs Mayweed might remember something about the death of young Stanley Bilston, some feature of the inquiry that had never been made public at the inquest. It would be worth having a chat and so he decided that it was time to meet Mrs Mayweed.

There was the matter of the pressed snowdrops to discuss too. He did feel it odd that she hadn't come direct to him about her complaint, particularly as she had known him for all his police career, but he never had understood women.

At this late stage of a Sunday afternoon, perhaps the time was right. He decided it would be wise to take a female officer with him, on the grounds that he was about to interview a female suspect in her own home. He had no idea whether Mr Mayweed would be there. Perhaps he was out selling kettles and Pluke did not want Mrs Mayweed to make false accusations of rape or indecent assault against him.

Accordingly, he asked Detective Constable Collins to drive him and Agar back to the Incident Room, where he explained his theories to Horsley, told him that Agar and Collins had all the relevant information about the child's drowning, placed the coroner's file on the desk and said he was going to interview Mrs Mayweed about the snowdrop letters. For this purpose he wanted Detective Constable Newton to be his driver and companion.

Minutes later, Pluke was being driven to the splendid detached house that was the home of the Mayweeds on the outskirts of Crickledale. He had the snowdrop file with him and as Anita pulled into the gravelled drive to park near Mrs Mayweed's BMW, the lady of the house materialised from behind a rose arch. She was pushing a barrow full of weeds, which she abandoned to greet her visitors.

'Mr Pluke!' she enthused. 'How nice to see you! And you have brought your young lady. Do come in. I was just attacking the border, dandelions you know, such persistent weeds ... they get everywhere...'

'Their juice is good for treating warts,' Pluke commented as he went after her into the house, beckoning Anita to follow. 'And the flowers are renowned for keeping witches away. There aren't many witches in prolific dandelion country.'

She led them through the front door, kicking off her gardening shoes and replacing them with slippers, as she said, 'The library is on your right. Do go in. I will just wash my hands and I shall be with you in a few seconds. Find yourselves chairs, then perhaps, some sherry?'

'We are on duty, Mrs Mayweed, thank you very much, so we must decline,' he said, having no wish to accept favours from a suspect under investigation. 'But I do not object to you enjoying sherry in your own home.'

He removed his panama but retained his ancient coat as he examined the rows of volumes, ancient and modern. Anita was not wearing either hat or coat, since it was a warm spring evening.

Looking rather massive in her casual gardening clothes, Mrs Mayweed made her stately entrance bearing a schooner of sherry, then sat down to enjoy Mr Pluke's company. 'Tea, Mr Pluke? Or coffee? You must have something!'

'No, thank you, we are fine. Now, this is Detective Constable Newton, she is one of the detectives engaged on the inquiry into Mr Gallholme's death.' He introduced Anita. 'You are aware of his death?'

'It is the talk of the town, Mr Pluke.' Her

face was pale, he thought. 'I heard at church this morning, Millicent told me. I nearly fainted, I really did, it was such a shock. A murder in Crickledale! Well, nearly in Crickledale. How terrible!'

'Like you, he had received a pressed snowdrop.' Pluke decided to test her reaction to that comment.

'That's why I was so horrified, Mr Pluke. I mean to say, I know and you know that a single snowdrop is an omen of death and now he has been killed... I mean, what does that mean for the rest of us? I have been worrying all day, regarding with fear every man who's passed my house. I shall make sure I lock my doors tonight.'

'Mr Mayweed is away, is he?'

'Yes, he goes away a lot, you know, on business. He is visiting a potential new customer for our kettles, a shop in the Shetlands.'

'Mrs Mayweed.' Pluke decided to mention the death of Stanley Bilston. After reviving her memory with a brief résumé of the child's death in Trippingdale, he went on, 'You were working for Heathcock, Hockday and Haydock at the time, I believe? Certainly you were there when I started my career as a young constable in the town.'

'Yes, I was, Mr Pluke. You remember me then? I was a secretary. My father was a partner, you know, he was the coroner too.

A solicitor of some renown in his time, was my father. Very highly esteemed.'

'I am trying to recreate the flavour of the investigation into the boy's death, Mrs Mayweed. I have talked to Augustus Hockday and he has been most helpful, but I wondered if you, with your close relationship with the work of the practice at that time, could recall any of the doubts being expressed.'

'Oh yes. There were considerable doubts, Mr Pluke. There was even talk of murder, you know. My father studied the file and was most unhappy about it. He thought the boy's body had been placed in the stream after death but could never prove it. All his clothing was soaked, you see, and it was such shallow water. At one point he wondered if the boy had been held down in the water until he drowned. There were marks on the body, you see, and bruises. He ordered the police to make more enquiries, but they found nothing. It was all very odd. He talked about it in front of us all at work, in confidence, of course. I think he wanted us to suggest how it might have happened, but we had no idea. It was a very small boy lying face down in a stream and he had drowned with no one around. Those were the simple facts. Hardly a mystery, on the face of it.'

'Can you remember if the Giant's Trough

featured in the investigation?'

'Giant's Trough? No, I'm sure it wasn't mentioned. I do remember the statement from the boy's mother, about him going to play at the Hall and being told not to play in the castle. You'll remember how it was, Mr Pluke, as children we were all warned to keep away from the castle. They said it was dangerous because a giant lived there! That's what I was told when I was little. I was too terrified to go and play there. You could get into the parkland in those days, even though it was private, but I never went. And I knew nothing about a trough.'

'The trough is as large as a swimming pool, Mrs Mayweed, a danger to children I am sure. It is still there, a unique edifice, I might say. A national treasure, in fact.'

'I do remember discussions about the boy's movements, whether or not he'd actually been to the Hall to play with Stephen Gallholme, but Mr Gallholme senior said not. And so did Stephen, who was only seven at the time. Nobody asked if the boys had been into the ruined castle and no one mentioned the huge trough.'

'There were gaps in the official account, yet your father did not call Stephen as a witness, Mrs Mayweed. I'd have thought he was vital to the inquiry.'

'The boy couldn't help, Mr Pluke, he had seen nothing. He'd not seen Stanley that morning, he'd not been up the dale or to the stream. My father felt it would be a very gruelling ordeal for such a young child to be questioned in a coroner's court; apart from that, you and I know that the evidence of young children is never reliable, a fact recognised by the courts. Besides, my father had the evidence of Stephen's father, which was identical, and he did give evidence at the inquest, on oath. There was no reason to doubt his evidence. He said Stanley had not arrived at the Hall and Stephen had never gone to the stream.'

'Did Mr Heathcock visit the scene, is that something you would know?'

'No, he didn't. In fact, he rarely if ever went to the scene of a sudden death. There was no need, most were very ordinary events, Mr Pluke, like people dying in their own homes of coronaries, having mishaps like falling down stairs or being the victim of a traffic accident. Coroners did not concern themselves with that aspect of the inquiry.'

'That was considered the job of the police?'

'Yes, it was. Examination of the scene was their responsibility. My father would never have interfered.'

'I was thinking more of a visit than an examination.' Pluke smiled. 'To get a feel of the place, to know the layout of the land and so on.'

'Oh, no, he never did that, Mr Pluke, he did not visit Trippingdale, I know that. He told us in the office.'

'So, can I put this to you? What was the general consensus of opinion, within your office, about the death of young Stanley Bilston?'

'I do hope you don't think I am betraying confidentialities, Mr Pluke!'

'Good heavens, no, Mrs Mayweed, particularly not when the participating parties are dead, your father and the boy. And both Stephen Gallholme and his father too. And, of course, I am engaged upon a murder investigation.'

'So you are. Well, both the Gallholmes – father and son, that is – denied seeing Stanley that morning,' she said quietly. 'I think they were lying.'

'And Mrs Gallholme?'

'She was away, Mr Pluke, visiting friends in London, that was confirmed.'

'So why do you think the Gallholmes were lying, Mrs Mayweed?'

'I think Stanley did ride his bicycle to play with Stephen at the Hall. I think both boys then went to play in the castle, Mr Pluke, even though it was forbidden due to the danger of falling masonry or open dungeons or something. Now you have told me about the giant trough, it all makes more sense. Because the general public weren't allowed in, few knew what it was like inside. I do know my father felt Stanley might have fallen into something like an old well and drowned, but it was a puzzle as no wells were known locally. We were sure Mr Gallholme had transferred the body to the stream, perhaps to remove any suggestion of negligence. Landowners do owe a duty of care to all who visit their property, even trespassers, Mr Pluke.'

'That's interesting,' murmured Pluke, 'very interesting. So even the coroner thought the boy had died elsewhere and that his body had been moved to the stream to make it appear he had drowned there. To avoid criticism, you think, or something more serious, like liability for the death? An accusation of negligence, perhaps?'

'Yes, something along those lines, but the difficulty was that no one could prove it. There were no witnesses, you see, no one would talk. We all thought Mr Gallholme made sure his son gave a negative statement and he himself made one.'

'Hence the open verdict?'

'Hence the open verdict, Mr Pluke. Does that agree with your views?'

'It confirms what I have concluded. Mrs Mayweed. I believe the two boys were playing in the castle, messing about on the rim of the trough, perhaps, or even on the thick covering of briars and undergrowth. I think Stanley either fell in or was pushed in – as a boyish prank, I might add, with no malice intended. But once in the water, he'd not be able to get out. There were briars and weeds in which to become entangled and, of course, the sheer deep sides, very high to a small boy. I think he drowned in the old trough, Mrs Mayweed.'

'It does make sense, Mr Pluke, now I know about the trough and its massive size. The police should have found it, shouldn't they?'

'In hindsight, yes, although no one appears to have mentioned it, not in their statements anyway, and not at the inquest. But even a careful look into the old castle might not have revealed the trough. I'd heard rumours of its existence but even I had difficulty recognising it beneath its camouflage.'

'Then I fear an ordinary constable might not have seen it, Mr Pluke.'

'Very true, Mrs Mayweed. You'd never notice it unless you were looking for it with determination. One does need to be very observant to track down missing troughs, Mrs Mayweed. I do think Stephen Gall-holme was with the boy when he got into the water but I believe he wouldn't help him out.'

'Wouldn't? You mean couldn't, don't you, Mr Pluke?'

'I mean wouldn't, Mrs Mayweed. There is a very old superstition that you never go into water to help a drowning person. The belief was – and still is in some places – that if you save the victim, then the water will avenge itself by taking you. The belief is that the water spirit is determined to have a victim, you see; if it is denied its intended victim due to a rescue it will take the rescuer. And it is true that very many attempted rescues from drowning have resulted in the loss of the rescuer, Mrs Mayweed.'

Anita chipped in: 'But, sir, a seven-year-old boy wouldn't know that!'

'No, but the household in which he lived was very superstitious. You only need to look at the horseshoe motifs and other charms around the place, on their coat of arms, on the tower in the trough and so forth. And on top of that, there were horror stories to stop children going into the castle, tales of giants et cetera. If Stephen's mother believed the legend of the water spirit and was worried he might play near the old trough, she would fill his head with even greater and more fearsome stories to keep him away from it. The lad would have been conditioned by his surroundings and family; he'd never admit to being in the castle ruin.'

'You're saying he'd be frightened to admit he'd been there, Mr Pluke?'

'Yes, he'd be terrified of the trough, afraid of the consequences of disobeying his mother and, once there, he'd be too scared to attempt to rescue his friend if he fell in, He might have developed a serious fear of deep water. Or he might have been unable to lift his friend out – I know how difficult that is.'

'So what do you think happened, Mr Pluke?'

'Inevitably, it is speculation, but I do think Stanley fell in. An accident, I am sure, the sort that can befall a child. I think Stephen was either unable or afraid to rescue him so he ran to summon his father. I think Stephen would have been retained at the Hall while his father rushed to the castle to see what had happened. He'd get there too late; if Stanley had been in the water for several minutes, he would be dead. At that stage, realising the boy was beyond help, I think Stephen's father removed his body and carried him to the stream, probably in an estate vehicle and taking the boy's bike with him. You can easily fit a cycle into a pick-up truck or Landrover. Once there, he placed him in the water face down to make it look like a simple drowning accident and returned the bike to Moorend Cottage. The presence of the bike would suggest the boy had returned home, then met with his accident. Gallholme had to risk being seen,

358

but he would know the boy's grandparents were in York, it was their Saturday ritual, and the lad's mother was in the buildings of Home Farm, working. He knew that too. The chances of anyone else being around in that part of the dale was remote. He gambled that no one would see him, but in any case who would be suspicious of the boss driving his own vehicle around the estate? Anyway, I'm sure the boy's body would be hidden during that journey. And what about his attitude? Well, I'm sure he'd think that a drowning is a drowning, wherever it happens. He could even lie to his own son; a child would believe his dad and if he told Stephen that Stanley had disappeared from the castle by the time he arrived to help him out of the trough, how could Stephen know otherwise?'

'But why do all that, Mr Pluke? It does seem a drastic reaction to what was really no more than an unfortunate accident. He wouldn't do that sort of thing just to maintain the family's image and reputation, would he? Or to avoid compensation for the death, or public criticism from the coroner?'

'He might, but I believe there is another much stronger reason. I have some further enquiries to complete before I dare venture that opinion to others. But, having said all this, Mrs Mayweed, I must add that it is all speculation.'

'That unfortunate child is buried locally, you know that, Mr Pluke?'

'I do, Mrs Mayweed, thank you. I have seen his grave.'

'His family keeps it in immaculate condition, Mr Pluke, such a good example to the rest of us.'

'Clearly, his death has devastated those who still care for him, Mrs Mayweed. Sadly, as your father realised, there is no evidence to support any misgivings about the case but these thoughts and my discussions with you do help in my investigation of the murder of Stephen Gallholme.'

'But it shouldn't be allowed, should it, Mr Pluke?'

'What shouldn't, Mrs Mayweed?'

'People of such high status getting away with evil things, Mr Pluke, not being found out in their deceptions. It happened so often when I was working in that office: guilty people getting away with their crimes, not being prosecuted for all sorts of reasons. Mr Gallholme senior was no angel, either. He had a reputation, you know, with his maids. No woman was safe alone with him, so they said. It really does make me angry, Mr Pluke.'

'Angry enough to send a token of death to those whose standards fall below what you consider necessary or desirable?' he put to her with startling suddenness.

'Mr Pluke!' And her face flushed a deep crimson. 'Mr Pluke, I do hope you are not accusing me of sending those snowdrops.'

'My officers are investigating the private lives of the recipients, Mrs Mayweed. We believe that most of them have some scandalous conduct or sexual secret to conceal, not necessarily criminal behaviour but perhaps things that are morally wrong. Maybe the vicar has been spending too much time with that charming lady editor of the parish magazine, for example, or perhaps there is a suggestion that Jeremy Dramjoy, treasurer of the Crickledonian Society, has been dipping into official funds without authority – which could be criminal – and there might be a hint of an unsavoury relationship between Mr Hosegood and his neighbour, Mrs Plodger...'

'They need to be stopped, Mr Pluke, they should set an example to those less fortunate than themselves.'

'In a murder inquiry, Mrs Mayweed, we know that the killer often tries to deflect suspicion from himself or herself by reporting the discovery of the victim's body. In the case of the pressed snowdrops, it would make sense for the sender to claim also to be a recipient; in that way he or she would hope to deflect suspicion from her own actions.'

'Oh, dear, Mr Pluke.'

'And you have done that, haven't you? You claimed to have received a pressed snow-drop, which allowed you to mention it to the other victims and to tell them its significance. That was vital, if it was to have an impact. And your victims were all known to you – you'd been secretary, treasurer, chairman, chairwoman, president or on the committee of many, if not all, the associations and societies to which they belong or belonged. You knew them all and their weaknesses, and you had access to their home addresses.'

'I did not kill Mr Gallholme, Mr Pluke, if that is what you are suggesting.'

'I am sure you did not, but I will have to check your movements for yesterday morning between six and ten o'clock, and I will require a sample of your handwriting on this envelope.'

From his file he produced a clean en-velope, a small brown one of the type used to send the snowdrops, and he asked her to write her own name and address, in block capitals, and provided a blue ballpoint pen for the purpose. He watched as, white-faced, she wrote her name and, when she had finished, he eased from the file the letter she had given to Millicent.

'They match, Mrs Mayweed. Look at the style of the figures in the post code... I think any court would agree that the writing is identical. And I note you have a splendid library here, books are ideal for pressing flowers of all kinds, like snowdrops, Mrs Mayweed. Would you permit my officers to examine your entire library? Perhaps we might find more snowdrops awaiting despatch to other sinners?'

'I don't know what to say, Mr Pluke, really I don't. What can I say, except I did not kill Mr Gallholme. I do admit sending the snowdrops but I bitterly regret sending one to poor Mr Gallholme.'

'Why did you send one to him?' asked Pluke.

'Because of the scandal that was covered up, Mr Pluke, the truth about Stanley Bilston. I mean here was he, heir to a fortune, a leader in the community, coming back home to occupy a position of honour and trust and esteem, while all the time he'd been party to a cover-up even if he was a child at the time. He's an adult, now, and then there was that business about the woman he allowed to drown after the car accident. I have a cousin living in the south and she told me about that. He let her drown, Mr Pluke. He watched her die! Two questionable drownings, Mr Pluke. Really, how can such a person be acceptable as a good and honest example?'

'Why send pressed flowers, Mrs Mayweed? Why not send originals?'

'I was going to send originals, Mr Pluke, they are much more effective, I am sure. Then, as I was nurturing my crop of snow-drops Mrs Gallholme died. I knew Stephen would inherit and wanted to send him one as a gesture of my disgust at his past behaviour, so I decided to press a flower for him.'

'Just for him?'

'That was my original idea, after his mother died. Then I thought I would press all those from my garden, keeping them for use throughout the year ... am I so very dreadful, Mr Pluke?'

'It is not a nice thing to do, Mrs May-weed.'

'What are you going to do with me? Arrest me and have me thrown into the Tower of London or something?'

'It is not a criminal offence to send such flowers through the post, Mrs Mayweed, nor does it appear to infringe the provision of the Post Office Acts. However, a court might decide to bind you over to be of good behaviour, should I decide to seek such an order from our local Magistrates Court. I have yet to decide on an appropriate course of action. My immediate response, however, is to do nothing more than let all your friends know about your behaviour – and your victims, too.'

'You wouldn't do that, Mr Pluke!'

'First, though, I must eliminate you from our enquiries into the murder of Stephen Gallholme. To enable me to do that, Mrs Mayweed, I need to know what you were doing yesterday morning between the hours of six and ten o'clock.'

Mrs Mayweed said she had been in bed until eight thirty, when she had risen to have breakfast, then she had stripped the bed and prepared the washing machine for its Saturday spin. Those chores and the re-making of the bed, with some dusting and hoovering, had occupied her until ten o'clock, when the butcher's van had called.

She'd obtained a joint for Sunday and then Mrs Plodworthy had come for coffee at ten thirty until eleven, after which she had spent time preparing for her outing and lunch with Millicent Pluke. 'So you see, Mr Pluke, even if my husband is busy with his kettles, I do have an alibi.'

'With no witnesses to confirm it during the very early hours. If need be we shall talk to the butcher's van driver and Mrs Plodworthy, but I am sure that is not necessary. I do not regard you as a suspect for the murder of Stephen Gallholme.'

'Er, now, Mr Pluke, the matter of the snowdrops ... if I am not a murder suspect, do you need to take things further? I mean, if I had to appear in court to defend my actions, it would be mortifying...'

'I did receive several formal complaints about the letters, Mrs Mayweed, which means I must initiate the necessary enquiries. Perhaps if the recipients withdrew their formal complaints, I too could withdraw the matter...'

'Could you do that, Mr Pluke? Ask them to withdraw their complaints?'

'I think that is for you to arrange, Mrs Mayweed. I think you have to call on each and every one of those to whom you sent a snowdrop, explain things to them and ask them to withdraw their complaints. I think an apology in every case is called for, don't you? And I do not want to consider prosecuting you for wasting police time...'

'It will be so embarrassing, Mr Pluke, facing my victims, but you know that, don't you?'

'Confession is good for the soul, Mrs Mayweed,' he said, getting up to leave. 'I shall wait to hear from each of your recipients – a letter will suffice, they need not call on me in person.'

'I think she has learnt a lesson,' said Anita Newton as they drove away from the Mayweed residence.

'I shall not prosecute for such a thing. She has committed no offence for which a prosecution could succeed in a court of law, but she was useful to me. She did give me a contemporary insight into the thoughts surrounding the death of young Stanley and for that I am grateful. It has been of enormous help to me; it was useful to have the opinions of a person who could actively recall the events surrounding his sad death.'

'You really do think the two drownings are connected, sir, don't you?'

'Three, don't forget the girl in the sports car, the one called Ann.'

'I can't see how that was linked, sir? It was a long way from here, the aftermath of a piece of bad driving.'

'Stephen let her drown, Detective Constable Newton. It supports my belief that members of the Gallholme family would never go to the aid of a drowning person. If he let Ann die, it's likely he did so for the same reason he let Stanley drown, even as a child. His father covered up his childhood actions but he was not around to do so when Stephen abandoned Ann to her fate. He was convicted of manslaughter for that.'

'So you believe Stephen was responsible for two deaths by drowning. And now he himself has drowned, sir. How very odd.'

'Not all that odd, Detective Constable Newton, more a form of poetic justice, some might say, or the water claiming its own as the ancient belief warns us. The water always get its victim, you see. But one must not take the law into one's own hands. We cannot dispense our own justice. The law must take its course and we must find the killer of Stephen Gallholme. Now, we will go to the supermarket.'

'The supermarket.'

'They are open, are they not? On Sundays?'

'Yes, sir, until eight o'clock.'

'And Besco is the only supermarket in Crickledale, I believe?'

'It is, sir.'

'Then that is our next stop, Detective Constable Newton. I shall be pleased if you will drive me there.'

The huge car park at Besco contained a handful of vehicles. Pluke, with Anita at his side, entered through the revolving doors and made for the desk marked 'Customer Reception'. A young woman was in attendance. In her mid twenties with fair hair and blue eyes, she was dressed in her smart red-and-white overall with her name on a badge sported above her left breast. It said 'Debbie'.

'I am Detective Inspector Pluke of Crickledale Criminal Investigation Department,' was his opening line, one which was guaranteed to produce a response. 'And this is Detective Constable Newton.'

He showed his warrant card and Anita produced hers, to provide the necessary proof.

'So how can we help?' asked Debbie. 'A

shoplifter, is it?'

'I would like to speak to the manager please, in confidence,' said Pluke.

'I'll get him,' she offered. She pressed a button on her console and spoke into the microphone, whereupon the entire store was filled with her voice, saying, 'Mr Brisket to Customer Reception please. Mr Brisket to Customer Reception.'

'He'll be here in a moment, you can wait over there.' She pointed to two chairs as another customer arrived to complain about a leaking jar of pickles.

Within five minutes a dark-suited man, pale-faced and forty-something, arrived in front of them, anxious to help. 'Brisket,' he said. 'Dean Brisket, the store manager. How can I help?'

Pluke made the necessary introductions and asked if they could talk in the privacy of his office, and Brisket agreed. He led them through the check-outs and into his room, tucked away behind 'Fresh Fruit and Vegetables'. 'So?' He offered them seats as he sat on the edge of his desk, swinging an elegant, black-socked ankle and polished black shoe.

'Were you on duty yesterday morning?' began Pluke, while Anita wondered what on earth his line of questions would be.

'I was. Eight o'clock, Mr Pluke. Eight till eight.'

'I believe you had problems.' Pluke smiled.

'We had. The power went off during the night: a circuitry malfunction, so the Electricity Board said, whatever that means. I think it was a mains fuse somewhere, it cuts us off completely. Happily, we've standby generators for our freeze cabinets, so we didn't lose much stock. But is that of concern to the police, Mr Pluke?'

'Are you responsible for the staff, Mr Brisket? In particular, the morning cleaners?'

'Ultimately, yes, but we do have a supervisor to take direct charge of them, to allocate duties and so on.'

'And if I wanted to check upon the attendance of a particular cleaner yesterday morning, could you help?'

'Yes, we have staff rotas. Yesterday, you say? But none of them worked yesterday, Mr Pluke, they couldn't, the place was in darkness. Except for a few emergency lights about the place that is, powered by generators. No mains power, you see, nothing to plug their cleaning machines into. They were all sent home. We didn't get things put right till very late in the morning, getting on for lunchtime, in fact.'

'Was Mrs Pinder supposed to be on duty yesterday morning?' was Pluke's next question.

'Margot Pinder, yes, I'm sure she would be. She's one of our regulars – a good worker, by the way. Hang on, I'll get the rotas.'

He lifted a clip of papers from a hook on the office wall and flipped back just one sheet. 'Saturday.' He was talking to himself. 'Oh, no, Mr Pluke. Margot swopped, she asked Betty Gribbins to cover for her. Betty came to work and was sent home. We allow them to swop shifts, provided they let us know for pay and insurance purposes.'

'So even if the power had not gone off, Margot Pinder would not have come in to work?' Pluke wanted that kind of clarification.

'Right, Mr Pluke, she'd made arrangements well beforehand, it shows here. We weren't expecting her yesterday morning. May I ask what this is all about?'

'We have a major inquiry in Trippingdale, Mr Brisket, and we are making confirmatory checks of all the residents, checking their statements. For elimination purposes.'

'Oh, I see. Well, yes, I can confirm she wasn't in yesterday.'

'Thank you,' said Pluke. 'That is just what I want to hear. Now, I will trouble you no more.'

'Sir,' said Anita Newton as they were

371

leaving. 'Am I right in thinking you suspect Mrs Pinder of the murder of Stephen Gallholme?'

'You are right,' confirmed Pluke. 'And I have suspected her for some time. I just need more information before I put my allegation to her.'

'But how did you know about the super-market, sir?'

'Mrs Pluke told me she could not shop yesterday because of the power cut and yet Mrs Pinder claimed she had gone to work. She did not mention the fact she had exchanged duties nor did she speak of the power cut. I think she did not know about it. She would have known, if she'd been to work as she said.'

'But, sir, if she changed duties for yester-day morning, it looks as if she had pre-planned the killing.'

'My thoughts entirely,' said Montague Pluke.

'But why, sir? Why do that to a man who was going to make things better for her and her husband, and the whole of the estate?'

'I will know that answer very shortly.' He smiled mysteriously.

'So where are we going now, sir? Back to the Incident Room?'

'I would like to see if the Registrar of Births, Deaths and Marriages is at home. I need to look at her records before I speak to Mrs Pinder.'

And so Anita turned left out of the supermarket car park and made for Crickledale.
The Registrar lived in Holywell Lane.

17

The Registrar was called Marcia Craven, Mrs Marcia Craven, and she was at home when Pluke called. In view of the nature and importance of his request, she agreed to escort him to her office immediately, where she claimed she could find the relevant certificate. Inside, everything was clinically tidy and she had no trouble locating the register he sought, i.e. births in Crickledale and district during 1958.

'It is concerning the death of Stanley Bilston,' began Pluke.

'Oh,' said Mrs Craven, 'I thought you wanted births.'

'Ah yes, I do. It is his birth that interests me. He was born on the twenty-third of February 1958.'

'Knowing the date makes things so much easier. Now, what is it you wish to know, Mr Pluke?'

'I'd like to see the birth certificate, please. Does it name the father?'

'It may do, but perhaps not if it's an illegitimate birth.'

This one didn't. It recorded the birth of Stanley Bilston on Sunday, 23 February

1958 at Crickledale Maternity Hospital. The mother's name was shown as Margot Bilston, born in Trippingdale, Bilston being her maiden name. The father's name was not given and Margot's address was shown as Moorend Cottage, Trippingdale Estate, Crickledale. The registration information had been provided by the mother and she had signed the register 'Margot Bilston'. Pluke studied the Margot part of the signature for a moment, then nodded to himself in some satisfaction.

'Mothers of illegitimate children are not obliged to provide the father's name,' Mrs Craven reminded them. 'Clearly, the child was illegitimate. It seems the mother was not married, you can see that by her maiden name. Although, I suppose, it is possible for a woman to marry a man bearing her own maiden name...'

'Thank you,' said Pluke, scribbling the salient details in his pocketbook. 'If I need further information I shall contact you during office hours. Thank you for being so courteous to me in opening like this.'

'You wouldn't have asked had it not been important, Mr Pluke,' she said.

'We'll run you home,' offered Anita.

'No, it's a nice evening. I shall walk, the fresh air will do me good.' And so they departed.

'Incident Room next,' Pluke instructed his

375

chauffeuse. 'Then I think it is time to call on Mrs Pinder.'

When they arrived at the Incident Room, Pluke recognised an air of excitement. The place was buzzing – something had happened. He walked across to his desk in the corner, removed his coat and hat, then asked Horsley, 'Has something important happened, Inspector Horsley? I sense a charged atmosphere.'

'We've found the murder weapon, Montague. Or, to be precise, we have recovered a straw-fork from one of those deep holes in the Giant's Trough.'

Discovery of the weapon was always a major breakthrough in any murder investigation and the fork was now standing in a corner of the Incident Room, safely sealed in a plastic cover.

Soon, it would be examined by the forensic lab or the Scenes of Crime officers and it had been labelled as *Exhibit – Murder of Stephen Gallholme. Pitchfork.* Pluke went to examine it, not touching anything but looking at it fairly closely. It had a broomlike shaft, which appeared to be made of ash. It was perhaps a fraction shorter than something like the handle of a garden hoe or household broom and it was rather sturdier. The shaft would have to be strong enough to allow the twin prongs to carry heavy loads of straw, he knew. The prongs themselves were made of iron and they were part of a one-piece iron unit into which the handle was slotted. A screw helped to secure the wooden shaft in place. In Pluke's opinion it appeared to be very old, an antique example of a pitchfork, and that might explain the shorter-than-usual shaft. People were shorter in bygone times; they wouldn't want a very long handle.

'Where was it found?' Pluke asked Horsley.

'In one of those deep well-type hollows,' he said. 'The Fire Brigade used grappling irons. They pulled out all sorts of stuff including a lot of ancient horseshoes but they managed to haul this to the top by getting the teeth of their grappling irons between the prongs and easing it upright, very gently, to the surface, letting the handle slide up the side of the well. It was a tricky operation, but they did it. It had sunk when thrown in, Montague, the prong unit was heavy enough to drag down the wooden shaft. It's going for forensic examination first thing tomorrow.'

'Any chance of fingerprints on it? Or DNA samples?' asked Pluke, eyeing the smooth wood of the shaft.

'There's always a chance. We'll do our best.'

'A wallop from that handle could be serious,' murmured Pluke, 'in the hands of a strong person.'

'It's short enough for the tool to be very manoeuvrable. I can imagine someone using this like a fighting stave and those prongs would go either side of a man's neck, eh?'

'Indeed they would,' said Pluke. 'I know our forensic experts will produce the necessary evidence from it. Now, I have some news too. I have identified the woman who sent the snowdrops. I have interviewed her and she had admitted doing so.'

'You have? Well done. So who was she?'

Pluke provided his explanation and detailed his action, saying that the snowdrop letters now formed no further part of the murder inquiry, but they had helped point him towards the killer.

'Well, Montague, we've had a call from Australia. We can rule out the Australian cousins as suspects. They're still in the dark about their new role but their movements can all be accounted for. And we've not found any other horse riders who might have used the castle and its stock of hay and straw – nor the hay-fork, of course.'

Following these matters, Pluke told Horsley of his visit to the Registrar's office too, then announced that he was going to interview Mrs Pinder.

'*Mrs* Pinder?' asked Horsley, showing the same curiosity as Anita.

'And because she is a woman I shall require the presence of a female police officer. Detective Constable Newton has been with me, she is a driver and I think she should now drive me to the gatehouse.'

'But why Mrs Pinder?' persisted Horsley. 'Have we missed something? I thought her husband was in the frame.'

'I think she is higher in the frame, if that is the correct expression.' Pluke smiled. 'I think she killed Stephen Gallholme.'

'You do spring surprises on us, Montague. But why her? If I remember correctly from reading the statements, she was at work yesterday morning. She couldn't have done it.'

'She wasn't at work, Inspector Horsley. She lied. She asked a friend to stand in for her at work that morning and, in any case, the supermarket was closed due to a power failure. She did leave the house early, her husband told us that, and she did return with some shopping, which she could have bought elsewhere in Crickledale. She told Detective Sergeant Wain she had shopped in the market place and she had also visited Crickledale churchyard to put flowers on a family grave. Being a driver, she would have the time to do all that. Her car is kept in the buildings at the Hall, making it easy to drive through the Hall grounds and out to the castle without anyone seeing her. I think she planned the killing and I am sure she knew Stephen would be in the castle at that time. Perhaps it was part of his regular routine? Maybe she'd asked him to meet her there. Possibly the trough and castle produced terrible childhood memories and he went there regularly to repent – it was the anniversary of Stanley's death, remember. But the fact is that Stephen was there and, I suggest, Mrs Pinder went to find him. She left home, got her car and drove through the Hall grounds and out to the castle. No one would see her, there was no one about at that time on a Saturday morning. She confronted Stephen and it seems she persuaded him to go to the edge of the trough – perhaps she even forced him with the points of the pitchfork at his throat – to see the place where Stanley had died. Anyway, I think she hit him with the heel of the shaft and swiftly followed that attack with the prongs, forcing his head into the water. She was a shepherdess, you see, accustomed to doing similar things with stubborn ewes and powerful rams...'

'Margot Bilston!' said Horsley. 'Mother of the drowned child?'

'I have her signature,' added Pluke, 'on an envelope and I have seen her maiden name – it forms her signature in the Register of Births, Deaths and Marriages. Margot, the same name, written in the same hand, as I am sure any expert would testify.'

'Is being shepherdess very relevant, sir?' asked Anita.

'Have you see how shepherds and shepherdesses handle sheep when they are being dipped?' asked Pluke. 'Using their crooks? They hook the handle end around the horns or the necks of the hornless animals and, with astonishing dexterity, thrust the head and the entire body into the bath of sheep-dip, holding the powerful and struggling animal under the surface for the required period ... and all done with a crook or sometimes with a forked implement specially made, one with wooden prongs. I was reminded of the skill when I saw the disused sheep-dip trough up near the deserted village. Mrs Pinder is a powerful woman – you can see that by her build – handling a strong sheep or obstructive ram would not be problem for her. With her strength and skills, I think she is quite capable of dealing with an off-guard man in just the same way ... hurtling him off balance and into the trough, then holding him down until it was all over...'

'I thought you were just looking for litter, sir.' Anita recalled their seemingly pointless trip.

'I was,' he said. 'The sheep-dip trough was a bonus. It showed the value of visiting the scene, Detective Constable Newton, looking at it in its entirety, not necessarily just for clues to the crime. But the litter was important too.'

'In what way?' asked Horsley.

'Pinder takes his duties very seriously, letting nothing get past him. He obeys orders, Mr Horsley. He is that sort of person. He did let the post lady through. He allowed her into the private dale but it seems he is permitted to do that, to admit friends. A sensible thing – I am sure he must have friends who call on him from time to time.'

'Right, but that doesn't explain the litter.'

'And there were other signs of many visitors,' Pluke reminded him. 'Muddy footpaths, car-parking areas and so on. Lots of people have been visiting the dale. I think Mrs Pinder was letting them pass through the gate when she was in charge, often on Saturday and Sunday afternoon when her husband was having time off to watch football or cricket. Weekends are when the place gets busy; Pinder himself said that. I think he had trouble warding off visitors his wife had previously allowed through or friends of those visitors who expected access.'

'Why would she do that?' asked Anita.

'To earn some extra money,' said Pluke. 'Secretly. They are poorly paid; she works as a cleaner to help make ends meet; she has to run a car to get to work, which I am sure they can ill afford. They have no pension to come from the estate when they retire. I think she managed to charge visitors a small amount for entry... I might be wrong, but it makes sense to me. When opening the gate, it would be so easy to accept money from someone wishing to drive into the dale, especially as no one was there to check on her. And it explains the rubbish and possibly her husband's attitude to people who arrive thinking they can gain entry. People do talk about where they've been over the weekend; I can imagine someone arriving at Trippingdale Gate expecting to be allowed entry for one pound or something, as their friends did on a previous occasion, and then being told they can't ... no wonder poor old Pinder maintained his angry stance!'

'All right, Montague. Let's agree the Pinders have fallen behind in the wages race and she's been on the fiddle to make ends meet, getting what she felt was due. Stephen's new regime would have stopped that little earner, I can see that. She'd lose a useful bit of extra cash even if she pretended to welcome the change. And she has the strength and skill to deal with the unfortunate Stephen as if he were a recalcitrant ram objecting to a bath in a smelly sheep-dip. But that doesn't mean she murdered him.'

'It is pure speculation on my part, so far, anyway.' Pluke smiled. 'But I do feel she has been brooding, for years possibly, about Stanley's awful death and the injustice of it all. Look at the way she's tended his grave all these years ... and then, when Stephen was set to return in what might be termed a blaze of glory...'

Horsley nodded. 'I can see she had the opportunity and ample time to complete the foul deed yesterday morning. And you might have hit on a motive. But she made no attempt to move or hide the body, did she?'

'I think she thought it would be regarded as an accident, a riding accident or something. People like Mrs Pinder have no concept of modern detective skills or scientific advances. And even if the riderless untethered horse didn't prompt a search, she knew that by letting in a tourist or two later in the day the body would be found. A bad riding accident, that's how she saw the interpretation of the outcome, that's why the saddled-up horse was left to wander about. Being used to dealing with animals, she would surely have placed the reins in a position least likely to result in danger to the horse when it was running loose, hence the reins over the horse's neck.'

'But you upset everything by finding the body, a detective of all people, one who smelt a rat...'

'It was Detective Constable Helston's observations relating to the horse that prompted further thought,' said Pluke.

'I'd say she has a promising future in the world of crime detection, has that young woman, if she can keep out of Wayne Wain's clutches.' Horsley smiled.

'You will note I have not used him as my driver and deputy during this investigation,' Pluke told him. 'He will be wondering why, and he will begin to see Detective Constable Newton as a threat to his position, I would think...' and he smiled at Anita. 'And she has a bright future too.'

'You do like grooming youngsters to take over from you, don't you?' Horsley laughed.

'Wasn't it Browning who said "Let age approve of youth"?' Pluke sighed. 'I shall not be here for ever, someone must take my place ... but enough of that. We have a murder investigation to conclude.'

'So tell me, Montague, in spite of Mrs Pinder's brooding revenge over the years, why kill the man whom most people welcomed as a bringer of change and improvement? I'm sure he would not have allowed her and Pinder to become destitute; like his father. He would have cared for them. Broadbent suggested as much.'

'Her son drowned in that trough all those years ago, I am convinced of that,' said

385

Pluke. 'He might have been saved but who-ever was with him at the time did not save him. Perhaps he did not even attempt to save him. Her son died.'

'I've got that,' Horsley told him. 'And I know about the old superstition, how some people would never rescue a drowning person.'

'I think Stephen was with him. I think Stephen, only a child himself, was terrified of the castle, thanks to fears placed deep within him by his mother, but I think Stephen was afraid of attempting a rescue. He might even have been frightened of water. He knew about the old superstition, his mother had seen to that in her warnings for him to keep away from the trough. So when Stanley fell in, Stephen did nothing – except to run for his father. That's how a child would react, after all. By the time Gallholme senior reached the trough it was too late – and I think he got there alone, he left Stephen at home. Stephen would never know what had actually happened, so I don't think his statement was a lie. He told what he thought was right.'

'But Stephen could have pushed his pal in,' protested Horsley. 'If so, he would have panicked once Stanley couldn't get out. He'd have to run for his dad, there was nothing else he could do.'

'He might indeed have pushed his pal in,

it is quite possible. Hence his presence at the trough yesterday morning, the anniversary of the tragedy, a form of penance or reparation, or even an attempt to revive a buried memory of exactly what did happen.'

'And for those reasons you think Gallholme senior removed the body to the stream to make it look like an accidental drowning there instead of the castle?'

'That is one of several reasons for his action,' said Pluke.

'But why?' persisted Horsley.

'I have a theory,' said Pluke.

'You and your theories! What is it this time?'

'Stanley was born in February 1958,' Pluke reminded him. 'Stephen was born later the same year, in June. Stanley was illegitimate, we know that from the birth certificate. He was not Pinder's son. Pinder and his wife have no children, he has told us that. Stanley was born – and died – before the Pinders got married. So who was Stanley's father?'

'No idea,' said Horsley. 'It could have been anybody.'

'Yes, it could,' admitted Pluke. 'But imagine a young shepherdess, out in the fields and on the moors all day alone, with a handsome master paying her regular visits...'

'Are you suggesting it was Gallholme senior?' cried Horsley, who then said, 'Well, yes, I suppose it could be true. Master and servant – it happened all the time.'

'We have no proof, not until we talk to Mrs Pinder,' Pluke acknowledged. 'But old Mr Gallholme had something of a reputation with women and he did look after the Pinders rather well, under pressure from Mrs Pinder perhaps? But suppose Gallholme *was* Stanley's natural father. It means Stanley was an heir to the estate, by blood, if not by legitimate means.'

'He'd never inherit, not being illegitimate, not the son of a woman who worked in the fields!' cried Horsley.

'Right,' said Pluke. 'Now consider Stephen.'

'His parents weren't married either, were they?' Horsley nodded. 'So he was illegitimate as well, even if his parents did everything to make it seem he wasn't.'

'Right.' Pluke smiled. 'But he was younger than Stanley.'

'God, yes. So if there had been a battle in the courts, a contest between the two, then Stanley, the elder son, might have had the stronger claim!'

'It's a thought,' said Pluke. 'If that prognosis is correct, then Stephen Gallholme was no more an heir than Stanley and yet he got everything. That's the unfairness of it. I think that notion would rankle with Stanley's mother.'

'She would know, wouldn't she? The truth about the Gallholmes? Margot Pinder, I mean. She'd lived on the estate for most of her life.'

'I would think she knows more than anyone else about the estate and its personalities,' Pluke agreed. 'So, Inspector Horsley, there you are, as owner of the estate, with one of your illegitimate sons failing to save the life of the other, the elder, in fact. What are people to think?'

'That the elder claimant was bumped off?'

'Right. That's what the talk would be, the mystery of the death in the trough, whisperings of murder by drowning, getting rid of an embarrassment. So Gallholme senior, thinking and working fast, decided to forestall those rumours by making the death look nothing more than a sad drowning of a little boy in a moorland stream. His own "marriage" would not have stood up to a criminal investigation, he knew that. He took the only way out, a piece of quick and positive thinking, in my view.'

'And do you think Margot knew the truth?'

'I do. I'm sure there was rumour and speculation among the staff. There was the business of the bike, too, and the thorns in the boy's clothing. If their significance wasn't immediately apparent, I'm sure Margot would later realise things weren't right. The coroner also smelt a rat, but lacked the evidence to clarify things in his mind.'

'And yesterday was the anniversary of Stanley's death,' whispered Horsley.

'It was, to the day if not the precise date,' said Pluke. 'At some stage yesterday morning Mrs Pinder went to put flowers on her son's grave. After killing Stephen, perhaps? One can only ponder about the thoughts going through her mind at that time. But she must have considered that the man who failed to save Stanley or who possibly killed him, even as a child himself, should die in exactly the same place and by the same means – by drowning in the giant trough. And she was quite capable and determined that he should. As I said earlier, the water in the trough got its victim after all.'

'Is this all guesswork, Montague? Or do you know more than the rest of us? Have you asked Mrs Pinder about any of this?'

'Not yet. I want it to be a surprise, but I do keep my ears and eyes open, Mr Horsley. I cannot think of any other scenario which would provide all the answers. But now it is time to talk to Margot Pinder.'

'Mind if I come?' asked Horsley.

'Not at all,' said Pluke. 'Come along, Detective Constable Newton, to the car. We have work to do.'

It was mid evening when they approached the now familiar outline of the gatehouse. The gate was closed and as they came closer the sturdy figure of Aaron Pinder emerged. He recognised Pluke in the front passenger seat and prepared to open the gate, thinking the wanted admission to the parkland. But Anita drew the car on to a parking area and they all emerged.

'Evening, Mr Pluke, and others,' said Pinder, no longer the angry gateman they had come to know. 'You're not going through, then?'

'We'd like to talk to Mrs Pinder,' said Pluke. 'Alone.'

'Well, she's in the house. I'll go and lose myself, I could do with a walk. She'll see to the gate if anybody comes. I'll tell her.'

They waited. In a moment Mrs Pinder appeared in the doorway and beckoned them inside, apologising for the cramped space and saying the fire had made it very hot. 'A cup of tea?' she asked.

'No, thank you,' said Pluke. 'We want to have a word with you, Mrs Pinder.'

She looked him directly in the eye, as if challenging him to make his accusation. He felt she knew why he was here, but for the moment she said nothing. She pointed to the chairs but Pluke remained standing and then began with a thunderbolt.

'Mrs Pinder. Stanley Bilston was your son,

wasn't he? The boy who drowned all those years ago, in 1966.'

'Thirty-four years ago this weekend, Mr Pluke. I've always tended his grave and remembered his anniversary.' She was almost staring at him, defying him to put the tough queries.

'And who was his father?' was Pluke's next very direct question.

'That's nothing to do with you,' she snapped. 'Nothing at all.'

'I think it was Mr Gallholme senior, Stephen's father. He did look after you and Aaron very well.'

'You can think what you like, Mr Pluke.' But her face told him the truth.

'We could exhume Stanley to obtain a DNA sample for comparison with similar samples from a member of the Gallholme family, Mrs Pinder. That would establish whether or not Constantine Gallholme was Stanley's father.'

She said nothing, merely continued to look him straight in the eye.

'You told me you were at work yesterday morning, Mrs Pinder, at the supermarket.'

'So?'

'You weren't at work, Mrs Pinder. We've checked.'

'I'm saying nothing.' And now, very rapidly, her face began to show dismay.

'We've found the weapon that was used to

kill Stephen, Mrs Pinder. A straw-fork, a pitchfork, some people call them. Hidden in the old trough, deep down one of the internal wells. We've managed to retrieve it. We are going to examine it for fingerprints and further DNA samples. It will show whether or not it was used to kill Stephen. It will also show whether you handled it. And we would like to examine your car, the tyres especially, to see if they bear earth from the area around the castle, earth from yesterday morning. We have taken samples.'

She began to cry now, her large body bowed in her misery. Anita went to comfort her, placing an arm around her shoulders.

'He had everything. He was a louse, Mr Pluke, like his father. Stephen let my son die. He let that other woman die. He thinks nobody up here knew about him letting her drown. How could he? Scared of water, was he? When she died I realised what must have happened to my Stanley all those years ago. And he's illegitimate as well, I bet nobody knows that. He's no better than my Stanley was and yet he comes back here like God Almighty to run the place: owner of all this lot, owner of me and Aaron even, and he begins to tell me what to do, to move us out of here, taking our jobs away...'

'So you hit him? You knew where he'd be yesterday morning?'

'You know everything, Mr Pluke. You

know I did. He died like he let others die, in the water, terrified of it. He deserves every last drop that's in that mucky old trough. I didn't mean to kill him, just to give him a taste of that water. But if my Stanley couldn't inherit – and I know he couldn't – why should Stephen? It's so unfair, so dreadfully wrong... Aaron doesn't know I did it, though, I hoped nobody would know...'

'I think you did mean to kill him. I think you planned it very carefully. You'd better come with us to the police station, Mrs Pinder,' said Pluke. 'The car is outside.'

She left the house in tears as Anita went to find Aaron Pinder.

The publishers hope that this book has given you enjoyable reading. Large Print Books are especially designed to be as easy to see and hold as possible. If you wish a complete list of our books please ask at your local library or write directly to:

Magna Large Print Books
Magna House, Long Preston,
Skipton, North Yorkshire.
BD23 4ND

This Large Print Book for the partially sighted, who cannot read normal print, is published under the auspices of

THE ULVERSCROFT FOUNDATION

PB

NEATH PORT TALBOT LIBRARY AND INFORMATION SERVICES							
1		25		49		73	
2		26		50		74	
3		27		51		75	
4		28		52		76	
5		29		53		77	
6		30		54		78	
7	10/17	31		55		79	
8		32		56		80	
9		33		57		81	
10		34		58		82	
11		35		59		83	
12		36		60		84	
13		37		61		85	
14		38		62		86	
15		39		63		87	
16		40		64		88	
17		41		65		89	
18		42		66		90	
19		43		67		91	
20		44		68		92	
21		45		69		COMMUNITY SERVICES	
22		46		70			
23		47		71		NPT/111	
24		48		72			

ℰω